Her daughter was gone.

"Teegan?" Liz's voice was low the first time she said it. Not so much the second. "Teegan!"

Harley appeared back in the doorway then, his face far, far too still.

A thousand furious butterflies beat inside Liz's stomach, and when she spoke, her words came out in a cracked whisper. "Where is she?"

Harley started to shake his head, and Liz saw the answer in his eyes. Her daughter was gone. Taken by whoever had assaulted poor Miss Wilma and left her unconscious.

Liz wanted to scream. To cry out. To pound her fists on the wall. To shake the old woman awake and demand to know what had happened.

Minutes, she thought desperately. *We were in the other room for five minutes! Ten, tops.*

She didn't realize she'd said it aloud until Harley answered.

"That's all it takes," he said. "But we'll figure this out, Liz. We'll get her back."

"How?" Now her voice was shrill.

Where was her daughter?

* * *

Undercover Justice: Four brothers-in-arms on a mission for justice...

* * *

If you're on Twitter, tell us what you think of Harlequin Romantic Suspense! #harlequinromsuspense

Dear Reader,

I am so excited to introduce you to Harley and Liz. I love them both to bits.

Harley, though, is extraspecial to me. He's a big bear of man on the outside, but he's sweet and soft on the inside. You'll get to see lots of that as he interacts with Liz's little girl, Teegan! As with the rest of the brothers-in-arms in my Undercover Justice series, Harley became a detective to make sure his father's killer was put behind bars for good. But unlike the other guys, Harley might've chosen a different path if he hadn't been so focused on justice. So in addition to working with the police, he has a degree in art, he sculpts and is a computer whiz, and he's delighted to put those talents and interests to use.

I hope you fall in love with him as much as Liz does!

Happy reading,

Melinda Di Lorenzo

UNDERCOVER PASSION

Melinda Di Lorenzo

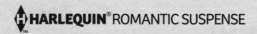
HARLEQUIN® ROMANTIC SUSPENSE

Recycling programs
for this product may
not exist in your area.

ISBN-13: 978-1-335-45665-6

Undercover Passion

Printed in U.S.A.

Amazon bestselling author **Melinda Di Lorenzo** writes in her spare time—at soccer practices, when she should be doing laundry and in place of sleep. She lives on the beautiful west coast of British Columbia, Canada, with her handsome husband and her noisy kids. When she's not writing, she can be found curled up with (someone else's) good book.

To Mr. and Mrs. O., for your invaluable help with my "police" work.

Chapter 1

Liz James flicked the cash register shut with a barely stifled sigh. She handed the customer her wrapped sculpture and a receipt, then mustered up a smile.

"Thanks so much!" she said. "I'm sure it'll look great on your son's fireplace mantel."

The woman—a tourist in from Freemont—nodded her appreciation, tucked the package under her arm and exited the store. And Liz let out the sigh, glad that the clock over the door read three minutes past five. She slid out from behind the counter, quickly flicked the lock shut, then stole a quick glance outside before she began the roll-down of the shutters. Hers was the last building on the block, which meant she had a good view of the rest. They were all already closed and dark. She was, as usual, the slowest at getting things shut down. She fought yet another sigh.

She usually loved her job. She loved the art. She loved

the customers. She *really* loved being her own boss. But today had seemed especially long. Her biggest supplier—the man who also held the lease on her art store and the apartment above where she and her daughter lived—had dropped off a dozen extra paintings first thing in the morning, and Liz had spent most of her hours trying to find a home for them. As always, the stock sent in by Jesse Garibaldi wasn't particularly high-end. But she knew it would move quickly, anyway. The man seemed to have an endless stream of interested parties who were willing to pay top dollar for the pieces.

She'd asked once where they came from—both the paintings and the buyers—and Garibaldi had explained that an anonymous local artist did the work. The pieces were nice, but not high-end, so Liz just assumed they were a side job for someone who didn't want his name associated with the work. They sold exclusively through Garibaldi, with 50 percent of their profits going to one of his own local charities. Liz could hardly say no to the sudden influx of new pieces and the guaranteed profit.

She took a step back and studied the most prominently displayed one. It wasn't anything terribly exciting. Well done but not outstanding. A landscape piece. A mountain in the background, a stream in the forefront and trees dotting the horizon. Except for the water, it could easily have been the view from a dozen different spots on the outskirts of Whispering Woods. The blue trickle told Liz that it was somewhere farther up the mountain.

Though she'd never ventured up the slope herself, she knew from one of her customers—a retired engineer—that a glacier-fed lake existed on a plateau, and that the river sloped down the other side. According to the engineer, the river was somehow the main source of water for all of the town. Liz couldn't remember the details. Her eyes had glazed over and her ears had shut down when the engineer attempted to explain how it all worked. Liz could talk about art history for hours. She had museum layouts memorized. But pipes and water pressure were a whole other story. The engineer had laughed and waved his hand in front of her face to check for signs of life, then called her a hopeless artist. And Liz had agreed. Engineering wasn't her forte or her passion. But for some reason now, staring at the painting made her wish she'd paid just a little more attention.

Whoever the painter is, he or she is a heck of a lot more adventurous than I am.

For a second, the thought gave Liz a twinge of longing. Unconsciously, she reached up her hand toward the swirl of blues and greens and grays. As soon as her fingers met the canvas, she realized what she was doing and started to jerk back. Then stopped, frowning. Even though the pad of her index finger had just barely brushed the surface, the texture struck her as odd.

With a guilty look toward the door—pushed on by a ridiculous feeling that someone might actually be peering in and watching what she did—Liz pressed her fingers to the painting again. When no one burst through the door, she pushed a little harder. It felt…off. She dropped her hand and stepped back to study the painting again, this time for non-aesthetic reasons.

It was watercolor, she was sure. But also not.

Definitely strange, she thought.

Liz had never gone to school for art—life had had other plans for her—but if things had turned out differently, it was what she would've studied for sure. Not the means of creating it. She didn't consider herself to be talented in that way. But the mediums and movement, the artists and their expressions…those fascinated her.

She'd read hundreds of books. Spent countless sleepless nights combing through them. So, while she might not be a formal expert, she was at the very least an extremely well-read amateur.

Frowning, she moved from the first painting to a second and gave it a quick once-over. The scenery was similar to that of the first, though more of a close-up. Like someone had zoomed in to a small section of the first to showcase the details. The mountain peak wasn't visible, but a bird could be seen on a tree branch, and rock sharply parted the river. Likely done by the same artist. Was the paint the same? Liz felt compelled to find out.

When she reached out this time, it was with far less hesitation and only a cursory glance around. Sure enough, it had the same texture. Not quite right. Not quite smooth enough.

"So weird," she muttered, then blew out a breath, wondering why it was stressing her out so much.

The artist probably had some kind of special mixing technique. Or added some secret ingredient to the paint to make it feel a certain way. She'd read about all kinds of unconventional things, and God knew plenty of the stuff she carried in her shop was unique. That was just art.

Which is what you love about it.

"Maybe I've finally cracked," she said aloud to the empty store. "I mean, really? The paint *feels* funny?"

She definitely had more important things to worry about. With a headshake, she stepped away from both pieces and turned back to the cash register. Cashing it out and storing the money from the day's sales was one of the last things on her to-do list. Then she could get back to the part of her day that she loved infinitely more than she loved her job. And that was saying something. Because she really did love running Liz's Lovely Things.

Her eyes sought and found the one non-artsy picture she kept in her little store. It was a framed shot of her eight-year-old daughter with eyes closed, tongue out and a ladybug headband askew on her head. It was Liz's favorite. It perfectly captured the zany essence of her kid. Teegan would be in the apartment upstairs now, bouncing on her heels as she counted down the seconds until Liz came up, too. Driving the sitter crazy, probably.

With an affectionate smile, Liz turned away from the picture to jab her finger against the computerized register to punch in the closing code. The machine came to life with a *tick-tick-ding*, then began to automatically reconcile the internal receipt totals. Liz snorted as the little shop filled with the noise of it.

Even though it was the same every night, she always wondered why the people who created such an efficient piece of equipment hadn't found a way to get rid of the old-fashioned sounds. As she grabbed the broom and started her quick sweep of the hardwood floors, she considered—not for the first time—whether or not the designers had left the noisiness that way on purpose. Some kind of nostalgic throwback. Then, as if to emphasize—or maybe mock—her thoughts, the cash register let out a weird groan. A crack followed the groan, and Liz sensed imminent disaster.

"Oh, you are so *not* going to break down right now," she called out from across the room.

But as she set down the broom and moved toward the register, she saw that the strange sounds weren't coming from the register at all. The machine had finished its cycle already and sat slightly ajar, waiting for her to pull out the tray and lock the money in the safe.

Liz frowned. She stepped nearer again. Then realized her mistake. The door to the storage room—which had its own exterior entry on the other side—hung open, its lock dangling uselessly to the side. Panic hit Liz hard, and she tried to turn and run. But it was too late. A sharp point pressed to her throat, and a gravelly male voice filled her ear.

"Move more than an inch," he said, "and I'll put a nice little hole in your jugular."

Liz let out the smallest, shakiest breath. "Just take whatever you want."

"Good choice," replied her assailant. "Where is it?"

"Right there. The register's open. Take it all. Please."

There was a pause. "The money? I don't want the money."

The statement intensified Liz's fear. "You don't?"

"Where're the damn Heigles?"

"What?"

The knife pushed in a little hard. "The Heigles? Which ones are they?"

"I don't know!" Liz gasped.

"I know he brings them to you."

Him.

Did the knife-wielder mean Garibaldi? Did he mean *those* paintings? After a heartbeat of consideration, she decided she didn't care.

"There," she said, lifting her finger just fractionally.

The blade eased. "Where?"

"The one with the river."

The knife dropped off completely, and Liz found herself fighting a need to sag down and close her eyes. And she knew she couldn't. She made herself watch as the man abandoned his hold on her, and she tried to commit every detail to memory.

There was the way he shuffled a little, favoring his

right foot. How that shuffle masked his height and gave the impression that he was so much shorter than he was.

There was the fact that even though his face was covered by a ski mask, she could see a mottled mark on one eyelid. Maybe a bruise, maybe a birthmark.

She saw his jeans, and how dirt permeated the denim—not just near the bottom, but all over.

But when he stepped up to the painting, those observations kind of slipped away. Because he lifted his hand and touched it, just like she'd done minutes earlier. And he seemed…satisfied.

Fear gave way for a second. Curiosity took its place. Liz genuinely wanted to know what it was that he felt. What it was that made him nod, ever so slightly.

But when he angled his gaze back in her direction, renewed fear sliced through her. And his words turned the fear into terror.

"You have a daughter," he said.

A whimper threatened. "Please. Take the painting. Take them all. And the money."

"Believe me. I'd like to." An unpleasant hunger laced his tone.

"Do it."

"Not what I came for, unfortunately." He stepped back again, his eyes running over Liz.

Panic hit her. "Don't—"

He cut her off with a dark chuckle. "No. Not that, either. But consider this a warning. For you and your kid. You're going to want to call the cops. You're going to want to run to someone and tell them I was here. But I guarantee you that doing either will result in bad things happening to the both of you."

He gave another head-to-toe stare, his expression so cold that Liz had no doubt he was telling the truth.

Bad things.

Just vague enough to be even more terrifying than the man's presence.

"Do we have an understanding?" he asked.

Liz managed a nod. "Yes."

"Good."

He at last turned away and limped out at a jog. Liz started to draw in a semi-relieved breath, but as he disappeared through the storage door, her daughter's laugh echoed from the same direction. Oxygen forgotten, Liz's feet hit the floor at a dead run.

Detective Harley Maxwell paused in his chase and scanned the building in search of his target. Except for the buzz of a neon shop sign a few doors up, the air was silent.

Which actually might work in your favor.

Keeping very still, he strained to hear a sound—the crunch of gravel, the creak of a door—that would indicate the correct direction. Then it came. The light brush of feet on pavement from around the side. Harley pushed down his triumph. He'd celebrate once he had his hands on his wily escapee.

He moved to the edge of the building and pressed himself against its side with practiced stealth. He knew he wasn't the fastest runner on his team of partners, but what he lacked in natural athleticism he made up for in cunning.

Slow and steady, he cautioned himself as he inched along. *Surprise is your friend.*

He reached the edge of the building then and paused again. He started to ease forward. Before he could make it even a single step, a figure came stumbling around the corner.

Prepared for victory, Harley reached out. "Aha! Now I've got— Whoa!"

He froze midgrab, as he realized his hands were clasped to someone other than the person he pursued. Not that he didn't recognize her. The short curvy woman with her untamed head of brown curls was more than familiar to him. His cover story—that he was an aspiring artist in the small town, trying to find his muse—included subletting the studio beside her apartment. The fact that his short-term apartment rental had gone bust in a flood meant temporarily staying in the studio 24/7. So he'd spent enough time close to her over the last week to have her smattering of freckles and full lips permanently etched into his memory.

Yeah, said a voice in his head. *Close to her. But not this* close.

He had to agree. He hadn't been near enough to know for sure that her skin would be warm and soft, and though he'd caught hints of her perfume before, its lightly floral fragrance hadn't ever filled his nose quite so thoroughly before.

Realizing he still held her arms, he dropped his hands and tried to take a cautious step back, but her hands came up to stop him, almost clutching at his shirt. Concern flooded through him. Automatically, he brought his fingers up to hers to offer comfort.

"Hey," he said as he gave her a quick soothing squeeze. "What's the matter? Something happen at the store?"

"No. It's Teegan." Her gaze darted around frantically. "Where is she? I heard her, but now I can't find her."

Harley relaxed a little. "Kind of the point of the game."

"What?"

"Hide-and-seek."

"She's hiding?" The tension in Liz's face eased marginally.

"Yeah," Harley replied. "And in case you didn't know, the monkey's pretty darned good at it, too. You'd think in a three-building limit, she'd be easy to spot, but I've been looking for her for a solid two minutes and haven't spotted her yet."

"I really did hear her a second ago, but—" The pretty brunette's eyes crinkled with worry again.

"What's wrong?"

"Nothing. I just need her to come in. Quickly. Please."

"All right." He cupped his hands around his mouth and called out, "Olly, olly, oxen free! You win, monkey!"

"Yes!" The little girl's triumphant cry came from above.

Harley tipped his gaze up, and rolled his eyes as he spotted a flash of purple on the side of the building. Like an actual monkey, she'd managed to scamper up the solitary evergreen tree there, then used one of its wide branches to tuck herself in behind the Liz's Lovely Things sign. Her grinning face popped out, and she offered a wave. Harley shook his head and smiled back. She had a right to be proud. No way would he have found her on his own.

He turned to say as much to her mom, but the words didn't make it out. Liz's posture was rigid, her eyes focused across the road rather than on her daughter. Automatically, Harley widened his stance defensively and craned his neck to see what she saw. He spotted the object of her attention right away. A man.

He stood near the end of the block, tucked against the door frame of a closed shop. There was something off about him. Harley had seen enough people who were up to no good to recognize one when they were standing

more or less right in front of him. This guy definitely
had that look. He held his hoodie-covered head down,
but still somehow gave the impression that he wasn't trying not to be seen.

Hiding. But not.

The contradiction puzzled Harley a bit, and he glanced
back toward Liz. Her cheeks were flushed, her chest rising and falling with short breaths. Her reaction clued
him in to the man's intent. The guy wanted to blend in
for the general public, but also to make sure one person
knew he was there.

And that person is Liz.

Concern drove away Harley's other feelings and made
his gut twist with protective instinct instead. His urge
was to reach out to the woman beside him—to defend
and soothe—but he stopped himself just short of doing it.

Instead, he tipped his head and—in a low voice—
asked, "Someone you know?"

"What?" Liz's response was at first startled, then too
innocent. "Who?"

"The guy over there who's making you look like you
swallowed something sour."

"I don't know what you're talking about."

The stiff defensive tone and the blatant lie put an idea
into Harley's head. "Look. I'm not here to judge. If you
need help…if he's an ex, or—"

Liz let out a laugh that sounded genuine. "Oh, God
no. Nothing like that."

"All right." He knew his reply sounded dubious.

She clearly picked up on it, too. "Look. He was just
an unhappy customer."

"A *really* unhappy customer?"

"It happens."

"Okay." He paused, and he noted the way her eyes

flicked back to the hooded figure. "But if you did need help…"

"You're the knight in clay-stained clothes I'd call first," she assured him before she turned to call out to her kid. "Teegs! Anytime you come down from there would be good!"

Harley smiled as the little girl started to expertly scamper down. From the corner of his eye, though, he watched Liz, searching for another sign of fear. Even though he'd had the pretty woman and her activities under close surveillance for the last two weeks, this was the first hint that there was even something to watch. He'd actually been questioning whether or not he and his partners were way off base in having him in to keep an eye on her. Was this a sign that they were right after all? Was Liz's obvious fear of the hooded man related to the case they'd been investigating for the last fifteen years?

Even though she'd already denied knowing the shadowy figure, Harley wished he could ask a more pointed question without giving himself away. Something told him that even if he'd been able to, drawing attention to the situation right that second might backfire anyway. Liz was too on edge, the man close enough to see if she reacted poorly. The last thing he wanted was to put Teegan—who was now using cartwheels to propel herself toward them—or her mother in danger, so he kept his mouth shut and turned back to the other man to assess for any immediate danger. The hooded figure was on the move now, his head still down as he shuffled out of the doorway.

Harley tensed automatically, preparing for a fight. Preparing to tell Liz to grab Teegan and run. He was hyperaware of the fact that he'd left his gun in a coded lockbox high on a shelf in his closet. A safety precaution, which now seemed like an *un*safe choice. He wished he had it strapped to his side in easy reach.

But it only took a second to realize it wouldn't be necessary. The man was headed in the opposite direction.

Still uneasy, and with his hands flexing, Harley took a quick inventory. He noted the fact that the guy was too covered for the late-spring warmth. He saw his limp and tried to mentally calculate whether it was a fresh injury or something older and more permanent. Before he could reach a conclusion, though, the guy disappeared around the corner.

Just in time, too.

Teegan's fresh giggle filled the air as she flung her arms around Harley's knees. "You lost! I totally beat you!"

Harley gave the street corner a final glance, tucking what he'd seen into the caches of his memory for future perusal, then smiled and turned his attention to the little girl.

Chapter 2

Liz exhaled, overwhelmingly glad that her shaggy-haired neighbor had shown up. She didn't know Harley all that well, but just his brick-wall appearance was enough to make her breathe a little easier.

As he bent to speak to her Teegan, she gave the back of his head a surreptitious, grateful look.

In the week and a bit since he'd been staying at the studio adjacent to her apartment, he'd been friendly and helpful. Ready with a smile, but not overbearing. He had a nice-guy vibe that she'd liked since the second she'd met him. His wide shoulders and solid build weren't exactly off-putting, either. And at the moment, not only was his presence a soothing buffer but he was also a good distraction for her too-intuitive daughter.

"You completely kicked my butt," he said to Teegan, before shooting a conspiratorial wink Liz's way. "Don't tell your mom I said that."

Teegan gave him an eye roll. "I'm pretty sure she can hear you."

"Darn it. You might be right."

Harley grinned, and Liz did her best to smile back. She knew her effort was probably lacking. Her teeth felt wooden, and the rest of her mouth was still dry with fear. Being held at knifepoint and having her daughter's life threatened wasn't exactly something she would forget anytime soon. In fact, she was pretty sure her brain hadn't even started to process it, let alone figure out what to do about it. The adrenaline still coursed through her body. And she knew that the second it stopped, she'd probably collapse, if not physically, then at least emotionally.

Which you don't need to do here.

"Teegan," she said, her voice shakier than she would've liked, "I think we should go inside and get cleaned up for dinner."

"Did you even *see* me, Mom?" her daughter countered, still clinging to Harley.

"I did. You were so high up that I just about had a heart attack."

"Mom! That is *not* true, and you always say—"

Teegan's protest cut off in a giggle as Harley stood up with her still attached to his arm. She dangled from his bicep, her bare feet almost a yard from the ground, utterly pleased by the situation. Harley spun, and Teegan sailed in a circle. The spinning motion gave Liz another few seconds to scan the surrounding area.

Was her assailant still watching from somewhere she couldn't see? Had he spied Harley's broad shoulders and goofy display of strength? Did it make him think that she and Teegan weren't completely unprotected?

God, she hoped so.

She turned her attention back to Teegan and Harley.

The well-muscled man spun in a final slow circle, making her daughter's laughter echo through the otherwise quiet street. As he came to a stop, his sleeve slid up, revealing a circle of scrawling ink around his arm. The tattoo was distracting. Sexy, even. For a moment, it actually held Liz's attention long enough to keep her from her worried thoughts.

Crashing into Harley the way she'd done just a few minutes earlier had emphasized the quiet strength he possessed under his clay-speckled T-shirt. She couldn't say why, but it'd been almost unexpected. It seemed silly, really. His body was visibly tanklike. Liz had admired it more than a few times. So why it stuck out now was a mystery. But it was definitely not unpleasant.

Unless the guy with the knife thinks he's a threat, said a voice in her head. *Then it'll be anything but pleasant.*

Liz fought both a shiver and a stab of guilt.

"Come here, baby," she said to Teegan, her voice not quite as firm as she would've liked. "Let Mr. Maxwell go. Contrary to popular belief, he's not a jungle gym."

Her daughter finally disentangled herself and moved to stand in front of Liz, her eyes still sparkling. "Were you watching, Mom? I was practically flying."

"Uh-huh. And between that and the climbing, I think we should probably go inside before one of the neighbors comes out and complains about *my* parenting and *your* safety." She said it lightly, but she couldn't quite keep from shooting another nervous look up the street.

"You can use me as your scapegoat," Harley offered. "Bad-news artist influencing your daughter's precious mind."

Liz couldn't help but smile. "You're the least 'bad news' artist I've ever met."

He grinned back. "I feel like I should be insulted by that compliment."

"Don't be. It's refreshing to see someone with more talent than ego."

Teegan groaned. "Are you guys just gonna stand there all night talking? Because if you are, I'm gonna go climb some more."

"No!" The word came out of Liz's mouth a little sharply, and both Teegan and Harley blinked at her.

The big man recovered quickly, his surprised look relaxing into a smile. "Well. Since apparently you *really* want to get the kiddo home…mind if I walk with you up to the apartment? I think I might've dropped my phone in the hall between your place and the studio."

"Sure." She wondered if the relief she felt was evident in her reply.

But if he noticed, he didn't say. Instead, he offered her a grin and gestured toward their shared building. "Women and children first."

Teegan immediately took off at a happy skip, and Liz's heart thundered nervously in response to the open space between them. She took a step forward without even realizing she was doing it until Harley spoke.

"You want me to catch her?" he asked.

She didn't stop walking, but she made herself answer calmly. "She'll be fine. It's only a hundred feet between here and the door. And Lord knows she's done more dangerous things in the last five minutes."

"True enough. Guess I'll just have to settle for protecting you instead."

He said it teasingly, but she noticed that he was quick to step between her and the road, and she couldn't help but wonder if it was on purpose. Had he picked up on her distress? She suspected she hadn't hidden it very well.

She'd been so worried about watching the man who was watching her that she hadn't even stopped to think if Harley was paying attention.

He gave her shoulder a nudge. "I sometimes think I *might* be one, by the way."

"One what?" Liz replied, puzzled.

"A jungle gym."

She let out a genuine laugh. "I'm sure Teegan agrees. I'm sorry if she's bugging you too much."

"I don't mind. She's got enthusiasm."

"That's a nice way of saying she's a pain in the butt, huh?"

"I can *hear* you!" called Teegan from a few steps in front of them.

"Well, there wouldn't be much point in saying it if you *couldn't* hear me, would there?" Liz called back.

In typical Teegan-style, her daughter turned and stuck out her tongue before flinging open the door that led to the units above the shop.

"Still think she's just 'enthusiastic'?"

Harley grinned. "I plead the Fifth."

"Yeah, I don't blame you." Her tone was ruefully amused. "And speaking of self-preservation...any idea where the sitter disappeared to? Did Teegan scare her off?"

"I can *still* hear you," her daughter yelled from the top of the stairs. "And I didn't scare her away. You were late, and Miss Wanda had to go pick up her *boyfriend* from work."

"Late by five minutes," Liz muttered under her breath. "I think I pay her enough to cover that."

Harley took the handrail and gestured for her to take the first step. "To be more accurate, Wanda's boyfriend had some kind of emergency—sliced finger or something—so I volunteered to bring Teegan down to you."

"It doesn't make me feel any better than my sitter left my kid with a strange man."

"I'm not all that strange."

"Ha ha. You know what I mean."

"I do," he agreed. "But Teegan assured Wanda that I was—and I quote—the best old man ever. And she was happy to remind Wanda that I was the one watching her the other day when you ran to that store."

"I forgot about that." She smiled ruefully. "I think my kid would make one heck of a lawyer."

"She would. And she also used her powers of persuasion to rope me into the hide-and-seek."

Liz sighed. "You really don't have to indulge her like that. Because I promise you, she'll take full advantage and have you wrapped around her little finger faster than you can blink."

"I don't mind. Really. I needed a break from work anyway."

"Sculpture's not coming along?"

"Sculpture's actually shaping up well."

"So you made some progress?"

"Well. I don't know what it *is* yet. But yeah. The clay's slightly more than a lump now."

Liz laughed again. "I guess that's good."

"It's awesome, Mom," Teegan interrupted. "It looks like a mountain. But also a dragon."

She groaned. "You have *got* to stay out of Mr. Maxwell's workspace."

"Since we rent it to him, isn't it really *our* workspace?" countered her daughter.

Liz's face heated. "Teegan!"

But Harley just chuckled. "Kid's got a point."

Liz shook her head as they started up the stairs. "Kid's got an opinion. About everything." She paused, then projected her voice toward her daughter. "And if you want to get technical, we sublet to Mr. Maxwell. But we lease the building from Jesse Garibaldi, so it's *his* workspace, and his shop and his apartment, not ours. So just stay out of everything!"

She turned back to Harley and was surprised to find that his expression had gone stiff.

The sound of the so-called business owner's name dug at Harley in an unexpected way. Not unexpected in that he was surprised to hear it. After all, Jesse Garibaldi had his finger in every pie Whispering Woods offered, and Liz's Lovely Things was no different. Harley had known the man held the deed before he ever set foot in the building. The pretty brunette's financial ties to the man were one of the main reasons she'd come under the microscope in the first place.

So, if you knew all that…then what's bothering you?

It only took Harley a moment to answer his own question. It wasn't hearing Garibaldi's name. It was hearing it from *Liz*. He didn't like the way she dropped the criminal's name so easily. The way she made him a part of her light-hearted joke.

No one knew better than Harley that there was nothing funny about Garibaldi. A person responsible for so much death and chaos couldn't provide any amusement. And for some reason, the way it just rolled off Liz's tongue made it even worse.

You don't want her to be involved.

The acknowledgment gave Harley serious pause. Obviously, he preferred it when people weren't involved in illegal activities. Especially where Garibaldi was concerned. This felt different.

It was a part of his job to determine Liz's guilt or innocence, not to be biased on whether it turned out one way or the other. Impartiality was the name of the game. Developing an emotional opinion would seriously hamper his ability to keep things as they should be.

"Are you all right?" Liz's voice yanked him back to the moment.

He blinked, realizing the pretty brunette was three steps above him because he'd come to a complete stop in the stairwell.

And you're probably not covering up your feelings very well, either.

That didn't mean he could stop himself from staring at her for a second longer, wondering if he'd be able to get back that necessary neutrality. If his short time across the hall from Liz had already swayed him away from that even hand of justice, he had to consider whether or not he could maintain a professional distance. Or re*gain* one, as the case might be.

"Harley? Seriously. Are you okay?"

He forced a rueful headshake and answered in a light tone. "Sorry. Spaced out. Guess the amount of work I did today wore me out more than I thought."

Her face relaxed into a sympathetic smile. "It probably doesn't help that you've been sleeping in the studio."

"No. Not much. Mattress on the floor never quite cuts it."

"Any news on when they'll have the apartment fixed?"

"Not a word."

"Well. I'm sure you know, but you're welcome to stay at the studio as long as you want." Her smile changed into a teasing one. "I might actually miss you a little when you go. It's only been a week, but I'm already way too used to having a handyman around."

"One unplugged toilet doesn't make me a handyman," he assured her.

"There was also the picture frame."

"I caught it before it fell. That wasn't handy. That was lucky."

"But then you hung it back up again more securely."

"I think you just have low standards."

She laughed. "Even if that's true, I'll never admit it."

They argued good-naturedly about it the rest of the way up, with Liz compiling a list of tasks Harley had completed for her since the flood had forced him from his rental unit in town. In their shared hallway above the shop, Harley finally lifted his hands in mock defeat.

"All right," he said. "I'll let you have this one. I've been mildly helpful since I've been stuck here."

"Good. I hope you'll continue to be mildly helpful for the duration of your stay."

"If you need anything, you just let me know."

"I will."

He continued to stand there for a second, looking for a reason to continue the conversation. Thoughts of the hooded figure in the street below nagged at him and kept him from simply turning and walking through his own door. There'd been genuine fear on Liz's face when she'd seen him. That alone was enough of an excuse to prolong their interaction.

Too bad you can't just ask outright what it was that scared her.

A direct approach would've been smoother. Easier. A glance toward Teegan—who was hanging off the door handle with a bored look on her face—reminded Harley that even if he *had* been at liberty to ask, he wouldn't have done it. That didn't mean he felt right about just letting the little girl and her mother disappear into their apartment alone.

Will asking if they currently have any loose floor-boards seem like a put-on?

He shifted from foot to foot, but no subtle segue came to mind. Not one that didn't sound like a line, anyway.

"Well," he finally said. "I guess this is good-night?"

He thought Liz looked a little disappointed, too. "I guess it is."

"So."

"So."

"Good night."

"Good night."

"Good niiiiiiiight," Teegan sang, breaking the awkwardness in the air.

Harley grinned, and Liz laughed, then tugged her kid close.

"We'll probably see you tomorrow?" she said.

"Here's hoping," Harley said back.

As he turned to go, though, another worry occurred to him. What if Liz's fear wasn't limited to the man outside? What if it carried over into her home? Or worse. What if the hooded figure wasn't alone, and the danger as well as the fear carried over?

After a nanosecond of consideration, he decided he didn't care. Even though he'd only known the woman a short time—and in spite of the fact that her alliances in Whispering Woods were under his own scrutiny—he had an obligation to keep her safe.

Not just because it's her. *Because of the general protect-and-serve thing.*

He rolled his eyes inwardly at his own need for re-assurance, then started to turn back, a lie about hearing a knocking in the pipes springing to mind—*and where was* that *ten seconds ago?*—but Liz spoke first.

"Wait."

"Yes?"

"Your phone."

He frowned for a second before remembering his claim about dropping it somewhere in the hall. "Oh. Right."

It wasn't an invitation in, but at least it bought him another minute or two.

"Maybe that exhaustion is affecting your short-term memory," Liz teased.

"More than likely."

She gestured to the kid. "Come on, Teegs. Help Mr. Maxwell look for his phone."

The little girl executed a perfect eye roll. "Mom. It's a tiny hallway."

Harley stifled a laugh. "Yeah, but I'm old, so my eye-sight's bad. You know I wear glasses when I'm sculpting, right?"

"Yeah."

"So, I need your eagle eyes. Or I'll probably never find it."

"Fine."

Teegan made a big production of dropping to the ground and squinting at the carpet.

"Do you want me to describe it to you?" Harley asked, amused by her antics.

"I know what a *phone* looks like. Duh."

Liz sighed. "Sorry. I don't know where she gets the attitude from."

Harley swiped his hand over his mouth to cover his

smile. "She must be a future artist. We're all full of bad attitudes, aren't we?"

"I wish that particular bad attitude had been passed down from me to her," said the pretty brunette. "But sadly, this one has it in her head that she should do something science-y."

"That's not a word, Mom."

"Of course it's not."

"It actually makes you sound really *un*-science-y when you say it," Harley added.

"Ugh! You guys are—"

"The grown-ups?" Liz lifted an eyebrow at the kid, then smiled. "Or close enough, anyway."

"Guess that'll have to do." He paused, then prepared to drop the lie about the knocking in the pipes, but once again, she spoke first.

"Beef stew," she said.

He felt his brow furrow. "Uh?"

Liz laughed. "Sorry. Apparently, I'm terrible at inviting a man for dinner."

Relief—and true pleasure—rushed in, and he grinned. "Lucky for you, I'm very good at accepting poorly executed dinner invitations."

"I won't even make you clean up," she teased.

He cast a rueful look down. "Whoops."

He'd forgotten about the fact that he was wearing "work" clothes. In addition to providing him with a good excuse to stick close to Liz, Harley's cover story had also given him a chance to do something he hadn't done in far too long. Create a small amount of *actual* art. And he was enjoying it. As was evidenced by the mess on his T-shirt and jeans.

"I can get changed," he offered, hoping she'd say no.

Thankfully, she shook her head. "And miss the chance to have evidence of a *real* artist in my house? No way. Don't worry about your shoes, either. The only place we don't wear them is in the bedroom. Old carpet."

"Gotcha."

"*Now* can we go inside?" Teegan pleaded.

"Now we can," her mom agreed, then turned to Harley. "Unless you want to keep looking for the phone?"

He feigned a groan. "You know what? I just remembered that I stuck it in my back pocket."

"In your pocket?" said Teegan. "Isn't that where it usually goes?"

"Not for me, smarty-pants. I keep it in my coat. Which I'm not wearing, because someone insisted we hurry."

Liz laughed, seemingly unaware that the lost phone had been a ruse. "Okay, you two. I'm going inside. You can stay out here and fight, or you can come in with me."

"In!" said Teegan right away.

"Same," Harley agreed with a wink.

He tensed a little as Liz moved to stick her key in the door handle, but the click of the lock reassured him enough that he kept down an urge to push his way through first in the name of safety. The dimness inside was reassuring, too, as was the evident tidiness when Teegan reached up to turn on the light. All were signs that no one had broken in or left in a hurry.

Unless he's a very practiced stalker.

Harley gritted his teeth at his habitual detective brain. Liz didn't seem worried about letting her daughter barrel through into the apartment, and she was the one who'd seemed so scared outside. He knew he could take his cues from her. Whatever her affiliation with Garibaldi, he couldn't imagine—not for a second—that she'd put her daughter in harm's way.

Okay, Detective Maxwell, he said to himself, *time to stow away the mental badge and be a little more Harley-the-artist. At least until the beef stew is done.*

Chapter 3

As Liz lifted the last dish in the pile and started to scrub, a knot of worry made her stomach ache. It'd been surprisingly easy to bury the earlier frightening events. Between Harley's ease with small talk and Teegan's nonstop chatter, the intruder and his knife had fallen miraculously to the back of her mind. But dinner had gone by quickly, and now the dread of being alone crept up a little more with each passing second. Even dragging the meal out to include pie and ice cream hadn't slowed things down enough. In a few moments, the last drops of soapy water would be dry. The big dark-haired man—who'd taken a break from drying duty to read Teegan a noisy story in the other room—would probably yawn, thank her for dinner and be on his way. And while he might then be stationed directly across the hall, it wasn't the same as having him just a holler away.

So tell him what happened, urged a little voice in her head. *It might make him stay.*

But she shook off the thought. The thug in her shop had said it clear as day. Mentioning his strange and violent query about the painting would endanger her daughter. And until she had time to think it through, she didn't want to be reckless about a single thing. Liz needed to weigh her options. And she didn't need to involve an innocent bystander. She couldn't. Because she was sure that—like any reasonable person—Harley would want to call the police.

The little voice piped up again. *Because that's what makes sense.*

And under normal circumstances, that would be true. Crime equaled calling the cops.

But what would you tell them? That a man who didn't rob you expressed an aggressive interest in a painting while making vague threats?

Liz shook her head to herself. The breaking and entering was enough to warrant a police visit. Logically, she knew that. And if they took it seriously, it might earn her some round-the-clock protection. But the idea that it might backfire was enough to make her hesitate. What if they *didn't* take it seriously enough? What if they just took their notes and called it a night?

She thought she was probably better to sit on her hands for a bit. Keep Teegan out of sight. Maybe even ask the two part-time employees she had if they wanted to do some extra work, then head out of town for a couple of days. Pay a visit to some friends down in Freemont City. Whatever it took to convince herself that the shop below was safe.

You could call Garibaldi, instead.

That thought gave her pause. After all, the painting in question was his. And so was the building that housed her shop and her apartment. So, if something funky was up, he might want to know. And he certainly had more than his fair share of influence in the town, so if anyone could guarantee her and Teegan's safety…

Liz shook her head again. He was probably *too* entrenched in Whispering Woods politics to move subtly.

Frustration and fear battled in her head. She'd always been critical of the call-the-cops or don't-call-the-cops moment in movies. Involving the authorities seemed like a given. But now that she was in the thick of that exact moment, she understood. Just that tickle of doubt was enough to make her think twice. A move in either direction could result in disaster. Her stomach roiled at the thought of making the wrong decision.

Liz didn't realize how vigorously she was scrubbing the plate in her hands until Harley's teasing voice carried over her shoulder.

"Hey," he said. "Careful with that thing, or it might not make it to the cupboard in one piece."

His nearness wasn't quite enough to ease her tension, and she had to force a laugh. "Just being thorough."

"Thoroughness like that could clean the shellac right off." He stepped closer and grabbed the tea towel from the counter. "And besides that. I'm waiting."

"You're that excited to dry a dish?"

"To dry the *final* dish. Unless you want to keep washing it."

Liz stilled her hands, which had started to scrub again all on their own. "Okay. Maybe I'm going a *bit* overboard."

"Just a bit," he joked. "Now hand it over before I call Teegan for backup."

"Right. She's always so eager to help with the cleaning."

"You're underestimating my ability to bribe."

"Ah. Is that the trick, oh, ye of no kids?"

"Hey. I might not have kids, but I know what worked for *my* mom."

"Yeah, right. I bet you were a naturally well-behaved little boy."

"You think?" He tugged at a piece of his shaggy hair. "That's not the usual rep an artist like me goes for."

"I don't think there's much that's usual about you." As soon as she said it, she realized how it sounded, and she quickly added, "After all, you volunteered to both wash *and* dry."

He chuckled. "Okay. So I might've been a Goody Two-shoes. In the most masculine way possible, of course."

"Of course." ·

"But that doesn't mean I won't call that little angel of yours in here and offer her a pile of sugar in exchange for coercing you into giving me the plate."

With an exaggerated sigh, Liz dipped the dish to rinse it, then held it out. As Harley reached for the plate, though, Liz lost her grip, and it slipped from her hands and plummeted toward the tile. Knowing she wouldn't be quick enough to grab it before it hit, she braced herself for the shatter. But Harley moved like lightning. He bent low, shot out a hand and snagged the plate just before it hit the ground. And for some inexplicable reason, the slick move made Liz's throat constrict, and unexpected tears pricked at her eyes.

Maybe it was his easy grace. Or the fact that he was able to sweep in and avert a minor disaster while she decided before it even happened that there wasn't a damn thing she could do about it. It was a stupid analogy for the situation with the man who'd held her at knifepoint. But it fit, nevertheless. And as Harley stood, brandished the plate and grinned triumphantly at her, Liz thought she might actually cry. Something she hadn't let herself do in years. Something she didn't want to do now, if she could avoid it.

Harley picked up on it, too. Or some of it, anyway.

"Don't look so sad," he said to her. "I saved the plate."

Liz swallowed. "I know."

"So I'm gonna guess that something more than the plate is making you make that face." He gestured to the table. "You wanna sit?"

"I feel like *I* should be making that offer to *you*."

"We can both sit. I hid five bucks in Teegan's room and told her I'd double it if she found it in no less than ten minutes and no more than twenty."

In spite of the watery feel in her eyes, Liz laughed. "For real?"

"Yep. Figured you might want some recovery time." He pulled his phone from his pocket and set it down. "Even set a timer."

She eyed the countdown clock—it had just rounded the three-minute mark—and sank into the chair. "You're a magician."

"Superhero is what I was going for," he joked.

"Either way, I don't know what I would've done without you tonight." She blushed as soon as she said it, but it didn't seem to faze Harley.

"Probably the same thing you always do. Be an extraordinarily competent mom."

"Or a mom with one less plate, a pile of dishes and no time to rest her feet."

"Okay. I guess I *am* indispensable. I'm adding this to my résumé."

Liz laughed again, and the urge to tell him about her confrontation with the man in the shop reared up once more. He was just so easy to talk to. And it didn't help when Harley's hand slid across the table to clasp her own. Shots of warmth—both attraction and comfort—sparked up through her palm and arm, then settled in her chest. She lifted her gaze to meet Harley's, and she found him staring back, concern playing out through his brown eyes.

Harley gave Liz's hand a reassuring squeeze. He knew that from a professional perspective, he should probably pull away. Hand-holding with a person of interest wasn't exactly police protocol. From a human perspective, though, he was sure that the physical contact was what the pretty brunette needed.

And it's not exactly unenjoyable, either, is it?

He shoved aside the snarky question in favor of studying Liz's posture. It had become closed off, all of the relaxation that had built up over the course of the meal slipping away. Harley suspected that her earlier apparent fear had wormed its way back in. He also thought she might be fighting an internal battle. If she was on the edge of telling him the truth—or even a small piece of it—he didn't want to spoil it by breaking contact. In hopes of getting her to talk about whatever it was that had rattled her, Harley had deliberately bought them some one-on-one time by keeping Teegan occupied. What he needed to do now was to use it effectively. To get her to trust him and open up even more. If that meant some literal hand-holding, then so be it. So, instead of pulling away, he ran his thumb over the back of her hand.

"Hey." His voice came out a little huskier than he'd meant it to, and he had to clear his throat before adding, "My head might look thick, but I can tell something's bothering you."

Her eyes, which had been focused on their clasped

hands, flicked up to rove over his face. "Your head's not thick."

He feigned surprise. "It's not? Well. That's going to be a big shock to my brother. He's been telling people for *years* just how thick it is."

Liz laughed, her shoulders loosening visibly. "Let me guess. An *older* brother?"

Harley nodded, wondering if he should feel less comfortable with telling her a few true details about his life. But who was to say that Harley-the-artist and Harley-the-detective didn't have things in common?

"Not even two years between us," he told her. "Thinks he's pretty smart, though."

"Well, trust me. If he's calling you thickheaded, he's not the smart one." She blushed. "Sorry."

"What for? Complimenting me?"

"For insulting your brother."

He shrugged. "Don't worry. He can't hear you."

"I know," Liz said ruefully. "And that makes it worse. I'm talking behind his back, and I've never even met him."

"Feel free to send him an apologetic email. He likes that kind of thing."

She started to laugh, but the sound cut off as quickly as it had come. Her expression sobered, and she bit her lip, hesitation clear on her face.

"Harley?"

"Yes?"

"I—" She stopped, then pulled her hand away and shook her head.

Harley quashed a stab of regret at the loss of contact, flexed his fingers and made himself smile. "You what?"

"It's nothing."

"Nothing usually means something."

"Says who?" Her reply had a forced lightness to it, and Harley responded in kind.

"Every man since the dawn of time," he teased. "And just FYI, I have it on good authority that I'm an excellent secret-keeper. I mean, have I even *once* mentioned that secret stash of chocolate-chip cookies in Teegan's sock drawer?"

"She has a—" Liz groaned. "Ha ha. Very funny."

"Made you laugh, though, didn't it?"

"You realize that saying 'ha ha' doesn't count as a laugh, right?"

"No?"

She smiled. "Afraid not."

"Hmm," he replied. "I guess it's an imperfect talent. I'll keep working on it."

"On the other side of things…you're pretty good at the rest of this stuff."

"That's great." He leaned forward and, in a conspiratorial whisper, added, "But you're going to have to define 'this stuff.'"

Her smile widened. "Talking. Listening. Making me say 'ha ha' and generally distracting me."

"In that case, I'm happy to help. Even if I don't know what it is I'm distracting you *from*."

She opened her mouth, and Harley expected to hear another denial, but instead she let out a vague affirmation that sounded like a sigh. "Yes."

It's a step in the right direction, Harley thought to himself, while out loud he stated, "You know, not too long ago, some woman I know told me I'm a good listener."

She smiled. "Some woman, huh?"

"Mmm. You may have seen her around. Has a noisy kid. Owns an art shop. Pretty blue eyes." The last bit slipped out before Harley could stop it, but she blushed in response, and he was glad—just this once—that his mouth was working faster than his brain. "Anyway. This woman. She'd probably tell you it's okay to use me as a sounding board."

"This woman might be right, but she might not have the whole story."

"Try me."

Liz's mouth worked for a second, like she was trying to find a way around his words. "You know, Mr. Maxwell, I get the feeling that you could charm your way into anything."

It was Harley's turn to laugh. "Well, Ms. James, if my brother could hear *that*, he'd be even more shocked than if he heard you say I wasn't thickheaded."

"He doesn't think you're charming?"

"I'm pretty sure he thinks I'm still an awkward kid, doodling in a notebook."

It was a bit of an exaggeration. Harley knew that Brayden appreciated his talents, and also took advantage of them whenever needed. But he couldn't very well tell Liz that he'd morphed from doodler into detective, so he just offered a grin and let her doubtfully sweep her gaze over his chest and shoulders.

"You know what?" she said after a second. "I just can't picture it."

"What? My doodling?"

"You, being awkward."

"Perfect. I've got you fooled. My work here is done." He pretended to stand, and Liz's face abruptly crumpled.

Under other circumstances, her obvious distress at the thought of his leaving would've been a huge fan to his ego. Right then, it just deepened his concern. He dropped back into the chair and slid it closer to Liz, then reached out with the intention of putting his hands on her wrists and offering a word of comfort. Instead, she leaned into his chest, and his only choice was to either push her away or wrap his arms around her. He picked the latter without even thinking about it. As she clung to him without any sign of letting go, her body shook a little, and he knew she had to be crying.

Automatically, Harley's hands started to move in a soothing circle over her back. "It's all right. I'm not going anywhere."

When she answered, it was without pulling away, and her words were small and muffled. "I'm scared."

The statement tugged at him. "I can see that."

She held tightly for a few more seconds before finally easing back. Harley couldn't help but note that she didn't pull away fully—their knees still touched, and the tiniest move would propel her into his arms once more. He could also see the streak of tears down her face, enhanced by the transfer of clay from his shirt, and it took real effort to keep from reaching up to brush them away in a too-intimate gesture. In the end, she beat him to it. She lifted up her thumb to wipe at the damp spot she'd left on his clothes.

"Sorry about that." There was a mix of regret and frustration in the apology.

"Don't be sorry," he said back. "It's probably cleaner now than it was before. I should be thanking you."

"Thank the woman you barely know for literally crying onto your shoulder? That's gotta be a new one."

"I know you at least a little." He gave her knee a squeeze.

"Well enough to let me sob on you?"

"I know that you work hard, make a killer beef stew and care more than anything about your kid. I'd say that's all the prerequisites needed for sobbing."

"Ah. If that's the measure, then I guess I'm okay." Her hand came up to rest on the back of his, and she spread her fingers over his knuckles. "It's not even that I don't want to tell you what's upsetting me. I *can't*."

The feel of her skin moving over his was distracting. "Can't?"

"Sounds crazy, right? It *feels* crazy." Her hand slid up his arm, and he wondered if she was even aware that she was touching him.

He swallowed, trying to focus on their conversation. "It's only crazy if you believe that the *can't* comes as a result of someone casting a magic spell on you, preventing you from spilling your guts."

"I actually wish it were that straightforward. An evil spell would explain so much." The tips of her fingers had reached the crook of his elbow, and she looked down as if just noticing their placement, then started to jerk them away.

Harley reflexively brought up his hand to grab hers and stop it from slipping away. For a second, they sat still, both their gazes fixed on their locked palms. Then—also together—they lowered their hands to rest together on the table beside them.

"Can I ask you something, Harley?" Liz asked softly.

"Definitely," Harley agreed.

"If you thought—even for a second—that me telling you what I'm worried about might backfire and hurt Teegan, would you still want to know?"

He didn't even have to think about it. "No."

Liz's eyes lifted to his. "That was a pretty quick answer."

"What kind of man would I be if I thought endangering a kid was the way to go?"

"Not the kind I'd want to have over for dinner, I think."

Unconsciously, Harley inched forward. "It'd be terrible to have missed that beef stew."

Liz's free hand came up to the outside of his thigh. "And the dishwashing."

Their faces were inches apart now, and detective-Harley was urging artist-Harley to put some space between them. But artist-Harley was too interested in studying the little flecks of gray in Liz's otherwise blue eyes. They were tiny. Unnoticeable, until he'd gotten this close. Just like the floral scent he'd observed earlier. He inhaled and wondered what else he might've been missing by keeping a professional distance for the last ten days. The warmth of her lips, maybe?

No. Not maybe. Definitely.

He could definitely feel the heat of her mouth now.

His detective side was fighting a losing battle.

He leaned forward. So did Liz. Harley heard her breath catch and saw her lids drop just a heartbeat before his eyes closed, too. He bent in, anticipating the soft, sweet taste of her kiss.

And for a moment, he had it.

Delicate heat.

A burst of need.

A desire to deepen it.

Then, as quickly as it started, the kiss was ripped away by an explosive bang that rocked the room and sent Liz flying from her chair.

Chapter 4

Liz's ears rang. Her eyes watered and her leg felt like it was on fire. Her head spun. And the world around her seemed to be moving in slow motion.

Plates spinning and wobbling.

A spice rack in pieces, green and brown particles settling among the shards of glass.

But in spite of it all, the only thing Liz could think about was Teegan. Where was her daughter? Still in her room? Was she hurt?

Oh, God. Please don't let her be hurt.

Liz tried to stand, but the pain—seemingly everywhere now—made her stumble. She wanted to cry. Not from the way she hurt, but from the sudden certainty that under the circumstances, she might not be able to reach her daughter in time. She wouldn't be able to protect her from whatever threat had just rocked their little apartment.

Maybe if I crawl…

But she no sooner dragged herself forward an inch than dizziness struck. The room swam, and her arms slipped, and her head started to slide toward the ground. She braced for impact. Thankfully, before it could come, a warm, rough hand landed on her shoulder and pulled her back. It only took her a second to clue in.

Harley.

Relief surged through her as he lifted her from the ground. Something told her he'd know what to do. So she let herself exhale as he pressed her body to his wide chest and carried her from her spot on the ground across the room.

Then panic hit again.

Across the room. No. That was wrong.

"Teegan!" Her gasp sounded far away and water-logged.

His voice, on the other hand, was low and rumbly, and right in her ear. "On it already, sweetheart."

Liz breathed out, and the world seemed to speed up again as Harley put her down and grabbed a hold of the small kitchen table, tilting it on its side right in front of her.

"Stay there," he ordered, sounding far more in charge than Liz would've been able to manage. "I'll grab the kid. If someone comes in, play dead. I won't be more than a heartbeat away."

Liz nodded her understanding. Partly because she couldn't form any words, and partly because Harley darted away so quickly that she wouldn't have had time anyway.

Play dead.

The only reason the frightening possibility didn't render her completely useless was that her mind was preoccupied with her daughter. She needed to hold on to some semblance of sanity. But it felt like a lifetime was passing as she waited. *Had* passed already. Liz knew that in reality it'd only been a minute. Maybe less. The proof was in Harley's phone. The black device had flown off the table, and it now sat on the floor, propped against the bottom of the stove. She could see that there was still almost a minute left on the countdown, and the pre-bang conversation had to have lasted for at least fifteen minutes.

But knowing just how short a time had actually passed did nothing to ease Liz's sense of urgency. She itched to get up and make her way toward the hall that led to Teegan's bedroom, and fixing her gaze on the doorway instead seemed like a shoddy substitute for action.

Please hurry.

She had to trust that Harley would be successful in retrieving her. He was stronger than she was. Obviously not as scared.

But he's not her mother.

The thought spurred her to try to push up from the ground, but pain shot up her leg once again. And a glance down told her why. An inch-long gash in her jeans glared up at her. Crimson liquid oozing out a slash in the denim. It looked bad. Maybe not deadly, but definitely stitch-worthy.

Wincing at the way it hurt, she reached across the floor and grabbed a wayward tea towel. She balled up the fabric and shoved it into the cut in her jeans to stanch the flow of blood. Thankfully, the bit of counterpressure offered a small amount of pain relief, too. She breathed out and gripped the edge of the table.

"Liz."

At the sound of her name, she dragged her gaze up, and her whole body sagged with relief. Harley stood at the edge of the room, one hand grasping Teegan's and the other holding her favorite purple backpack. Liz's throat constricted. Her daughter looked tiny beside the big man. An odd mix of safe and vulnerable at the same time.

Liz very nearly wanted to weep. And when Teegan disentangled herself from Harley's grip and launched herself across the room and into her arms, a few unstoppable tears managed to squeeze through. But not many. Harley was quick to remind her that she didn't have time to give in to the strong emotion.

"We need to move," he said. "If whatever that bang was started a fire, we only have minutes to get out."

"Right. Okay."

She gave her daughter a squeeze, then let her go, and braced herself for the pain of standing up. Sure enough, the fire bit into her thigh. But she refused to give in. She held her leg stiffly and raised her eyes to meet Harley's gaze.

"What're we waiting for?"

His stare dropped down. "You're hurt."

"I'm fine," she lied.

"You sure?"

"Yes. It's just a cut."

"So prove it."

"What?"

"Prove you're fine. Walk from there to here."

"I—" She bit her lip.

"That's what I thought," he said.

He stepped forward, and she prepared for him to offer an arm. She bit her lip and pushed her pride aside. She'd lean on Harley—literally—if that meant getting her daughter to safety. She turned her face toward him to admit she'd need assistance. But she didn't have to say it. Harley was already at her side, already bending down to scoop her up from the ground like she weighed nothing. It felt embarrassingly good to be cradled against his broad chest.

"You don't have to carry me," Liz protested, wiggling a little.

"I don't have to," Harley agreed. "But in the interest of expediency…"

"What's expediency?" Teegan piped up.

"Getting somewhere faster than a snail can," Harley replied easily.

"I think you should let him carry you, Mom," Teegan said.

"Two against one," he added.

"All right," he said, directing his words down to Teegan in a far more enthusiastic tone than Liz would've been able to manage. "Our mission is to get out. It might not be easy, but I have faith we can do it. What about you?"

Teegan nodded. "Me, too."

"Okay. You have to carry the bag, take the rear flank and protect us from back there. Oh. And hold on to the bottom of my shirt so you don't get left behind," Harley instructed.

"Got it!" Liz's daughter agreed, her small hand coming out to clutch tightly to the dark-haired man's clay-covered T-shirt.

But they only made it as far as opening the door a crack.

Acrid smoke was creeping up from the bottom of the stairs, blocking the escape route.

Harley stepped back into the apartment quickly, Teegan still clutching his shirt and Liz still held firmly against his chest.

He silently cursed the fact that he'd let his guard down

long enough to *not* predict that something was about to happen. He'd known something was wrong. He was sure it had something to do with both the hooded man and Jesse Garibaldi. It was the whole reason he'd been so eager to stay for dinner. Yet he hadn't pursued it. Hadn't pushed Liz to tell him what she knew, when he knew perfectly well that was exactly what he should've done.

But you had time to kiss her.

He growled silently at himself for his weakness.

Even now, as he carried Liz up the hall and toward the kitchen, her ample curves fit against him in the most distracting way possible. That hint of floral perfume swirled up and filled his nose, making him want to draw in a deep breath after deep breath. The way he held her meant the soft skin on the inside of her arm stayed pressed firmly to the back of his hand.

It was both a relief and a regret to set her down.

It made him irritated at himself. Not because it took away from his ability to do his job—though maybe that should've been more of a factor than it was—but because it hampered him in keeping Teegan and Liz safe. He'd let down his guard, and now they were in danger.

They were just lucky that whoever set off the explosion hadn't come upstairs first.

Or maybe luck has nothing to do with it. Maybe the culprits just didn't care what happened after.

After all, he knew from experience that Garibaldi had a thing for using pipe bombs to cover his tracks. It was what had started this whole quest for justice to start out with. What killed his father.

"Harley?"

Liz's small, worried voice drew him back to the moment and reminded him that he didn't have time for heavy musings.

"What do we do?" she asked.

"We come up with a plan B," he said. "Find another way out."

Five minutes had gone by already. Any second, the fire could make its way up. It was a little surprising that heat and smoke hadn't already permeated the apartment, really.

He needed to think. Fast.

Teegan tugged on his shirt, and he turned his attention her way, trying his damnedest to stay patient. The kid had a solemn expression on her face, and her finger extended toward the hall.

"What's up, monkey?" Harley asked.

Her little blond head swiveled toward her mom, then back to Harley. "Promise not to get mad?"

"I won't get mad," he assured her.

"Not you," said Teegan. "Mom."

Harley flicked a raised-brow look toward Liz, who shook her head.

"I won't get mad," she said. "But just be warned that the last time she asked for that promise, she'd cut all of her socks into dresses for her dolls."

"We'll take our chances." Harley smiled at Teegan. "Tell us."

"You know the big tree outside?" the kid replied, still nervous. "The one I climb all the time?"

"Sure do," said Harley. "Heritage oak."

Teegan's confession came out in a rush. "It has a big branch that goes all the way to my mom's window. And I climbed up. And there's a flower-thing under the window. But I *stood* on the flower-thing, and I could see into the window, so I think you could get out that way, too." She paused. "Are you mad?"

"Not right now," Liz said. "But I can't promise I won't

be grounding you later. Do *not* climb up that high. Ever again."

"Ever again *after* we've climbed down today," Harley amended. "Show us."

"Okay."

Helping Liz up and supporting her as they moved, Harley followed the girl down the hall to the bedroom. Once inside, he helped Liz to the edge of the bed, then stepped over to examine the potential escape route. Teegan stood close beside him, pointing at the places she'd described just a few moments earlier.

Harley nodded his appreciation. He could see the potential. It might not be the easiest thing for Liz with her injury, but it beat the alternative of fighting through smoke and flames.

He reached out, unlatched the lock on the window, carefully removed the screen and surveyed what he could see of the outside. The thick branches blocked a large portion of the view, but a glance down and to the side made him frown. He could just see the back end of what appeared to be a white panel van. If he had to guess, he'd say it was just about lined up perfectly with the rear door of Liz's Lovely Things.

And there's no smoke.

He leaned out to get a better look, pretending to examine the stability of the tree's branches. He still saw nothing.

What did it mean? And what was the vehicle doing there? Harley knew for a fact that Liz didn't accept after-hours deliveries. He felt sure that if she'd made an exception for this particular evening, it would've come up in conversation.

Hell. She let me know last week when she ordered a pizza because she worried about the door startling me.

He stared out the window, frowning even harder. Even if someone *was* at the store for a legitimate reason, why would they be going in instead of out?

The bottom line was that he *couldn't* reason through all of it. And that was saying something. His powers of deduction weren't exactly subpar.

Unless there is *no fire.*

The thought made no sense. Except it also made perfect sense.

"Is everything okay?" Liz asked.

He pulled himself back into the room and decided to go with the most obvious observation. "We can't climb down."

"We can't?" she replied, pushing to her feet a little unsteadily. "Why?"

He looked from her to Teegan, then opted for the truth. "There's someone—maybe more than one someone—down there."

"A bad guy?" Teegan asked.

"Well, hopefully not. But I'm not sure we can chance it."

Teegan sucked in her lower lip in a thoughtful way that made her look an awful lot like her mother, then shrugged a little. "We could go up instead."

"Up?" Harley repeated.

"To the roof," she told him, like it was the most obvious thing in the world.

"Have you climbed to the roof before?" Liz's voice was full of worry.

Blond curls bounced a negative. "No. Well. Not on the tree. But a bit up the ladder on the other side. Not *all* the way, though. But there's some awesome branches there. I don't think any bad guys could see us 'cause of the leaves. And the tree's really strong."

"Could that work?" Liz asked.

Harley took another look outside. He could see that a few bigger branches curved together overhead, forming a U-shaped bowl that stopped just a few feet from the roof.

"I think it could," he confirmed.

"Think?" Liz repeated.

He started to amend "think" to a much firmer "know," but before he could get the words out, a thump and a rattle from out in the apartment told him time had run out, and not in the form of fire.

Someone was breaking in.

Liz's heart thumped so hard that it hurt. Her gaze flicked around, rapid fire. Teegan. The bedroom door. Harley. Teegan again. But in spite of the rapid movement of both eyes and her pulse, her feet seemed glued to the spot.

She urged herself to move, wondering when she'd become so good at being a damsel in distress.

Maybe since something exploded in your store a few minutes ago?

She shook the sarcasm and the inaction off, stepping toward her daughter. Harley was moving, too, with surprising stealth for a man of his size. He strode smoothly to the door, closed it with no more than a whisper of a sound, then turned to Liz. He put his index finger to his lips, shook his head once and gestured to the window. Liz nodded her understanding. She took a breath and started to lift Teegan. But she'd forgotten about her leg. The tiny bit of pressure made her bite down so hard to keep from crying out that she tasted blood.

Harley was there in an instant. He scooped Teegan up, carried her to the window and placed her on the sill.

Liz's throat closed a little as she watched her daughter step out. But another noise out in the main area of her apartment, followed by what sounded like a muffled voice, made her sure it was better than the alternative. Harley was already back by her side, anyway. He slid his hand—warm, big and reassuringly solid—to her waist and helped her limp over to the window, then through it.

As she stepped into the cool air, she took a shaky breath, her eyes fixed on the spot where she stepped. A small modicum of relief hit her. The platform below—the "flower-thing," as Teegan had called it—was actually a two-foot wide ledge. Maybe it *was* designed to hold window boxes, but it was definitely not some flimsy little jut. She lifted her gaze and sought her daughter. Teegan stood to the side, her pose relaxed. Like standing on the side of a two-story building was the most normal thing in the world. She even smiled enthusiastically and offered a little wave as she caught sight of Liz. The height clearly didn't bother her tree-climbing daughter.

Liz breathed out, closed the gap between her and Teegan, then swiveled her attention back to the window. Harley was making his way out now, too. He paused to get his footing and set Teegan's backpack down on the ledge, then reached into the house. For a second, Liz was puzzled. Then she saw the screen in his hands. Carefully, he lifted it up and positioned it in the frame. There was a slight click as it found its place, and not a breath later, the sound of the bedroom door opening.

Harley spun. He stepped closer, then pushed himself flush against the brick exterior of the building. Liz followed suit, grasping her daughter's hand to encourage her to do the same. She no sooner had Teegan's palm pressed into her own than she felt Harley reach for her on the other side. His fingers threaded between hers and squeezed.

A near-hysterical laugh bubbled just under the surface

as Liz imagined what the neighbors would think if they spotted them up there. But the laugh died before it ever made its way out. Two men's voices came from inside the bedroom, close enough that it was easy to distinguish between the two. And the conversation made Liz shiver.

"Looks like the whole place is clear," said the first man. Then he paused and added, "Where the hell did they go, though? Awfully late to be out running around on a school night."

The second man was dismissive. "Who knows? Maybe they ran out of milk. Maybe the lady had a hot date and dropped the daughter with a sitter. I can't pretend to know a damn thing about what it means to have a kid. Nor do I want to."

The first man chuckled. "Amen to that."

There was another pause, followed by the sound of feet crossing the floor, and the first man spoke again.

"Window's open," he said.

His words were so loud that they might as well have been spoken in Liz's ear. She had a sudden feeling that if she turned her head and leaned forward to see around Harley, she'd be able to *see* the speaker. Which meant that if *he* turned, he'd be able to see them, too. Her hand tightened on Harley's, and his thumb stroked soothingly over her knuckles. She willed herself to stay calm. Prayed for Teegan's continued silence. And was utterly thankful for Harley's presence.

"It's a nice night," said the second man after a moment, his voice just as clear but less suspicious. "Probably wanted the fresh air."

"Wanted the fresh air, but went out?" There was more than a hint of doubt in the question.

"C'mon, man. She probably just forgot to close it."

"I dunno. What if she smelled the smoke and was trying to get away?"

"You think a woman smelled smoke, took her kid out a second-story window, put the screen on, then *didn't* call the cops about the smoke?"

The first man let out a rough guffaw. "Okay. When you put it like that, I just sound— Hey. What the hell is that?"

"What?" said the second man.

Liz tensed.

"There's a *car* down there." The first man sounded worried.

"A car?" repeated the second. "Where?"

"Right through the tree. A white— Dammit. That's not a car. It's a van. Someone's in the store."

The second man dropped a responding string of curses that made Liz cringe on behalf of her daughter. But her concern only lasted for a few moments before relief took over. Because judging by the quick, heavy footfalls, the two men were leaving at a run. When she couldn't hear them anymore, she pulled Teegan in for a sideways hug and sagged against the wall, tears threatening.

Chapter 5

Harley could tell Liz was nearing a breaking point. He couldn't blame her. In his four years as a detective with the Freemont PD, he'd rarely experienced such a high-octane series of events.

And going through it is one thing. Going through it while trying to keep your daughter safe...

Harley suspected it'd put him near the edge, too. And it wasn't over yet.

He gave her hand another squeeze and spoke in a low, gentle voice. "C'mon, ladies. Just a bit farther to go, and we can find somewhere to regroup."

Liz's blue eyes—shiny with unshed tears—found him and held him. "Regroup?"

Harley let his gaze tip Teegan's way for a brief second. She was a hell of a kid. Taking the frightening situation in stride. That didn't mean Harley wanted to expose her to anything more frightening than he had to. Announcing that he was pretty sure their lives were in direct danger didn't seem prudent.

"For lack of a better word," he added with false lightness.

Liz swallowed then nodded, seeming to understand. "Okay. Regroup it is."

Harley tipped a smile toward Teegan. "Your turn first, monkey princess."

The kid didn't hesitate at all. She scampered out quickly to the nearest tree branch, moving so fast that she might as well have been a monkey for real. In seconds, she'd clambered up and was waiting in the foliage nearest to the roof. Mildly amused, Harley shook his head, then gave her mom a nudge.

"All right, monkey *queen*," he said. "Think you're going to be able to manage?"

Liz looked up at Teegan before answering. "I guess I don't have much of a choice."

"Not so much. But I'm here if you need a hand. Just take it slow and hang on tight."

She turned her eyes his way again, then surprised him by lifting up to her toes to place a quick kiss on his cheek. When she pulled back, she placed her fingers on the spot where her lips had touched, and a pretty blush colored her face.

"Thank you," she said with feeling.

Harley smiled. "S'what I'm here for."

She smiled back—brief and nervous—then took a breath. "All right. Here goes nothing."

Harley watched her follow the same route as her daughter, assessing her movements. They weren't smooth, and she was favoring her uninjured leg a little, but other than that, her agility seemed reasonable. Satisfied that she wouldn't tumble out of the tree, he let out a relieved sigh, slung Teegan's bag over his shoulder and followed them up.

He was glad to see that the kid's assessment was right.

The thickness of the leaves provided ample coverage from prying eyes, the width of the branches provided more than enough stability, and the edge of the roof was just overhead. Eye-level for Liz, and just above shoulder-level for him.

He didn't waste any time.

"I'll boost you up first," he said to Liz. "Then I'll lift Teegan up, too, so you can pull her from the top."

"And then what?" she replied. "You'll just climb up on your own, superhero-style?"

"That's what I do best."

"I'm starting to think so."

He smiled, crouched down a bit and threaded his fingers together. "I'm ready when you are."

Liz took another breath—her signature stabilizer, Harley was starting to think—then stepped onto his hands. He lifted up while she gripped the roof. Between his pushing and her pulling, the top half of Liz's body quickly disappeared over the top. Her legs hung free for a moment, then followed the rest of her. There was a thump. Then nothing. Worried, Harley started to call out, but a heartbeat before her name left his lips, she popped up again.

"Sorry," she breathed. "There's a three-foot drop on the other side."

"You okay?" Harley asked.

"Yes. Just startled. Send Teegs up." Her arms stretched down expectantly.

Harley turned to the kid. "Acrobat time."

She gave him the thumbs-up, and he reached down to grab her by the waist. He lifted her to his shoulders, where she sat just long enough to grip his hair, then pulled herself to a standing position. Harley brought his hands to her calves to steady her, but only a moment went by before her weight lifted. He adjusted his hold to help propel her up, then stepped back, ready to catch her if things went wrong. Thankfully, she made it up and over without so much as a sound.

Harley cast a quick look down, then grabbed the ledge himself. With a grunt, he flattened one elbow along the width of it, then the other. When he felt stable enough, he hoisted his body up so that his weight rested on his palms. He winked at Teegan—who stood staring at him with her hands on her hips and her mouth open—closed his eyes, then tucked and rolled onto the gravel-topped roof.

"Not bad, right?" he said as he finished in a seated position.

His attempt at levity only lasted for a second. From his low position, he had a perfect view of Liz's thigh, and it didn't look good. The towel she'd used to cover up the wound had come loose. The denim around the cut was a jagged mess, and thick blood oozed around it, making Harley wonder just how the hell she'd managed to make it as far as she had.

He opened his mouth to say as much, but Teegan beat him to the punch. She stepped closer and bent down, her little face puckered with worry.

"Mom!" she exclaimed. "That's a *really* bad cut! Worse than the time I fell off my bike!"

Liz hastily adjusted the cloth. "It's fine."

"That's what you said before," said Harley.

"No."

"No?"

"I said *I* was fine."

"Right. Such a remarkable distinction," Harley said dryly. "Let me take a look."

Liz was quick to shake her head. "We don't have time. We're way past the five minutes of leeway you said we had."

"That was when I thought the shop might be on fire."

"You don't think so anymore?"

He shook his head and quickly recounted the observations he'd made as he'd looked out the bedroom window, finishing with, "And I have a hard time believing that our two friends back there would have been *able* to make it upstairs, let alone be willing. So we've got time to make sure you're seaworthy."

"Seaworthy?" Teegan repeated.

"That's right. Shipshape. In good working order. Not falling apart at the seams like an old ugly shirt. So shove over a bit, monkey. I wanna take a look."

The kid giggled, then moved aside for Harley to get in and take a closer look. Gingerly, he pulled the cloth free from the wound. It was a mucky mess. Bits of dirt and gravel from the roof caked its sides.

"Hey, monkey?" he called.

"Yep!" she replied.

"Pass me your bag."

She handed it over, and he pulled the partially full water bottle from the side pouch. Probably not the cleanest, but better than nothing.

"Hold your mom's hand, Teegan," he suggested.

The kid was there in a flash, her little fingers intertwining with Liz's long, slim ones.

"Hang on tight," Harley said, then poured a bit of the water over the cut.

Liz drew in a hissed breath, but didn't complain. Harley felt her leg tense under his fingers, too, as he dabbed the edges of the wound with the cloth. Once the gash was exposed, he could see that it was long but not terribly deep. Whatever had done the damage had been—thank God—buffered by the denim. But it was still serious enough that Harley knew it needed more than a Band-Aid.

He dragged open the backpack's zipper and rifled through, searching for something that could act as a temporary fix. His fingers closed on something soft and stretchy, and he yanked it out, then held it up for Teegan to see.

"How attached to this headband are you?" he asked.

She shrugged. "It's old."

"Good. Because it's about to be repurposed."

"You can use the T-shirt I put in the front pocket, too."

He smiled. "That'll be way better than the dirty cloth. Thanks, kiddo."

He got to work. First, he finished with the cleanup of the wound. Next, he folded the T-shirt in question into a small, tidy square. After that, he positioned the fabric gently over the cut and asked Liz to hold it in place. Lastly, he lifted her foot from the ground and slid the headband all the way up to cover the fresh bandage job.

"Fits just right," he said, and he leaned back, satisfied with his handiwork.

"Does it feel better, Mommy?" Teegan asked in a small, worried voice.

Liz let out a breath. "Much. Mr. Maxwell must be a doctor as well as an artist."

Harley shook his head. "Nah. I'm just clumsy. Had to learn how to patch myself up. Now you get to reap the benefits."

"Were you in the army?" Teegan asked suddenly.

The question startled Harley. "The army? No. Why do you ask?"

Liz supplied the answer. "Her dad was training to be a combat medic."

It was the first time either of them had brought up the other side of Teegan's parentage, and Harley sensed that he should tread lightly.

But the kid wasn't interested in being delicate; she jumped right in, full disclosure. "He died before I was born."

Harley lifted his gaze to meet Liz's eyes. "I'm sorry to hear that."

"It was a training accident," she told him. "A one-in-a-million piece of bad luck."

"You must've been young," Harley replied.

"Duh!" Teegan interjected. "I said I wasn't born y—" She cut herself off as Harley and Liz both laughed. "Oh. You meant *Mom*."

"I did," Harley confirmed. "But I bet you weren't any bigger than a button, either."

"Mom was a *teenager*," the kid told him.

Liz sighed. "I was *eighteen*. I'd just graduated high school, and I met Jason through a friend's brother."

"In Missouri," Teegan added.

"That's right," Liz said with a smile. "Jason had just completed basic training and managed to get lucky and have a two-week break before he went to Texas to start up the medic portion. We met at a party and spent the next fourteen days glued together. I was heartbroken when he left, but we wrote letters back and forth like nobody's business."

"The old kind of letters," the kid interjected. "Not the email kind."

"Right," Liz agreed. "The old kind. Anyway, I found out I was pregnant with this munchkin after Jason had been in Texas for about a month. He wanted to get married. For me to fly to him right that second. I refused. I didn't think we should rush into anything we might regret. I wanted some time."

"But you moved in with Grams and Pop-Pop," Teegan stated.

Liz nodded. "Yep. That's Jason's parents. I was on my own already, then. Lost my mom to cancer when I was a kid, and my dad faded away after that. He passed the week I finished my senior year. So Grams and Pop-Pop kind of forcibly took me—took *us*—in. Jason was killed a month later. As crazy as it sounds, I didn't even see him again. But we stayed on with Grams and Pop-Pop right until we moved here. It was hard to leave. But it was time."

"Grams and Pop-Pop sold their house and went on a *really* long vacation," said Teegan. "Without us."

"Because they *deserve* a really long vacation without us," Liz replied with a smile.

Harley looked from her to her kid. It was a hell of a story. A hell of a life.

An admirable one.

"You do it well," he said.

Liz's brows knit together. "Do what well?"

"Life."

Her mouth twitched in a smile. "That's pretty specific."

Harley shrugged. "All of it. Run a business. Take care of your kid. Make it seem like it's easy, even when I know it must be anything but."

She laughed. "Right. Except for the part where I'm stuck on the roof of that business with the kid in tow."

Harley blinked.

Somehow, in spite of the fact that they'd just been running for their lives, it felt…*normal* to be sitting under the stars on top of the roof with the pretty brunette and her daughter. As he pushed to his feet and offered her his hand, he spoke again, his voice a little rougher than he'd expected it to be. "Like I said…you make it easy."

Liz let Harley help her stand, his last statement rolling through her head.

You make it easy.

It was different than the first time he'd said it.

You make it look *easy.*

The distinction was small. Probably just the verbal equivalent of a typo. But it stuck out. It warmed her, even though it was just semantics. Just like holding his hand right then—probably a few seconds longer than was necessary to gain stability—made it easy for her to feel safe and secure, even though she was sure they were anything but.

What would've happened if he hadn't been here? she wondered, as they made their way toward the ladder that jutted out on the other side of the building.

The thought gave her a chill. She didn't even want to consider the possibilities. She somehow doubted that the two men who'd broken into her apartment had had good intentions. And they weren't even the only ones to worry about. Who had the van below belonged to, if not them? Not having an answer made her shiver.

They paused at the ladder, and Harley opened his mouth like he was going to issue some instructions. Liz cut him off.

"There was a painting," she blurted.

Puzzlement clouded her neighbor's features. "What?"

"In the shop. I noticed it a few minutes before I closed the store up."

"One that wasn't supposed to be there?" he asked.

She shook her head. "One that's for sale. It's done by a local artist. I touched it. Don't ask why. I wouldn't normally put my fingers anywhere near a canvas like that. But I did. And it felt weird."

"Felt weird how?"

"I don't know if I can describe it."

She closed her eyes for a second, remembering. But instead of the strange texture of the painting filling her mind, it was that hooded man's voice that dominated. His casual threat on her life. On Teegan's. The warning of what would happen if she told anyone.

Liz's eyes flew open, her heart thundering. Her gaze landed on her daughter. She hadn't forgotten the frightening warning. Not exactly. But Harley *made it easy*, too.

Easy to think it'd be okay to tell him what had happened.

Easy to assume he'd somehow take care of it.

And easy to forget that it wasn't really his problem.

Guilt wormed through her gut. In the last half hour— even more than that, if she counted dinner and dishes and his games with Teegan—Harley had done more than he had to for her little two-person family. Probably more than anyone else would've. And while there was nothing Liz wouldn't do to protect her daughter, she knew she shouldn't add any more danger to the brown-haired artist's life if she could avoid it.

"Liz?" Harley prompted gently.

"It's nothing," she lied quickly.

He frowned like he knew perfectly well she wasn't telling the truth. But he let it go anyway. Sort of.

"All right," he said. "Weird-feeling painting. Noted. But not terribly important."

Liz's face warmed. "Right."

He nodded once. "Okay, then. Here's the plan. I'm

going to climb down first to make sure it's all clear. You're going to wait until I'm safely at the bottom before sending Teegan after me. Once I have her, you'll follow. Make sense?"

Feeling even guiltier—both at his willingness to go first and take on the risk, and at the fact that he hadn't called her out on her lie—Liz nodded her agreement. Harley reached out to give her shoulder a squeeze, ruffled Teegan's hair, then stepped onto the first rung.

Liz's heart jumped into her throat as she watched him disappear over the edge. She had to force herself to step close enough to watch him make the descent, and she didn't breathe easy until he was all the way at the bottom, giving her the thumbs-up.

She turned to her daughter and tried to keep the concern from her voice. "All right, you. Mr. Maxwell is waiting."

Her daughter shifted from foot to foot. "Mom?"

"Yes, sweetie?"

"You like him, right?"

Taken slightly aback by the direct question—though maybe it shouldn't have surprised her, considering that her daughter was both intuitive and forthright about 100 percent of the time—Liz played dumb. "Who? Mr. Maxwell?"

Teegan offered up her best eight-year-old eye roll. "Yeah."

"Yes, I like him. He's kind and helpful. Especially right now."

"And handsome?"

Liz returned her daughter's eye roll. "Yes."

"So was it okay that I told him about Dad?"

"Absolutely. It's always okay to talk about your dad." Liz reached out and pulled Teegan in for a quick hug.

"Now, you'd better hurry down before Mr. Maxwell thinks we've changed our minds. And be careful."

"I will!"

She watched her daughter easily navigate the ladder. She waited until she was at the bottom, then climbed on to follow her down. She was far slower and more awkward because she had to take the rungs one at a time, but she was actually happy about it. She had an extra minute to think about the question Teegan had just asked.

It was true that Liz never shied away from discussing Jason. Thinking about his death made her sad. Often indescribably. Even though she'd literally had only two weeks with him, and had never had the chance to really get to know him, the seven years she'd spent living with his parents had been enough to give her a good feel for the kind of man he would've been. Caring and dedicated. A little hot under the collar, but quick to apologize when he was wrong. Great sense of humor. He would've loved his daughter, no doubt about it.

She hated that Jason never got a chance to meet her. For both his sake and for Teegan's sake. But she suspected the sorrow she felt for what *might've been* didn't measure up to the heartbreaking loss that his mom and dad had experienced. She was glad that she'd been able to give them back a small piece of their son through their granddaughter. And she had often wondered over the years if the whole reason she'd met Jason in the first place was to do just that. Hoped it, even.

Would Harley want to know that?

The thought caught her so off guard that her grip on the ladder rung slipped just enough that she gasped. But an increasingly familiar set of warm hands landed on her hips then, steadying her and letting her know she was nearly at the bottom.

"Almost there, honey," Harley said. "Your leg doing okay?"

"Not too bad," she replied.

It was true; the pressure from the T-shirt and head-band bandage had eased some of the ache. But the truth of that reminded her of the lie she'd told just minutes earlier. Her feet paused automatically.

"One more step," Harley said.

"C'mon, Mom!" Teegan added.

Liz shook off the renewed guilt and dropped to the ground, realizing a little belatedly the big man's hands were still on her. She bumped backward, straight into his chest.

His strong arms wrapped around her. His masculine scent filled her nose. And before she could stop it, the memory of his warm lips consumed her mind, nearly drawing a gasp from her throat. For a second, she thought she might actually spin around and steal another kiss. She was pretty sure she *would* have done it, if not for the fact that her daughter stood just a couple of feet away.

As it was, she felt compelled to turn slowly and steal a glance instead of a kiss. Second prize.

But not all that bad.

His brown eyes were nonjudgmental. They were also as warm as his hands. As warm as she remembered his lips to be. It made her tingle from the tips of her toes to the top of her head. When his fingers finally did drop away from her body, a stab of regret tugged at her. And as he bent to say something that made Teegan smile, Liz suddenly suspected something.

Harley wasn't just brushing off her deception. He wasn't ignoring it or bothered by it. He was purposely giving her space. Letting her choose what she told him, even if it meant not knowing something that could help their situation.

And maybe that realization should've made her feel even guiltier. But it didn't. Instead, it renewed the tingle she'd felt moments earlier. Only this time, it wasn't from her toes to her head. It was in her chest. Expanding outward like a firework.

Chapter 6

As Harley stood up and caught the look in Liz's eyes, he had to push down a sudden urge to drag her in for a deep kiss.

Sudden? Really? You've been wanting to do it this whole time. He started to argue with the voice in his head, but had to acknowledge that it was true. *Okay. Fair enough.*

Every time they paused in their escape, every time he touched her, he thought at least a little about finding a way to sneak in another kiss. But there was something a little different in the way she looked at him now. He wasn't sure what it was, only that it was there.

He told himself now wasn't the time and cleared his throat. "I was just telling Teegan that this situation calls for the grown-up version of hide-and-seek. And that we need the ultimate hiding place. She said something about Miss Wilma?"

Liz nodded. "Miss Wilma's a funny little old retiree who lives at the end of the street in a side suite. She's always joking that she wakes up at about the same time Teegan goes to bed."

"She's nocturnal," the girl added. "Like a raccoon."

"She's definitely a night owl," Liz agreed.

"Think she'd welcome a couple of evening guests?" Harley asked.

"Probably," replied Liz.

Harley's mind worked quickly to come up with a plan. "We'll sneak over there and give her a good excuse. That you thought you smelled a gas leak, so woke up Teegan, then came to get me. You knew Miss Wilma was usually up late, so you thought she might let you wait at her place while I went and checked out the issue."

Liz sucked in an audible breath. "Wait. *What?*"

Harley winced, thinking that he probably should've eased into the last bit. "I have to go back in."

"We just spent the last twenty minutes working to get *out*. Why would you turn around and put yourself in danger?"

"Liz."

"No."

He eyed Teegan. Once again, he didn't want to worry the kid any more than was necessary. But there was no way around investigating what was going on in Liz's Lovely Things. It was Harley's job. His whole purpose in being in Whispering Woods in the first place.

But you can't tell her that.

So, in the end, he settled for a cop-out response. "We can talk about it once we're at Miss Wilma's."

Liz stiffened, then grabbed Teegan's hand. "We're ready when you are."

Harley nodded. He felt like a little line had just been

drawn. It was right between the two of them and him, and it stung more than it should have. Maybe it was unconscious—probably, since she hardly seemed like the type to be petty—but he could still feel it. And it didn't ease any as he slowly and carefully led them from their position below the ladder to Miss Wilma's at the end of the block.

By the time they'd finished their short well-hidden journey, the pressure of that imaginary line made Harley's teeth grit together so hard that his jaw ached a little. He could barely get through the explanation to Miss Wilma—who was more than happy to take them in and offered biscuits and tea—before he came up with an excuse to speak to Liz in private.

"You have a first-aid kit in your bathroom, Miss Wilma?" he asked. "Liz snagged herself on a nail on the way out of her apartment, and I think my first attempt at patching her up is questionable."

The wizened woman glanced down at Liz's leg, and her eyes widened. "Goodness. That's a doozy. There's a kit in the bathroom. I can grab it for you."

Harley waved off the offer. "No need. I'll take Liz straight to the source."

"All right," said the old woman. "The munchkin and I will entertain ourselves out here for a couple of minutes, won't we, baby girl?"

Teegan nodded eagerly. "Checkers?"

"I'll see what I can come up with."

Harley slid a hand to Liz's elbow and guided her up the hall. Once they were in the bathroom, as seemed to be her habit, she spoke first.

"I get it," she stated immediately.

"You do?" The surprised reply came out before he could stop it.

She nodded. "You're a little too good at this."

He raised a silent eyebrow, then reached around her to open the medicine cabinet. She stepped to the side, then sank down onto the closed toilet. He could feel her eyes on him as he dragged out the labeled first aid and started rummaging around inside for the things he needed.

One tube of topical anesthetic and another of antiseptic.

A pair of scissors.

A long, narrow strip of surgical tape and a compression bandage.

And a bottle of painkillers, which he opened right away to dump a couple of pills into his palm.

"Harley?" she prodded as she took the medication from his hand.

"I heard you," he replied as he dropped down to his knees beside her and started to cut off the headband and T-shirt. "Just didn't know it was a question. Which part am I too good at?"

She watched him for another moment, then tossed the pills into her mouth and dry-swallowed them before speaking again. "All of it. *This.*"

"You're criticizing me for my triage work?" he replied teasingly.

"You know I'm not criticizing," she told him. "But I'm guessing you're slightly more than an artist."

"I can't tell whether or not I should be insulted by that," he said back. "The cut's actually not looking so bad. Clotted pretty well, but I'm going to slather on some of this topical stuff. It's heavy-duty. Not quite as good as what you'd get injected before stitches, but it'll still numb it pretty well. I'm going to butterfly it together with the tape and cover the whole thing with the compression bandage."

"Thank you."

"Moral obligation as a superhero."

She breathed out and closed her eyes as he started on the tasks he'd just outlined. "Why did you really pull me in here? And don't tell me it was to fix up my cut."

"Because I wanted to reassure you that I'm not running back to the shop just for fun," he said. "I want to keep you and Teegan safe. Wouldn't be able to do that very well if I got hurt, would I?"

"And?"

"And I'd feel a hell of a lot more confident protecting you if I grabbed my firearm from the safe in my studio."

She blinked up at him, and when her mouth opened, he expected a protest of some kind. Or at least a question about why he not only had a weapon but why he'd felt the need to keep it at the studio.

Instead, she asked, "Can I really trust you, Harley?"

He felt his eyebrows knit together in puzzlement. "Trust me? With the gun? It's a legal licensed firearm. And I'm fully trained. But if you're not comfortable…"

"No. That's not what I mean. I'm sure that you wouldn't do something reckless."

"I definitely wouldn't. So what *do* you mean?"

"I mean if I tell you about what happened today, can you promise not to go to the police?"

The question made him want to roll out his shoulders to relieve a sudden kink. If she was about to confess to some involvement with Garibaldi, he wasn't sure he wanted to hear it.

Because you already decided she was innocent based on the feel of her lips?

He shoved off the self-directed question and went back to work on her leg, cleaning it more thoroughly this time than he had on top of the roof. "That's a tough question to just give a yes or no to."

"Is it?" She sounded almost disappointed.

And he had to admit that he felt something similar. Tempting lips and all, he really *didn't* want her to be on the wrong side. It was the only small positive that he thought had come out of the current sequence of events. Knowing that her store was under fire had led Harley to infer that she couldn't be involved with Garibaldi. The possibility that whatever crime had been committed at Liz's Lovely Things was a third party seemed unlikely.

But not impossible.

He chose his next words carefully. "I think of myself as a decent guy, Liz. One who does the right thing whenever possible. So as far as trust is concerned…you can count on me for that, every time."

"And if it's not a black-and-white situation?" she asked softly, opening her eyes and directing a clear, serious look his way.

He met her gaze. "I think *a lot* of things fall somewhere in the gray spectrum, actually. You have to sort through it to figure out what's right and what's wrong. But doing things that could result in people getting hurt…that's a hard limit for me. I wouldn't ever endanger Teegan, or ask you to do anything that might. The cops are the good guys."

She bit her lip, looking like she was trying to hold back tears. Harley couldn't help himself.

Garibaldi be damned.

He pushed up and reached out to fold her into an embrace.

Liz didn't resist at all. There was no point. All she wanted to do was sink into the big man and his strong arms. To let herself be vulnerable and to admit that the last little bit—she didn't know how much time had actually passed—had been the most harrowing of her life. So she gave in. She leaned into him, her shoulders shaking. She let her sobs come as he ran his palms over her back in a soothing circle.

"It's going to be all right," he said into her hair.

"Harley…" she replied, her voice so small she almost didn't recognize it as her own.

"Yeah, honey?"

"What the hell's going on?"

He tipped back to look her in the eye. "I was kind of hoping you could tell me."

Liz swallowed. "He said that if I told anyone, he'd kill Teegan."

Harley didn't pull away any farther, and even though his eyes darkened, his voice was calm as he answered her. "This was the guy in the hooded sweatshirt?"

"Yes."

"And this is why you asked me about *not* calling the police?"

"Yes." She heard the quaver in her own voice. "You won't, right?"

Something flashed across his face, and he slowly shook his head. "I won't. But I need you to tell me what happened."

As she explained what the hooded man had said and done, relief made her feel ten pounds lighter. Especially since Harley listened so intently and showed no signs of forcing her to call the authorities. The feel of him—warm, strong and still holding her firmly—was reassuring as well.

"And you're sure he was looking for the painting that you said felt weird?" he asked when she was done.

She nodded, the relief infusing her response with enthusiasm. "I wasn't, when I pointed it out. It was just an impulse, because I'd just noticed it. But when he walked over and looked at it, I knew I was right."

"And what did he call it?"

"A Heigle."

"Is that the name of the artist?"

"I'm not sure," she admitted.

The smallest frown creased his forehead. "You don't keep track of the artists in the shop?"

"I do. But the one who does these particular paintings is a local who prefers to stay anonymous."

"So how do they get to the store?"

"Jesse Garibaldi provides them."

Now his expression changed again. And even though it only lasted for a second, the look was the hardest one Liz had seen on his usually kind face. It almost made her flinch. Then the apparent anger was gone as quick as it had come, the only evidence it had existed in the slight stiffness of Harley's jaw. Liz stared at the rigid line of it for a second, waiting for some kind of explanation. But before he could speak—if he was even going to—the hair on the back of Liz's neck stood up. She whipped her head toward the closed door.

"Did you hear something?" she asked.

Harley's gaze followed hers. "Like what?"

"I don't know. Something."

They both went still, but all Liz could actually hear was the light, nervous thud of her own heart and the low rhythm of Harley's breathing.

"Maybe it was nothing," she whispered.

"If it was nothing," he replied, "then why are we whispering?"

"I don't know," she said again.

The tingle of something being *off* didn't lessen at all. Maybe it wasn't that she'd heard something. Maybe it was that she *hadn't* heard something. Or to be more accurate… didn't *currently* hear anything. Noise followed her daughter wherever she went. Giggles and chatter. Things breaking or furniture thumping. But there was none of that now. And realizing it made Liz's throat close up with increased worry. And Harley seemed to sense it.

"I'll go check on them," he said in a low voice. "You wait here for a second."

She nodded, but he no sooner stood up and stepped toward the door than she realized she couldn't just stay behind. She pushed to her feet. Harley turned to give her a look. She shook her head at him, and he didn't argue as she followed him out the door and into the hall.

Liz drew in a sharp breath as she spotted the first confirmed sign that her intuition was right. The front door hung open. It swayed back and forth, somehow ominous in its movement.

Harley dropped a curse, and a horrible, light-headed feeling hit Liz. It was accompanied by nausea. And a prickling unpleasant heat that made her face ache. Her feet slowed, and thick gag built up in her throat. For a second, she truly thought she might faint. But a heartbeat later, Harley's hand found hers, and he pulled her to a position behind him.

A human shield.

The thought slipped in vaguely, and it made her even more grateful for his presence. But it scared her a little, too. And the fear only worsened when he stopped abruptly just outside the doorway that led to the living room. He bent forward. Cautious. Then dropped a curse word and stepped back so hard that he bumped Liz to the wall.

She anticipated an apology that didn't come.

Instead, Harley was busy springing into action. He

released Liz and closed the gap between himself and the front door in three wide strides. He stepped out onto the stoop, then leaped down the small staircase.

But panic made Liz move in slow motion. She dragged her eyes from Harley's frantic motions to the living room. From where she stood, she could see something that didn't quite jibe.

A shoe.

It was tan. Flat. A lace-up.

What the—

"Oh, no," she gasped as she figured it out. "No, no, no."

She knew why Harley hadn't wasted a second. She raced forward and confirmed her suspicions. Miss Wilma lay sprawled out on the floor, one tan shoe on, one tan shoe off. Her eyes were closed, her chest rising and falling as though she were simply asleep. But a spot of blood dotted the rug beside her head, and the weapon used to create the destruction—a small abstractly shaped statue—sat on its side just a few inches away from the old woman's face.

But all of that wasn't what made Liz's pulse thunder.

It wasn't the knocked-over checkers board.

It wasn't the upended plate of cookies.

It was the emptiness of the rest of the room.

"Teegan?" Liz's voice was low the first time she said it. Not so much the second. "Teegan!"

Harley appeared back in the doorway then, his face far, far too still.

A thousand furious butterflies beat inside Liz's stomach, and when she spoke, her words came out in a cracked whisper. "Where is she?"

Harley started to shake his head, and Liz saw the answer in his eyes. Her daughter was gone. Taken by whoever had assaulted poor Miss Wilma and left her unconscious.

Liz wanted to scream. To cry out. To pound her fists on the wall. To shake the old woman awake and demand to know what had happened.

Minutes, she thought desperately. *We were in the bathroom for five minutes! Ten, tops.*

She didn't realize she'd said it aloud until Harley answered.

"That's all it takes," he said. "But we'll figure this out, Liz. We'll get her back."

"How?" Now her voice was shrill.

Harley took a step toward her, but she jerked away reflexively. This was her *daughter*. She needed to take charge. And logically, she knew that staying calm was the best way to get answers. But her head and her heart had different ideas. Tears were already streaming down her face as she pivoted on the spot, searching for some sign of where Teegan had been taken, or a clue for who was responsible, or an idea on what to do next.

The hooded man leaped to the front of her mind. Was it him? If so, why take her? And if he *had*, did that mean he assumed that Liz had told Harley what had happened?

You did *tell him*, she reminded herself. *And then* this *happened.*

Guilt stabbed at her so hard it hurt.

"The police!" she gasped suddenly.

"Is that what you want to do?" Harley asked.

"It's what I *have* to do, isn't it?"

"A few minutes ago, you were dead set against it."

She whipped her head in his direction. He was on the floor now, carefully checking over the injured woman.

"Things have changed, though, haven't they?" Liz replied in what she knew was a babbling mash of out-loud thoughts. "They're the good guys, you said. What I said before. That was when it was just me, worrying about the guy in the hood. Why does that seem like *nothing* now? And Miss Wilma needs proper medical attention. But Teegan. Oh, God. We need to call the police *now*."

"Let's just take a second to—"

A tinny musical chime came to life from somewhere in the room, cutting him off.

"Miss Wilma's phone?" Harley asked.

Liz shook her head. "Definitely not. She doesn't have one."

"Not mine, and not yours."

"No."

The chime stopped. Barely a heartbeat paused before it started up again. And as Harley immediately moved away from Miss Wilma and started digging through the mess in search of its source, a bubble of hope percolated in Liz's chest. It was small. And somewhat inexplicable. But it was there. It grew even bigger when Harley pulled a generic black phone out from under the discarded chessboard.

He glanced from the screen to her. "Unknown number."

Liz inhaled, her mind racing. Then impulse took over. She rushed forward, snagged the phone from Harley's startled hand and darted out of the room, answering as she made her escape into the hall.

"Hello?" she greeted breathlessly.

The man's voice on the other end crackled, low and gruff. "Lizeth Pauline James?"

"Yes."

"If you want your daughter back, you need to bring us the Heigles."

A dozen conflicting emotions tumbled through her,

some stronger than others. There was relief that Teegan was alive. And fierce protectiveness. Terror at not knowing what the kidnapper's true intentions were, and apprehension at being separated from her daughter. And under that, further puzzlement at the interest in a series of mediocre paintings.

"You have thirty seconds to decide, Ms. James," said the voice.

She opened her mouth to agree—she'd do anything to get her daughter back—but before she could speak, one of Harley's hands landed on her wrist, and the other snatched away the phone.

Chapter 7

Harley met Liz's eyes as he stepped out of reach and spoke three words into the phone. "Proof of life."

He waited through the heavy pause on the other end of the line, careful not to break his gaze. He could see how close to the edge Liz was, and he couldn't blame her for the slightly unstable look in her eyes. But he also didn't want to do anything that would tip her over the brink. She needed to feel in control, fine. That didn't mean he was going to let his own experience go to waste. He'd help her, even when her completely understandable emotions were clouding her judgment.

At last, a male voice responded to Harley's curt command. "Who is this?"

He took a small amount of satisfaction in remaining an unknown as he provided his perfectly verifiable cover story. "My name is Harley Maxwell. And if you've taken

Teegan for some reason, we're going to need both proof that you have her and proof that she's unharmed."

There was another pause, and the man on the other end repeated his question, only with a slightly different emphasis. "Who *are* you?"

Harley knew what was really being asked, and he kept his voice even. "I'm an artist. A sculptor, to be specific. I rent the studio space beside Ms. James's apartment, and I've been spending the evening with her and her daughter. I can wait, if you feel like looking me up on the internet."

"Not necessary."

Harley could tell it was a lie; whoever the man was, or represented, would be looking him up. Thoroughly, if not immediately. Which was fine. He'd covered himself well. The online portfolio, a beefed-up following and a real link to his education in Fine Arts would probably satisfy them. There was nothing that tied him to the Freemont PD. Harley had been working in the system from behind a computer long enough for it to be a specialty. If not for the very real lives at stake—and his concern for Teegan, specifically—he might've smiled at knowing his story was impervious to scrutiny.

"Proof of life," he reiterated.

"Thirty minutes," muttered the other man.

"Thirty minutes until…"

"We'll call you back so you can speak to the girl. Tell her mother this changes nothing about the Heigles. And we don't want to see a single damn cop. Got it?"

"Thirty minutes, the Heigles, no cops." As soon as Harley had repeated it, the line went dead.

And Liz verbally pounced on him. "We *need* the cops. The guy on the phone wasn't the same one who harassed me in the store. I'd recognize his voice. Which means someone else has Teegan. And whoever he is, he can have every stupid painting in the store!"

"Liz."

"What?"

"We need to sit tight until he calls back."

"Are you crazy?"

Harley took a measured breath. "You know that I'm not."

"I don't," she argued. "You're supposed to be the artist next door. The nice guy making my daughter laugh. Instead, you're some kind of *escape* artist. And a hostage negotiator who won't let me call the police."

"Reason it through with me for a second," he replied calmly. "If it was so easy to take the paintings, why not just walk in there and do it? Why kidnap Teegan?"

She blinked at him. "What are you saying?"

"Something bigger's going on, Liz. I strongly suspect that if we were to walk back over to your shop right this second, we'd find out that the Heigles are already gone. That's why the white van was there. And I think whoever was just on the phone knows that, too."

"But…" She trailed off, tears in her voice.

"I know," Harley stated. "Teegan."

"The first twenty-four hours are the most important. That's what they always say on TV."

"That's a different kind of scenario, honey. In this case, we know Teegan's okay. Probably scared, but definitely alive. We know she'll stay that way."

"How can you be so sure?"

"Think about it. If she weren't okay, our friend on the phone wouldn't have bothered agreeing to negotiate. He would've just insisted on getting his way."

Liz drew in a shaky breath. "But you don't think we should call the police. Why?"

He avoided a direct answer. "Asking for proof of life puts us in control, at least temporarily. And the guy on the other end gave us more info than that, too. He wanted twenty minutes. That makes me think that Teegan's not with him. Not yet. So either he needs time to get where she is, or he needs to wait until she gets where *he* is. Either way, we can be sure she's somewhere close, because the next nearest town is over an hour's drive, right?"

Liz offered the barest nod. "Yes."

"We also know that this guy's not operating alone," Harley added. "He kept saying 'we' instead of 'I.' So either he's working for someone or with someone. My gut tells me it's for."

"Is that good?"

"Yes. Working in a group means more witnesses. Less likelihood of someone doing something stupid. And murder isn't their game. They could've killed Miss Wilma, but they just made sure she was out cold. And they didn't take her with them, either, so we know they really want Teegan alive and able to be used as leverage."

She lifted a hand and wiped away a few tears, and when she spoke again, it was in a slightly steadier voice. "What else?"

"We can use these thirty minutes to help Miss Wilma. She needs medical attention, like you said."

"But you don't want to call 911."

"I don't think it would help."

"How can you even say that?" The desperate edge came back immediately, and she sank against the wall. "Who are you, Harley? Really."

"Liz." He wished it sounded less like a warning than it did.

Her face went abruptly blank, and before he could think about what it meant, she pounced again—this time literally. For the second time, she caught him by surprise, snagging the phone out of his grasp, then backing away. She slammed her fingers to the screen, then lifted her chin at him defiantly.

"Tell me," she ordered. "Because I've got 911 lined up, and all I need to do is hit Call."

Her pointer finger hovered, waiting to make good on the threat.

Harley ran a frustrated hand over his hair. The first rule of undercover work was *not* to break cover. Not for any reason. But he and his partners were in a unique situation. Operating a sting that was supported by their captain, but not quite within the normal bounds of police work. His brother, Brayden, had been forced to blow his own cover during his initial scouting mission to find Jesse Garibaldi in the first place. Their third man, Anderson Somers, had come in to protect one of Garibaldi's targets, and the target, Nadine Stuart, had known from the get-go that Anderson was a detective.

Would it be so bad to just tell Liz the truth? he wondered.

Maybe not. Unless she was working with Garibaldi. Which he really didn't believe was possible. But he needed to *know*.

"Harley?"

Her tone was more worried than it was demanding, and he sighed. She'd had more than enough thrown on her plate over the last few hours, without the added stress of thinking about *his* motives. He knew he sure didn't like worrying about hers.

"Have you ever committed a crime, Liz?" he asked, more interested in the nuances of her reaction than in her actual answer.

She blinked again, her teary eyes filling with confusion. "What? No. I mean, I've had a speeding ticket. And probably jaywalked. Why?"

He answered with another question. "Would you knowingly enter into a relationship with a criminal?"

She inhaled sharply. "What does this have to do with— Are you trying to tell me that's who you really are?"

It was his turn to blink. "Me?"

"Whatever it is, Harley, just tell me. I'm not going to judge you. All I want is to get my daughter back." With a defeated expression on her face that made his heart ache a little, she glanced down at the phone in her hand, then back up at him and added in a softer voice, "Twenty-three more minutes."

She was right. The seconds were ticking by, and if she was in league with Garibaldi, he'd eat his damn badge.

"The reason I'm not pushing for the police," he stated evenly, "is because I *am* the police, Liz."

She stared at him for a moment, and he half expected her to come down on him for lying to her for the last ten days. Instead, she just nodded and exhaled at the same time.

"That actually…makes a lot of things about you make sense," she said.

He tried to smile, but couldn't quite manage it, so he settled for a sincere pledge instead. "We don't have time for me to go into detail, but suffice it to say that we've encountered some corruption on the local police force."

He gave her the world's quickest debriefing. He told her he had three partners. Rush, whom he hadn't heard from in far too long. Anderson, who'd actually fallen for Teegan's teacher, Nadine. And his brother, who was the one who'd figured out the corruption in the first place.

"I'm sorry it's not much of an explanation," he said

when he was done with the recap. "But to be up front, the Whispering Woods PD isn't equipped to handle a hostage situation anyway. They'd be calling in for help from one of the bigger cities." He paused. "Liz, I'm sorry for covering up what I really do for a living, but everything else I've said to you since we've met has been true. We can still do things the traditional way, if that's what you'd prefer. But it will mean taking my help out of the equation. And I'm very good at my job."

His words made Liz straighten her shoulders, and her eyes filled with hope and trust as she said, "Okay. Tell me the plan."

As Harley led her back to the living room, Liz wondered if she should be mad that he'd deceived her. But as she watched him check over Miss Wilma once more, she couldn't muster up even an ounce of anger.

She sank down onto the floral two-seater couch and watched him work as he outlined what he thought they should do. His hands were gentle and sure, just as they had been with her. Professional, but not detached. So she wasn't angry. She was just thankful. Glad that he had the authority and know-how to take charge of the situation. Because God knew if she'd been alone, she'd have felt helpless. And she was sure that "proper" authorities wouldn't be promising her that she would be involved in finding Teegan.

Oh, God. Teegan.

Just thinking her name sent a wave of nausea through Liz.

She's alive, she reminded herself. *Scared, definitely. But also whole. Harley said so.*

She wanted to look down at the phone in her hands to check the time again. But things were moving in slow motion. Every glance only yielded thirty seconds, when she could swear it had been minutes. Her head was starting to ache with a fierceness that matched the one in her heart.

The couch dipped down beside her, and she jerked her head up, surprised to see that the big man had joined her. Clearly noting that she'd zoned out, one of his hands came up to clasp hers.

"You with me?" he asked softly.

Taking solace in the strength of his grip, she nodded. "Yes."

"Good. You wanna repeat the plan back to me?"

"We're going to call someone to take Miss Wilma to the Whispering Woods Care Facility. The Frost guy." Her mind blanked for a second, and she realized she really *had* spaced out. Liz could swear she'd been listening to Harley as she watched him work. But now the two-minute-old conversation seemed fuzzy. She looked from Miss Wilma to the overturned checkers, then to Harley.

"I'm sorry," she said with a helpless shrug.

"Mr. Frost owns the Frost Family Diner," Harley filled in patiently. "I know him through my brother, Brayden."

Liz nodded again, her mind latching on to the few details she'd retained from what he'd just said. Brayden Maxwell was also a detective, who'd come into Whispering Woods as a scout for the case they were working on. He'd been sidetracked by saving the life of Reggie Frost, whose family owned the '50s-style diner just up the road. The couple were currently on an extended vacation in Mexico.

"Right," she said. "Mr. Frost. Your soon-to-be…uncle-in-law?"

"That's the one."

"Is uncle-in-law a thing?" she wondered aloud, then shook her head as she heard how trivial it sounded.

But Harley smiled. "I guess it's a thing now. You want me to go over the rest again?"

"If you could."

"I was saying before that, I think it's safe to assume that Miss Wilma didn't witness anything, so we're not going to tell her about Teegan, or any of the other things that happened."

"And if she asks, the statue accidentally fell off that shelf up there—" Liz pointed to the dust-free spot the size of its base, recalling that Harley had mentioned it just a few minutes earlier. "And smacked her in the head."

"Exactly. And when the call comes in four minutes?"

"Four minutes?" She was surprised to hear that so much time had already passed.

He inclined his head toward the clock on the wall. "Three and a half, actually."

Liz saw that he was right, and she realized a little belatedly that while all the talking might've been required for planning purposes, Harley had been also using it as a deliberate distraction. And it had worked. She'd been busy trying to follow along—mostly failing, but still making the attempt—and the seconds had managed to speed up again.

In spite of everything, a warm, grateful feeling spread out in her chest. It didn't overwhelm the anxious pit of worry. But it was welcome. A small buffer.

Harley offered her a smile. "And when they do call— less than three minutes now—you answer, in case they put Teegan on from the get-go. I don't want you to miss a chance to talk to her."

Liz's heart squeezed—at Harley's selflessness, in anticipation of speaking to her daughter and with nerves at the thought of being in contact with the kidnapper again.

Harley gave her hand another reassuring squeeze. "It'll be okay, Liz."

And in spite of how basic the words were, some of the tension in her chest eased. She believed him. Somehow, it would work out. They'd get the Heigles back. They'd exchange the paintings with the men who held Teegan; Miss Wilma would be fine; Harley would finish his case. What happened after that was full of endless, hopeful possibility.

Then, as if to somehow force her back to the reality of the here and now, the cell phone in her hand chimed to life with its musical tone.

Liz brought her gaze up to Harley, who nodded in encouragement.

With shaking hands, she pressed the button and answered. "Lizeth speaking."

Teegan's sprightly voice came back in a near-shout. "Mom!"

The tears came so quickly that Liz couldn't hold them in, and her response quivered. "Baby. Are you okay?"

"Fine." Her daughter's voice dropped to a whisper. "But I think these are the bad guys."

The comment was almost funny. But not quite.

Liz swallowed. "Did they hurt you?"

"Not really. But Miss W—" There was a muffled protest, and then the gruff-speaking man took over.

"Enough," he said, and it was impossible to tell if he was talking to her or to her daughter.

But it didn't matter anyway. Harley was quick to pull the phone from her ear.

"Tell me what you're after." His voice was somehow cool, sure and conciliatory all at the same time.

He held the phone out just enough so that Liz could hear the response.

"I already told the woman." There was a sneer in the words. "And I'm sure she told you. Don't waste my time."

Harley's reply was even-toned. "And I'm sure you know the paintings were taken from the shop this evening. So don't waste *mine*."

"Glad we're on the same page about the urgency of the situation," said the other man. "I'm giving you twenty-four hours to get me what I want."

Liz's heart palpitated. It was both too long and too short. A far greater amount of time than she wanted to be away from Teegan. But a too-soon deadline for what could only be an arduous task. But Harley remained unfazed.

"I want regular check-ins from the girl," he stated. "Hourly."

"Far too inconvenient," replied the other man. "Once every four hours, and I'm not waking her up if she's sleeping."

"Once every three hours, and *you* call, even if *she's* out cold," Harley said.

"You're an artist, you said?" Suspicion rang through, loud and clear.

"Since the second I could hold a pencil." Harley was utterly calm. "You give her food and water. And I don't mean vending-machine garbage. Stuff a kid *wants* to eat and stuff she *needs* to eat."

"How the hell am I supposed to know what that is?" was the reply.

"Try asking her," Harley suggested.

And Liz almost wanted to laugh. The kidnapper sounded clueless and put out by Harley's demands. And the guy was supposed to be the one in charge, which he seemed to have forgotten.

Then Harley tipped his face her way and shot her a wink—*a wink during a hostage negotiation!*—and Liz knew the table-turning maneuver was intentional. She wanted to laugh even more. And hug him. And cry.

Harley cleared his throat. "Put her on again."

The other man sounded surprised. "What?"

"The kid. Put her on for her mom."

"That wasn't a part of—"

"Now." Congeniality dropped out of Harley's voice completely.

And a moment later, Teegan was back on the line. "Mom?"

"I'm here, sweetheart," Liz said immediately, pulling the phone closer.

"I miss you," her daughter told her. "And I'm tired."

"I miss you, too," Liz replied. "And if you want to find a place to lie down and sleep, you should do it."

"Okay. The man wants the phone back."

"I love you, Teegs."

"Me, too, Mom."

The kidnapper spoke then, his gruff voice even gruffer. "All right. No more messing around. Get me the damn paintings."

Harley took over the conversation again. "Give me your word about the calls and the kid."

A grunt and sigh made the line crackle. "Fine. You've got my word. A call every three hours, and the kid'll be fine."

"We'll get you the paintings. Got a clue where we should start?"

"If I knew that, I wouldn't need you."

The phone went dead, and Harley set it down on the table, then turned Liz's way. He met her eyes and opened his arms. And she threw herself into his chest.

Chapter 8

Harley knew Liz was seeking comfort, but in all honesty, he was taking it as much as he was giving it. He was afraid for Teegan. He *had* to save her. He would. But he knew it wasn't going to be easy and straightforward. Nothing that involved Garibaldi ever was. And it was Liz who pulled back first, straightening her shoulders a little and looking him in the eye.

"The most detective work I've ever done has been via a board game," she said. "So tell me where we start."

Impressed by her emotional strength, Harley kissed her forehead, surprised at how natural the gesture felt. Like he'd offered her support and admiration that way hundreds of times.

"I'm going to give Mr. Frost a call first," he said. "While we wait for him to get here, we'll make a list of details that might be important."

She straightened up a bit more. "Like the white van?"

"Exactly. That's a good—"

A groan cut him off, and he turned to find Miss Wilma propping herself up.

"Did you say 'white van'?" she asked.

Swiping another kiss across Liz's forehead—because it really *did* feel right—Harley pushed himself off the couch to his feet, then bent to help the old woman from the floor and into her armchair.

"Not sure how much you wanna be moving around," he said. "Took a nasty bump on the noggin."

Miss Wilma made a dismissive gesture with her hand, but winced a little. "Been hit harder by worse, I'm sure."

Harley looked over the wizened woman's head to meet Liz's gaze as he answered. "A statue fell from the shelf and knocked you out for almost thirty minutes, Miss Wilma. That's riding the line between mild trauma and something a little more serious. Mr. Frost from the diner is going to come and take you to the care center."

Miss Wilma made a face. "That bad, huh? Where's the little monkey?"

Liz jumped in. "Teegan was complaining about being tired, so we tucked her into your bed. I hope that's okay."

"Totally fine. Probably scared her to see me like that," Miss Wilma said ruefully.

"She'll be fine," Harley replied, catching Liz's eye to let her know that he meant the words as more than just a cover-up. "As soon as Mr. Frost gets here, we'll make sure Teegan gets home safe and sound. In the meantime, have you got a landline I can borrow to call Mr. Frost?"

The old woman cast a puzzled look toward the phone in his hands. "Something wrong with that one?"

Harley forced an easy smile. "It's old. Reception's terrible here in Whispering Woods. I really need to upgrade."

Miss Wilma nodded. "I've heard that Jesse Garibaldi's looking into replacing the cell tower. Guess it's a good thing there's a few old-fashioned folk like me kicking around. My phone's in the kitchen. Even has a cord attached to the wall."

"Perfect."

Harley excused himself to make the call, glad that he'd made an effort to memorize the phone numbers relevant to the case. He paused, though, right before dialing. Harley rarely sought outside help. Computers were his usual area of expertise, and more often than not, he could find the answers he needed in the digital world. His connections were usually virtual, and on occasion, he'd been told he was known as "the guy who knows a guy." So it felt a little strange to have to reach out to someone else. Especially a civilian.

Gotta do it, he said to himself. *For Teegan's sake.*

Thankfully, it turned out to be pretty painless. Mr. Frost was awake, answered on the second ring and was willing to help out. The man was grateful to Harley's brother for the role he played in keeping his daughter, Reggie, out of harm's way, and had promised that if an occasion came where any of the four undercover detectives need assistance, he'd be there in a heartbeat.

When the call was done, Harley took a moment to breathe. To think. He felt like he hadn't spared a second for thought since Liz came crashing around the corner a few hours earlier in search of her daughter.

Action is good. Action means things are happening.

And really, he'd volunteered to step in. Just a few short weeks ago, his brother had found Jesse Garibaldi in Whispering Woods. For fifteen years, he and his crew— himself, Brayden and their brothers-in-arms, Anderson Somers and Rush Atkinson—had searched. For fifteen years, they'd been patient. The vow they'd made as kids—to seek justice for their murdered fathers—was at last coming to fruition.

First, Brayden had come in and successfully identified their target: Jesse Garibaldi. The man who'd used a pipe bomb to blow up an evidence room at the Freemont City police station, then been let off on a technicality. Now he masqueraded as a businessman with investments in the community, but in just days, Brayden had uncovered a greater conspiracy. A corrupt police officer, a murder and something they were still trying to unravel. Brayden had also met Reggie Frost, fallen in love and taken his leave from the investigation. Which was a bit of a necessity considering his cover story had nearly been blown.

When he left town, Anderson Somers had come in to protect Nadine Stuart from Garibaldi. Although Harley hadn't met her himself, he *had* spoken to Nadine on the phone while Anderson acted as her bodyguard. Even their brief interaction had told him she was gutsy, opinionated and determined. A perfect match for Anderson, whom they fondly referred to as Mr. Nice Guy. Together, he and Nadine had not only solved the murder of Nadine's father—another pipe bomb, courtesy of Garibaldi—but also connected the wily man's business to the art world. Unfortunately, they'd been forced to let the entire town assume they'd died in a house fire. But not before tipping off Harley to the fact that Liz's Lovely Things might be a front for whatever Garibaldi's grander scheme was. Which brought him back to the current moment.

Liz was just like the rest of the town—an unknowing pawn in Jesse Garibaldi's life. And now whatever it was that was going on had resulted in Teegan's kidnapping. So. Action might be good. But *this* wasn't the kind Harley was hoping for. He'd rather have stayed in the dark about Garibaldi than allow the kid to be in harm's way.

A fierce need to protect her stormed through him. It wasn't a feeling he'd ever experienced before. Just the idea that she might get hurt was enough to send a dark roil through his gut. He wasn't an angry man. He was calm. Logical. Good at mulling things over and coming up with amicable solutions.

So why is this different?

It wasn't just that she was a kid. There were plenty of times over the course of his police career that he'd had the unfortunate task of dealing with crimes that involved children. Yes, they could be heartbreaking. They evoked all kinds of emotions.

But this is personal.

It was true. Over the last week and a half, he'd developed a connection to Teegan James. Her creative spirit and quick little mind appealed to him on a level that was new to him. Though he'd always assumed he'd have kids one day, spending time with Teegan made him *want* to have them. Which was definitely different.

Add that to the fact that he'd experienced firsthand what it was like to lose someone as a result of Garibaldi's wrongdoings...

It was extra personal. More than personal. If that was possible. Maybe there wasn't a word for the way he was feeling.

With a sigh, he pushed himself away from the counter and made his way back into the living room. As he stepped in, he was surprised to note a genuine, excited smile on Liz's face.

"What's up?" he asked, frowning.

"The white van," she replied. "I told Miss Wilma that there was a delivery mix-up, and that was why we were looking for it. She said that when she woke up at her usual time this evening, she saw a white van pulling onto the street. It had a logo on the side."

"That's right," Miss Wilma confirmed. "Big pretty one."

"So I suggested maybe you could *draw* the logo, if she felt up to describing it," Liz added. "That could work, right?"

"Definitely," Harley agreed.

"Pencil and paper in the side-table drawer where I keep my crosswords," the old woman stated. "Better get to it before my personal ambulance gets here."

Harley smiled, then stepped to the table in question. He yanked out a flower-printed notebook, sank down beside Liz on the couch and got to work.

Sketching on command wasn't a task he'd done much of since art school, but Miss Wilma's recall was good, and her description was on point. In minutes, Harley had an outlined logo that the old woman said was even nicer than what she'd seen on the side of the van. He studied the finished drawing. It was simple. Overlapping leaves that curved into a circle. The left half made up a letter *e*; the right half made up the letter *f.* It was definitely distinct. Definitely a lead.

"Is it good?" Liz asked, her hope guarded.

Harley nodded and offered her his widest smile. "Better than good. In fact, I'm not sure who I want to kiss more. You or Miss Wilma."

Liz blushed prettily, but Miss Wilma snorted.

"I'm pretty sure I can answer that one," said the old woman, then tipped her head to one side. "And unless my hearing's going, that's my ride."

Harley started to say he didn't hear anything himself, but just a tenth of a second later, the bell rang once, then twice more in a row in the preplanned signal that announced Mr. Frost's arrival.

* * *

Getting Miss Wilma out of the house went by in a blur. If Mr. Frost hadn't been a dead ringer for Santa Claus, Liz might not have noted what he looked like at all.

She was eager. The knots in her stomach were there, and she assumed that they would be until she had Teegan in her arms, safe and unharmed. But now the hope she'd laid at Harley's feet was more concrete. They had something. And it seemed like something significant. Not just a single hair that needed some kind of complicated forensic analysis. Not just a vague footprint impression. *A company logo.* That was something even a layperson like herself could search out.

So when they closed the door behind Miss Wilma and her white-bearded "chauffeur"—as he referred to himself—Liz couldn't quite contain her eagerness.

"Where do we start?" she asked, grabbing the sketched logo from the side table. "We can plug this into the internet with a description."

Harley's response was far less enthusiastic. With a far too impassive expression on his face, he gently took the paper from her hand, folded it in half and stuck it into his back pocket.

"We start with getting you somewhere safe," he said, not quite meeting her eyes as he spoke.

Liz felt her whole body droop. She'd been so sure he wasn't going to dismiss her involvement.

"Please, Harley." Her words were a choked sob.

He stepped forward and clasped both her hands. "I'm not discounting your ability to help. But even under the best circumstances, it would be too dangerous for you to be directly involved."

She pulled her hands free. "What are the best of circumstances in a situation like this?"

He ran a hand over his mess of brown hair and sighed. "You know what I mean."

She shook her head. "No, Harley, I don't. Everything I know about kidnapping I learned from late-night crime dramas. I can only assume those are far from accurate."

"Not the most reliable source," he agreed. "And even if TV were accurate, this situation is far from an average abduction."

Tears pricked at her eyes. "Why is 'average abduction' even a thing?"

Harley reached for her again, this time closing his warm fingers around her elbows. "I'm framing this wrong. Every move has to be calculated just right. We can't trust the local authorities, and we don't want to take chances and wait for reinforcements. That ties our hands in terms of the usual avenues. No Amber Alert, no public appeal. It puts us in a tough spot, honey. We want to get Teegan back unharmed, so we need to do things with as much efficiency as possible."

"You mean like *not* wasting time by arguing about whether or not I'm allowed to help find my own daughter?"

"Liz. We really—"

She cut him off. "Stop right there."

He frowned. "Where?"

"You keep saying 'we,' but you're trying to take me out of the equation. I'm not helpless, and I'm not just going to sit on the sidelines. You either include me or I go out on my own."

He muttered something incomprehensible, then let her go and roughly scraped one hand over his jaw. "I need to go back to the studio."

Liz nodded. "To get your gun."

"You're hurt," he reminded her.

"I feel okay," she replied.

"And it's more than likely that someone is watching both the shop and your place."

"Okay."

"Multiple someones, probably."

"All right."

"There's a real possibility that we're looking at, at *least*, three separate adversaries." He lifted his fingers and started ticking off. "The two men in your apartment and their friend down in the shop. Whoever actually performed the heist with the van. And the guy on the phone."

Liz suppressed a shiver and said, "If you're trying to scare me, it won't work. However much I'm worried about my own safety, it's nothing compared to what I feel for Teegan."

His expression changed, and she saw a fierceness in his eyes that nearly matched the one in her heart, and his two-word response surprised her.

"I know," he said.

"You know?" she repeated.

"I'm no stranger to loss," he told her, pacing the small room as he spoke. "I don't have any kids, so I can't imagine how it feels to be you at this moment. But I know how it would feel if it were my mom or my brother. It would tear me apart. And I'm sure that the feeling is only multiplied when it's your own child. I want to get her back, too. I just don't want you to take an unnecessary risk."

For a second, Harley's declaration made Liz pause. She could hear the genuine pain in his voice, and she wanted to know the source. She wanted to soothe it away, too. And she didn't want to make it worse for him. She could tell that he felt responsible for her and for her daughter. It warmed her. Made her happy—a slightly selfish emotion in light of the circumstance, but not one she could deny.

Am I being unreasonable? she wondered.

Was the right thing to do to sit back and let Harley, who knew far better than she did, do what needed to be done? Would she just get in the way of the investigation?

She opened her mouth, an offer to try to find some kind of compromise on the tip of her tongue. But then another terrible thought crept in. What if something happened to *Harley* while he was searching for the paintings? The idea pained her in a surprisingly strong way. And she couldn't make the offer to just sit on her hands.

Instead, she said, "You're right. This *is* tearing me apart. And I already feel like there are things I can't do that I should be doing. I can't sit on my hands, Harley. Would you, if it were *your* family?"

He met her eyes, then shook his head like he didn't want to admit aloud that she was right. And Liz really sensed that there was more to it than just his agreement. Maybe it was because she was so accustomed to using her intuition where Teegan was concerned. She had to know when her daughter was holding back. To be aware of when reading between the lines was necessary. But whatever the source, she was sure of what Harley's nod really meant. Not that he *wouldn't* sit on his hands while his family was in danger, but that he *hadn't*.

"Let's get out of here," he said a little roughly. "We need a place that has more internet and fewer lacy doilies."

Grateful that he'd given in—but worried that he might change his mind—Liz kept her mouth shut as he led her from Miss Wilma's place and back out into the street.

As they made their way through the quiet night, she half expected him to find some door to shove her through. One he could lock, then throw away the key. But he didn't. He just stayed quiet, too. He held her hand and guided back toward her own building at the other end of the block, using the same stealthy path to get back as they'd used to get there.

If there *was* someone watching them like he'd warned, they stayed well hidden. The only cars parked on the road were ones Liz recognized as belonging to locals. The buildings were mostly dark. Liz felt like she should be cautious, but the hairs on the back of her neck stayed flat. And Harley's comforting nearness and strength kept her heart from flipping too nervously in her chest, even for the few seconds of full exposure as they moved quickly to the side of her building.

Harley was the first to break the silence, gesturing to the ladder as he spoke. "Not a ladies-first situation, I'm afraid."

"That's okay," Liz replied with as much lightness as she could muster. "I think chivalry's a little overrated, anyway."

His face stayed solemn. "Then you've clearly been associating with the wrong men."

And with that, he turned and started his ascent.

Chapter 9

Harley didn't turn around and check for a reaction. He knew he probably sounded annoyed, and he also knew that Liz might misinterpret it as irritation at *her*. Truthfully, he was drawing his own ire. And every few rungs on the ladder renewed it.

Rung one. *Should've been more insistent.*

Rung four. *Shouldn't be putting her in danger.*

Rung nine. *You thought it was wrong to call Frost because he was a civilian...but this...this is far worse.*

Rung twelve. *It's her daughter. That much is true. But what good will that do if she gets hurt? Or worse.*

At rung seventeen—the second to last—he shut down his brain with an out-loud growl, then pushed up and over the lip of the roof. The problem was that in spite of every reasonable argument against allowing Liz to accompany him came the reminder that if their roles were reversed, he would've felt just the same. What if he'd had some warning about his father's death? Would he have been content to let someone else take the lead? Even now, he—and Brayden, Anderson and Rush, too—didn't trust anyone else to investigate Garibaldi and his doings in Whispering Woods.

The difference is training. Experience. Having the tools to actually do *the job,* he told himself as he turned to call down to Liz.

He found her already at the top. Her pretty blue eyes met his, and she reached out a hand. She didn't look at all perturbed, so if his gruffness a minute earlier had bothered her, she wasn't letting on.

"You were supposed to wait until I told you it was safe," he stated as he took her fingers and helped her over the side.

"And what if someone was at the bottom, just waiting until you were out of sight?" she countered a little breathlessly.

"You've got an answer for everything, don't you?" he grumbled.

"Let's just say that Teegan comes by her sass honestly." Liz smiled, but the pleasure in her expression quickly faded, and she swallowed, her eyes growing a bit too bright.

Empathy hit Harley in the gut. He could read perfectly what had just happened. It had been a common thing for him after his father was killed. There'd be some happy thought, and then he'd remember.

But Teegan's alive, he thought firmly. *And that's how we're going to keep it.*

As was quickly becoming a habit, he tightened his fingers around hers and gave her a tug. "C'mon."

He was surprised to meet with resistance, and he turned to lift an eyebrow her way.

"Wait," she said a little belatedly.

"Wait for what?"

"Tell me."

"Tell you what?"

"What you meant when you said you know what it's like to experience loss."

He opened his mouth to tell her now wasn't the time. To add that they didn't *have* time. Instead, he gave her another little pull, and as they made their way across the roof, he started to talk.

"I was thirteen when my dad died," he said, his voice low. "He was a cop for the Freemont PD. My brother and I—especially Brayden, I think—hero-worshipped him. He worked long hours, but always made time for us."

He paused when they reached the other side of the roof, and he let go of Liz's hand to step onto the outstretched tree branch. As soon as they were both moving through the foliage toward the bedroom window, he started speaking again.

"He wasn't perfect. His work hours drove my mom crazy. I remember that well. But he was so dedicated to the job. I think he truly saw the police force as a way to make the world a better place."

"He sounds like a good man," Liz said.

"He was," Harley agreed. "Hardworking. Dedicated. Friendly neighbor. The works. The kind of guy that gets called 'salt-of-the-earth.'"

"I'm sorry you lost him so early." Liz sounded like she meant it, but Harley couldn't help but shake his head.

"We didn't lose him. He was taken." There was no bitterness in the statement, just matter-of-factness. "He and two other officers were in the evidence room, reportedly going over something. They were keeping the details under wraps, but my mom told us that what they were working on was a career-changing case. But it all ended abruptly when a pipe bomb went off, killing all three of them and destroying the evidence at the same time."

"That's awful, Harley," said Liz.

"It was. It is."

He stopped again, because they'd reached the screen-covered window. The room was still lit, just as the two men had left it, and it showed no further signs of disturbance. But Harley stared, unmoving, through the mesh for a long moment anyway.

"What's wrong?" Liz asked after a few seconds.

Shaking himself a little, Harley lifted his hands to remove the screen, then carefully set it just inside.

"I was just thinking that it feels like days since I pulled this thing off," he said, gesturing for her to go in first. "But it's only been a few hours."

"I guess time flies when you're having one of the worst days of your life," Liz replied as she stepped through.

Without realizing what he was going to do until his fingers were already on her elbow, Harley shot out his hand and stopped her from going any farther. She turned his way, eyes wide. One foot was inside, the other still on the branch.

Her lips dropped open. "What are you—"

Harley tugged her elbow and leaned forward at the same time. He pressed his lips to hers forcefully, kissing her far harder than he'd done before. For a second, Liz was still. Like he'd shocked her into immobility. Then she came alive. Her arms came up to his shoulders, and her fingers slid to the shortest part of his hair. Her mouth went from soft and yielding to alive and eager, and when he parted her lips with his tongue, a little moan escaped her throat. The sound was all the motivation he needed.

In a slick move that he was sure was superhero-worthy,

Harley bent one leg, straddled the window frame in the same way that Liz was, then dropped a palm under her knee and lifted her leg over his hip. He held her that way for only a moment before pulling himself—and her with him—through the window and into the bedroom.

Vaguely, he thought he should probably stop. Or at least slow down. But Liz showed no signs of wanting him to, and with both her legs now wrapped around him, Harley was probably going to have to force himself to cease and desist, cop-style. For right that second, though, he was content to ramp things up a little more.

He spun so that her back faced the wall. Then he pushed her *against* the wall. He kissed her deeper. Slower. Tasted every bit of her mouth until he was sure that she was 100 percent breathless. One hundred percent sure that if he took it further and she continued to meet his attention with such enthusiasm that he wouldn't stand a chance of cutting it off himself.

He pulled back, breathing shallowly himself, and put one final gentle kiss on her lips. "There."

Liz's eyes were glassy as she tipped her face up and echoed, "There?"

"One of the worst days of your life," he said. "Just wanted to give you one small thing to make it the tiniest bit better."

She lifted a hand and touched her mouth. "That was a small thing?"

"Small," he agreed, stepping back and letting her feet slide to the floor. "But not inconsequential."

"Thank you," she replied softly. "And I don't mean for the kiss."

"Why? Was it bad?"

"What? No. It was perfect. I just meant—"

He bent down and kissed her again—firmly. "I know what you meant. But no thanks are necessary."

"Even superheroes need the odd bit of gratitude."

"Not this one."

"Can you really live up to that impossible standard? Saving everyone and never getting the credit?"

He suspected she meant it to come out as a joke—there was a hint of humor in her voice—but he also detected a touch of concern. Like she really thought his expectation might be unrealistically high. He knew that keeping her faith high was going to be key in driving them forward.

"I come from a family of cops. Saving people is in my blood." He said it lightly, then brought up his hand and dragged it backward over her cheek. "So should we do this?"

She let out a relieved sigh—like his words and touch were all the reassurance she needed. "Yes, please."

"Can you pack an overnight bag?"

"We only have twenty-four hours."

"I know. But that twenty-four hours might feel long. You'll be tired. You might want pajamas. Or just to be able to clean up." Harley smiled. "Take the advice of a man who's been unlucky enough to spend time on more than a few stakeouts."

Liz nodded. "Okay. Anything else?"

He hesitated, not wanting to tell her that he needed her to sit tight—and out of sight—for a few minutes. And he hated the idea of leaving her as much as he hated the idea of telling her that that was what he was about to do. But he didn't have to. She read him perfectly.

"You're going downstairs, aren't you?" she asked.

"I need to have a look," he replied.

"For my sake or the sake of your case?" Her cheeks went pink. "Sorry. That sounded self-centered."

"There's nothing self-centered about putting your kid's life first," he said. "You want me to make a promise?"

Her responding expression was serious. "Only if it's one you can keep."

"That's the only kind I make."

"Okay, then…promise away."

"Getting Teegan back is my number one priority. Keeping *you* safe is directly below your kid on my to-do list. And somewhere way below that is my case. So I promise you that I won't do anything that will skew those priorities." He paused, then added, "But to be completely honest, my gut is telling me that they're connected. There can only be so many bad guys in a town this small."

She studied him for a second before conceding. "I guess that's true."

He didn't tell her that he was sure that her own landlord was the underlying connection. She'd probably find that out sooner rather than later anyway, but for the moment, that particular piece of information would only make her worry more. So instead of elaborating, he gave her a nudge, then moved through the small apartment, carefully checking every possible hiding space on the off chance that someone had holed themselves up inside.

Something you should've done before *trying to kiss her within an inch of her life?*

He mentally rolled his eyes at his own conscience. If he'd really thought there was a chance someone was inside, he wouldn't have stopped to steal a kiss and have a chat. He was just performing the search for Liz's peace of mind. He wanted her to feel safe while he slipped out.

When he'd proved that every nook and cranny was clear, he took Liz's hand and brought her to the door.

"I'll stand in the hall until the lock clicks," he told her. "You focus on getting your stuff ready. Leave the lights on that were already on, and the ones off that were off, and I'll be back so fast you won't have time to miss me."

She nodded, but as he stepped into the hall and started to close the door, her voice stopped him.

"Wait," she said.

He paused and fully opened the door again, noting that in spite of her ample curves, she looked small and vulnerable right that second. Maybe it was the way the dark hallway behind her nearly engulfed her. Maybe it was the clear concern in her eyes. Either way, an urge to crush her to his chest almost overwhelmed Harley. He had a feeling, though, that if he pulled her into an embrace now, he wouldn't want to let go.

So he settled for meeting her gaze and asked, "Something wrong? Besides all the obvious things, I mean."

She sucked in her bottom lip. "How long should I wait before I worry about you?"

Harley exhaled, trying to ease the sudden pressure in his chest. It was a strange achy feeling. Liz was worried about *him*. It made him want to tug her close even more.

"I shouldn't be more than ten minutes, fifteen at most," he told her.

Her expression didn't change. "Damn."

"What?"

"I was hoping you'd tell me I *shouldn't* worry at all."

"You shouldn't worry at all," he replied automatically.

The smallest smile tipped up her lips. "The reassurance kind of loses its impact when I know you're just telling me what I want to hear."

"You shouldn't, though," he replied. "I'll only be gone for a few minutes."

"Make me another promise," she said.

He knew he should hesitate—wait and find out what

it was before agreeing—but he found himself nodding instead. "Name it."

"Promise me you're going to be safe and actually come back." Her voice wavered as she said it, and Harley couldn't even pretend to say no.

"I promise, Liz. I'll be careful and safe, and I'll come back." He moved forward, ghosted a kiss across her lips, then stepped back and closed the door.

Liz stared at the door for several seconds before forcing herself to reach out and click the lock. She could feel her confidence threatening to ebb away the moment she couldn't see, hear or feel the big undercover detective anymore.

Stop it, she told herself sternly. *You can't give in to hopelessness, and you can't lay every bit of hope on Harley, either.*

Relying so heavily on someone else wasn't her usual MO. Even for all the years that she'd lived with Teegan's dad's parents, she insisted on contributing. When her daughter was an infant, she took a night-shift job at a local restaurant so she could contribute financially. Her in-laws—which was how they referred to themselves, even though it wasn't technically accurate—always told her it wasn't necessary. They'd have been happy to carry the complete load. They weren't wealthy, but they were comfortable, and had more than enough to support her and Teegan. But Liz was fiercely independent. She'd taken their help for her daughter's sake, and was grateful for having both a roof over her head and two extra sets of willing hands. That didn't mean she was going to just sit around and take advantage of them.

She needed to channel that inner independence now.

To be proactive in helping find her daughter, even when the surreal kicked-in-the-gut feeling wouldn't go away.

She counted off ten careful breaths, then swallowed against the weight in her heart and made herself move. Made herself do the busywork Harley had assigned her to do, grabbing a soft-sided bag from the little closet in the hall, then moving to the bedroom to toss in the essentials.

Toothbrush and paste.

Yoga pants and a baggy T-shirt.

Phone charger and deodorant.

Two clean pairs of underwear and some jeans, just in case.

When it was all piled haphazardly into the bag, Liz shook her head at how it looked. Like she'd hurriedly packed for a spontaneous overnight trip with her boyfriend.

Boyfriend.

The word sent an unexpected lick of heat through her. In the eight years since Teegan had been born, Liz hadn't dabbled much in the dating world. In the beginning, it was too impractical. At eighteen, she was a single mother. Almost a widow. And too utterly enamored with her baby to care much about finding a relationship. As Teegan got older, Liz *had* gone out occasionally. Setups, mostly. Blind dates. A tiny sprinkling of online romance. One brief fling with a fellow employee at the bank where she'd worked as a teller for a few years.

But ultimately, she always went home alone. Not that she was ever lonely. Her life was full. Between her various career endeavors and family, she was content. Always.

Until now? asked a little voice in her head.

She frowned down at the pile of items. It went without saying that tonight wasn't a night for contentment.

Every breath made her lungs burn with the ache of missing her daughter. The fact that she could even think about a single thing other than Teegan was a miracle. A self-centered one, at that.

So why was she wondering what it would be like if she were packing this bag for a *real* overnight getaway? Why was she thinking about how Harley would look in the morning, slightly sleep-deprived, wrapped in a sheet and nothing else? And more important, why didn't it make her feel guilty?

With a sigh, she zipped the bag up, then sank down beside it on the bed to wait. A glance at her phone told her that time had slowed down yet again. Only six minutes had gone by since Harley walked out the door.

She closed her eyes and willed the time to go faster.

Her mind slipped away from Harley and back to Teegan. Liz hoped to God she wasn't hurt. Or too scared. And that the men who had her were treating her as well as Harley had told them to. She was so thankful that he'd made the demands he had. And it was that exact kind of thing that heightened her attraction to him.

Maybe that's why you don't feel guilty, she reasoned. *It would be hard to feel bad about getting friendly with a man who is so clearly dedicated to your and Teegan's safety.*

The thought made part of her question whether her attraction was some kind of transference. She knew that was a thing. And there was no doubt in her mind that his true desire to protect her and save Teegan made him more appealing. But she'd noted his affability before that night. And she'd be lying if she said his good looks hadn't caught her eye the second he walked into Liz's Lovely Things and asked about the studio.

Romance had had zero place in her life for almost a

decade. The idea that it had popped up now was almost ludicrous. Yet there it seemed to be.

She appreciated everything she'd seen in Harley. Like the way he was with her daughter—genuinely interested and able to get right down to her level. And the way he looked just after he finished a sculpting session—all intense and a little puzzled, as though he was trying to figure out how he got from one world to the other.

In spite of the fact that his "job" as an artist was just his cover story, his passion was clear. It was a passion Liz shared. And kindness like his wasn't easily faked. So whether or not there *was* a little transference happening, the truth was that she liked him anyway. She was interested in this big protective man in a far more than friendly way.

As if that toe-curling kiss wasn't enough to tell you that?

A pleasant tingle crept up her body as she owned it.

"I like him," she said aloud.

And suddenly Liz *really* wanted him to come back. Eager to know how much longer she'd have to wait, she opened her eyes to take another look at her phone. Eight minutes now. So he'd be nearing the end of his little mission. She hoped.

She closed her eyes again, picturing his movement through the building. He was quick and efficient. He would've retrieved his weapon from the studio in only a minute or two. And maybe—if he was *really* quick and efficient—he would've also put on a fresh set of clothes. He'd have made his way down to the shop and looked around for whatever clues he was searching for. With any luck, he'd have found something that would help them find her daughter. And she hoped that whatever it was helped him with his case, too.

She frowned to herself. She hadn't thought too much about the comment about her daughter's abduction—*please, please let her be safe*—being connected to his undercover work. Now that it was on her mind, it struck her as a little odd. And piqued her curiosity. What Harley had said might be true. Whispering Woods was a small town, driven mostly by tourism. The crime rate was exceptionally low, and really only increased with the influx of people during the two peak seasons of summer and winter.

But just a few weeks ago, two people had been found dead in a house fire. The town was *still* reeling. Especially since it was the second fire within a few days. The first fire had destroyed an older fourplex. But the local police and National Park Service had investigated and closed off the case, blaming the same man—who was identified as one of the bodies in the second fire—for both incidents.

Liz frowned a little harder as she recalled something else. The fourplex that burned down had belonged to Nadine Stuart. The same woman who'd left town with one of Harley's partners. And Nadine had also been Teegan's teacher.

Her heart skipped a nervous little beat, and her mouth went a little dry, too.

"Not a coincidence," she murmured.

She didn't know what the connection was—she didn't have quite enough information to piece it all together—but she was suddenly sure there was one. Just like Harley had said.

What's the common denominator? she wondered.

With slightly sweaty palms making her fingers slick, she checked her phone again. Ten minutes had gone by. Harley was cutting it close.

Liz pushed to her feet, her mind flitting nervously while her stomach churned. She paced the room. What would she do if he really didn't come back? How would she find her daughter? Harley had both the kidnapper's phone and the sketched logo in his possession. Why hadn't Liz asked to hold both? Or even one.

He promised he'd come back, she reminded herself. But another reminder quickly followed. *Because you asked him to.*

She stole yet another look at her phone. Eleven minutes. She considered being proactive and heading downstairs now. Then reconsidered that as unreasonable. Maybe Harley hadn't checked the time. Maybe he was halfway back up already.

Maybe you should check the hall.

She bit her lips, then decided her peace of mind was worth taking a peek for. If Harley caught her, he'd be annoyed. But at least she'd know that much sooner that he was safe.

She took a step toward the bedroom door. Then froze as a sound carried in from somewhere outside her bedroom window caught her ear.

Footsteps hitting the concrete.

She turned and inched toward the screen. She took a breath and leaned forward.

And realized that she'd looked at just the right moment. A few seconds later, and she might've missed it. Missed *him*. The hooded man with the oh-so-distinct limp. Who stood at the end of the alley, his attention focused straight toward the back door of Liz's shop.

Chapter 10

Harley took a step back from the empty space where the large paintings had to have been on display. It was the third time he'd come back to the spot, and the third time he'd found nothing of true interest.

He sighed and ran a frustrated hand over his hair.

He'd grabbed his gun quickly, then taken about thirty seconds to slip from his clay-and-dirt-covered T-shirt into a clean one. He'd snagged the small bag he always kept at the ready, stuffed his laptop into it and then made his way downstairs without a hitch.

It wasn't until he'd actually hit the inside of the store that he'd slowed down. And now his movements felt stagnant. Stalled.

The first thing that'd struck him was that there'd been signs of a struggle. Shelves askew, a can of paint knocked over. It wasn't particularly surprising. The men who'd broken into Liz's apartment had rushed down to confront the painting thieves.

Harley scratched at his chin. Who were they? Why were two separate groups breaking into the shop at the same time?

Not two, he corrected silently. *Three. There was the hooded man, too.*

He spun in a slow circle, feeling like he was missing something. Aside from the mess, he'd found very little hint as to what had gone on inside Liz's Lovely Things. Or at least very little that made any more sense of the situation.

Then there was the residual smoke, which had the same acrid scent he'd noted before. For a minute, he'd actually thought the gray-tinged air might lead him somewhere. With no evidence of any actual explosion, he'd quickly concluded that the smoke wasn't a by-product of something else, but rather the primary intention. A smoke bomb, most likely. So he'd gone in search of the smoke detectors to find out why they hadn't gone off. It'd been a disappointingly fast puzzle to solve. The three separate devices were hardwired into the ceiling, and whoever had disarmed them had done so without too much care. They'd punched a hole through the paint and drywall, then clipped a wire, which still hung loosely from the opening. Not bothering to disguise it, which meant not caring if they got caught, adding yet another question.

So he'd come back to the empty space that had housed the Heigles. He'd already known to expect the paintings to be gone. *Why* they'd been taken remained a mystery. What made them so important that someone was willing to steal them? To kidnap to get them? To threaten a woman and her child's life over just knowing which ones they were?

Though several things his partners had found—both Brayden *and* Anderson—hinted at the fact that Garibaldi's wrongdoings were somehow connected to the art world, which was what'd led Harley to Liz in the first place, the actual motivation behind it was unknown. Art theft and forgery were a highly specific tangent in the criminal underworld. Practically heart surgery. Jesse Garibaldi had cunning and cash, but being involved in some kind of art-thievery ring hardly seemed up his alley. He was a man who liked things quick and dirty, with the blame laid at someone else's feet.

And on top of that, Harley thought, *Liz said the paintings weren't worth much.*

Harley rolled his stiff shoulders and did his best to shrug off the fact that his little trip down to the shop hadn't yielded much, if anything at all. He tucked the few details to the back of his mind to peruse later. Right then, he needed to get back to Liz.

Even though he didn't have a watch, he knew he had to be nearing the time limit he'd set. If he didn't head back upstairs in the next thirty seconds or so, she would likely chase him down. She'd be glad to see him alive. At least for the thirty seconds it took her to realize he was just running behind and not lying dead in the shop. Then she'd be mad. And rightly so. She didn't need to add worrying about *him* to her already-full plate of concerns. On top of that, he had no desire to heighten her fear. Just the opposite.

So hurry up, he urged.

With a final frustrated look at the empty space, and another scratch at the day-old stubble on his chin, he started to turn. He only made it halfway before a creak in the floorboards alerted him to the fact that he wasn't alone.

Acting on instinct, he ducked low and sought cover behind one of the shelves of small framed prints.

And this is why we have partners or call for backup, Harley thought, wishing like hell he'd been paying a little less attention to the paintings and a little more attention to his surroundings. *First-day rookie mistake.*

He stabilized his footing and freed his weapon at the same moment. His body was on alert, but no assault came.

Instead, a familiar, nervous voice said, "Harley? Please don't shoot."

He immediately dropped his arm and stepped out. Liz stood in the doorway that led from the store up to her apartment. Her blue eyes flicked from him toward the back of the store, then back again. Fear was etched into her face.

He took an immediate step closer. "Honey. What's wrong? What are you doing? You shouldn't—"

She cut him off and moved into the store at the same time, her gaze going to the back of the store again. "I know. I'm sorry. But there's no time to give me heck."

Harley frowned, following the spot that seemed to hold so much interest for her. The only thing back there was excess inventory and the delivery entrance.

The delivery entrance.

"Liz," he said. "What's going on?"

"Hurry. Please."

The urgency in her voice spurred him to grab his bag from the countertop. By the time he had it slung over his shoulder and had started to holster his weapon, she was at his side, her warm fingers sliding into his.

"Hurry," she said again, tugging his hand so hard that he almost dropped his weapon.

His heart beat a solid nervous thump against his chest as she pulled him at a near-run across the sales floor. She barely paused to unlock the door before slamming her free palm against it to force it open. Together, they tumbled into the street. Harley expected her to stop. To give an explanation. But she kept going, pulling him across the street. And thank God she did, because they no sooner stepped into the door frame of one of the shops there than something inside of Liz's Lovely Things exploded.

The glass door they'd just come through shattered outward, shards flying. Seconds later, a lick of orange flames became visible through the opening, and only a moment after that, smoke—real burning smoke this time rather than the chemical stuff from earlier—blew out from the store in the night air.

Twenty seconds later, Harley thought, *and I could've been a dead man.*

He turned to say as much to Liz—to point out that she'd probably just saved his life, and also to ask how she'd known something was about to happen—but stopped when he saw the heartbreak in her eyes as she watched the flames grow steadily higher. So, instead of throwing gratitude her way in the wake of her enormous loss, Harley pulled her to him. He pressed her back to his chest and ran his fingers down her arms. It probably wasn't much comfort. An embrace hardly seemed like a good enough buffer when faced with losing a home and a business. But he still felt it was a hell of a lot more genuine than offering her trite comments about everything being okay. Lord knew he'd heard enough of that when his father died. People meant it when they said it. Harley knew that. But he was also a man who valued action over words. So he continued to hold her tightly.

"It was the man in the hood," Liz finally said, her voice nearly drowned out by the sudden blast of sirens somewhere in the distance. "I saw him coming off the street. I knew he was headed toward my store, but…"

As she trailed off, she drew in a wobbly breath, and Harley pulled her against him even tighter.

The sirens grew louder. Any second, Whispering Woods' two fire trucks would be on scene. Liz seemed to realize it, too.

"We shouldn't stay," she stated.

Harley nodded, his chin brushing against her curls. "You're right. We shouldn't. And I've got an idea about where we should go. Your leg up for a walk?"

She glanced down at her patched leg. "I guess there's not much choice."

"Not much," he agreed. "Unless you want me to carry you the whole way."

The joke earned him a tremulous smile. "I'll let you know if it becomes a necessity."

"Promise?"

"Yes."

"Okay. Let's move before someone notices we're here and thinks it's a good idea to ask questions."

For a few minutes after they left the area, neither said a word. Harley led the way, keeping quiet to give Liz space. And he suspected she kept quiet because she *needed* that space he offered.

The silence was comfortable, though, even if it was also heavy. It gave Harley time to think about what he'd just witnessed. He made an effort to filter it through his critical investigative lens rather than through his sympathetic feelings for Liz. A theory immediately came to mind—aided by the night air clearing his head a bit—and his gut told him it was the right one.

It started with the smoke bomb. A prank. The kind of thing that high school seniors threw into the concourse to delay exams. A distraction. Which Harley suspected was its purpose in this case as well. It made sense now

that it occurred to him. If someone—Garibaldi's enforc-
ers or guards or whomever he currently had under his
thumb—was physically watching the shop to protect the
man's assets, smoke leaking out of the building would
definitely attract some attention.

And it did. *From the two men who broke into Liz's
apartment*, Harley remembered.

At the moment it happened, he hadn't had time to
think too much about their role in the whole situation. On
first appearance, he assumed they were working *with* the
person who lit off the smoke bomb, but with the new idea
in mind, it made more sense that they might actually be
Garibaldi's men, sent there to keep an eye on his paintings. Assuming Liz's information was accurate—and
Harley didn't doubt her eyewitness account—it was more
likely that the hooded man was working with the thieves.

He went over the scenario in his head.

Mr. Hoody had come in to verify the location of the
Heigles. Taken that info back to his crew. The crew had come
in to do their part, fully prepared to confront Garibaldi's
spies. When it was all said and done, Mr. Hoody came
back. He cleaned up their mess, destroying evidence of
the struggle, the smoke bomb and the theft.

So what had happened to Garibaldi's men? Harley had
a hard time believing they'd come out unscathed. With
such a sophisticated plan in place, he couldn't imagine a
loose end. If they *had* somehow escaped, they would've
alerted Garibaldi by now. Garibaldi would be acting on it.

A chilling thought occurred to Harley. Maybe Garibaldi
was acting on it. Maybe taking Teegan was his way of getting the paintings back without ever getting his hands dirty.

But if that's true…what happens after?

The question—which made his hands want to ball
into fists and filled his chest with a terrible mix of icy

fear and heated fury—no sooner came to him than Liz broke the silence, and her words startled Harley so badly that he stumbled.

"It's Garibaldi, isn't it?" she asked softly.

Liz could tell that her question had thrown Harley for a bit of a loop. Not just because of the way he tripped over his own feet in what was undoubtedly an uncharacteristic moment of clumsiness for the big man, but also because of the extra moment he took to recover. Like he was using those few seconds to formulate an appropriate response.

And sure enough, his tone was utterly neutral as he replied, "What makes you say that?"

Liz knew she was right. That the puzzle piece that had clicked into place as she raced down the stairs to warn Harley of the impending danger was the exact right one. But she was pretty sure Harley wouldn't admit it unless she could show that she was already sure.

So she took a breath and gave him a quick rundown of the connections she'd made, and how she'd finally come to the conclusion. "While I was waiting for you to come back, I was trying *not* to make myself crazy by worrying about Teegan, and I was trying to be proactive. Helpful. So I was thinking about what you said about there being a connection between everything, and how there could only be so many bad guys in a small town. And I remembered about that house fire a few weeks ago. Did you hear about it?"

Harley nodded, his face impassive. "Yes. Murder-suicide."

Liz swallowed. "That's the one."

"What about it?"

"Jesse Garibaldi owned that house. He owns *all* the

houses in that neighborhood. One of the moms from Teegan's school told me that he was going to demolish them and build some higher-density residences."

"Okay." His voice was still even.

"And there was a cop who died a short while before that. His name was Chuck Delta."

"He was killed in a car accident."

She didn't ask how he knew, because she had a feeling he knew *everything* she was telling him. "Yes. He swerved to avoid hitting an oncoming car. Nadine Stuart was driving that car. Teegan's teacher. Who ran off with your partner Anderson?"

"And Garibaldi factors in how?"

"The whole town attended Chuck's funeral," she told him. "Which was *paid for* by Jesse Garibaldi. And I know he does stuff like that sometimes. He considers it to be a contribution to the community. But it kind of stuck in my mind. And all of this made me think of it again."

"What else?" Harley asked, his brown gaze probing.

"Your brother... Brayden?"

"Yes."

"He and Reggie Frost are a couple, you said. And the building that the Frost Family Diner is in is owned by Garibaldi. I know, because the whole block is."

"That's right."

"So he owned the burned-down house. He paid for the funeral for the officer who died. He owns the diner. And he owns the building where my shop is." She exhaled heavily as her chest compressed with the slap-like reminder of reality. "Where it *was*, I mean."

Harley reached out to take her hand again. "We don't know how much has been ruined."

She shook her head. "Fire and smoke? It's *art*, Harley. Even if the whole thing doesn't burn, I doubt much can be salvaged. Maybe something upstairs. But everything in the shop will be completely unsalvageable."

He was quiet for a minute, and when he spoke again, he didn't deny the truth of her statement. And it made her grateful.

"You're probably right," he said. "And whatever the smoke and fire didn't wreck will probably be destroyed by the efforts to put out the blaze."

In spite of everything, a small laugh bubbled to the surface at his blatant honesty. "What…you're not going to make me feel better? Tell me it's going to be fine?"

His fingers rubbed across the back of her hand. "If you want me to, I will. But when my dad died, that was all people said to me. 'Things happen for a reason.' 'Everything will work out.' Don't get me wrong. I do believe those things. But hearing it never did me much good. I wanted to *act*. Not sit back and let things just slide over me."

"Is that why you joined the police force?"

"Exactly why," he replied, then paused in his walking to give her a funny smile.

She frowned at his expression. "What?"

"I don't think I've ever really explained that to anyone before," he confessed.

Liz smiled back. "Then I'm honored."

He stared down at her for a second. "You have no idea how badly I want to just stand here and kiss you right now."

She felt her face warm. "I have *some* idea."

His brown eyes—which had been warm a second earlier—heated with desire, and Liz's breath caught as he closed the gap between them and tipped his mouth to hers. The contact was too brief by far, and when Harley pulled back, Liz wished she could drag him back again. But she knew they didn't have time. He clearly did, too. His eyes lingered on her lips for a second before he let out a regretful sigh.

"Time to move again," he said. "We're almost there."

"Where are we going, by the way?" Liz asked as she remembered that he hadn't yet disclosed their destination.

"My apartment."

"Isn't flooded out? Or was that just a part of your cover story?"

He chuckled. "No. Unfortunately, the burst pipe in the kitchen was real. Too real, probably. And it's still pretty disastrous inside. Plastic sheets and a slight lack of proper flooring. But I think that makes it a good place to hunker down and get to work. Unlikely to attract any unwanted attention."

Unwanted attention.

Liz had a feeling that the phrase was a euphemism for thieves and kidnappers and God knew what else. And it was a reminder. A kick in the stomach that renewed the knots there. Tears pricked at Liz's eyes, and she lifted her free hand to wipe them away before she sucked in a breath, then took his hand and pulled him to resume walking.

But she obviously hadn't fooled Harley, because they only made it a couple of steps before he gave her hand a squeeze and said, "It's gonna be a hell of a thing to rebuild, Liz, assuming that's what you want to do. And you're going through a hell of a thing right now, which is going to make it even harder. But you and Teegan can do it."

The ache in her chest expanded. "Are you telling me what you think I want to hear?"

"No, honey."

"So you really believe that we're going to get Teegan back?"

"We're going to track down those paintings, and we aren't handing them over until that kid has cartwheeled herself back over to us." His voice was fierce and sure. "If they harm a single hair, I'll do everything in my power to make them pay. I'm the kind of man who spends fifteen years chasing justice. No way can these guys outsmart us."

Liz breathed out. His reassurance was starting to feel like a lifeline. And also to feel like a habit. She tipped her head to the side to steal a glance at his profile. His jaw was stiff, and she suddenly felt self-doubt creep in. Was she in his way? Was her flux of emotions wearing on his nerves?

Like he could read her mind, his expression softened, and he glanced her way, then spoke again. "I'm just thankful that I was here when it happened."

"You are?" She sounded surprised, even to her own ears.

"I hate the thought that you could've been alone in this," he said with a headshake.

She bit her lip. It was a terrible thought, and even though it wasn't the first time it had crossed her mind, hearing him say it just renewed the realization that she was terribly lucky. What if Harley *hadn't* been there? She couldn't quite fathom it. Or maybe she just didn't want to.

"Actually…" Harley added. "Remember a minute ago when I said I didn't like that whole everything-happens-for-a-reason speech?"

"Yes."

"I take it back. That pipe bursting definitely happened for a reason. Bad plumbing and the forces of good united to put me in the right place at the right time."

Once again, Liz found herself laughing unexpectedly, but she sobered quickly. "Did I say thank-you?"

He smiled. "A time or two."

"I don't know if I can possibly say it enough times."

"Tell you what. I'll take every bit of gratitude you can offer once we've accomplished our goal."

"Well. I'm sure I'll be able to come up with *some* kind of creative way of expressing all that pent-up thankfulness." Her own reply caught her even more off guard than her laughter had, and an all-over blush crept up under her skin.

And his response—accompanied by a low, sexy chuckle—didn't help. "So that whole superhero-getting-the-girl thing is true, huh?"

Liz tried to fight her continuing blush. "Maybe you should've tried the upgrade from detective sooner."

They reached his apartment building then, and he stopped in front of it and turned to face her. His face was serious, and so was his tone.

"As it so happens, I'm pretty damn glad I waited until now," he stated.

The words warmed Liz from the inside out, and rendered her pleasantly speechless, too. She settled for nodding, then watched in silence as Harley dug a key from the bag he carried.

It wasn't until they entered the building—on one of many streets in Whispering Woods that housed apartments catering to short-term tenants during the tourist season—that she realized the conversation had been steered away from Jesse Garibaldi.

Chapter 11

As Harley led Liz into his apartment, he weighed his options for what to tell her. Or maybe not so much *what* as *how much*. Honesty was best. Harley believed that. But he had an obligation to his job, and he had an obligation to Liz's emotional well-being, too. Both those things worked against full disclosure.

But Liz had put together Garibaldi's involvement with impressive ease. Harley knew cops who didn't make accurate leaps so fast. In fact, he also knew cops who'd broken under less pressure than Liz had. Her kid had been taken. Her store robbed, then bombed. Her life wasn't just turned upside down—it was on the brink of complete destruction. Yet somehow, she was holding it together. Even in the moments when she could've let it overwhelm her—those few seconds where the worry shone through and her fear was evident in the quaver of her voice or the pinch of her eyes—she still pulled herself back and didn't topple over that edge. Tough as hell on the inside.

So Harley was sure that she wasn't going to let the Garibaldi thing go, either. Not so long as she thought— *knew*, he corrected mentally—that the man's business was connected to her daughter's abduction. He wouldn't have, if their roles were reversed.

Still, it was a short enough ride up to his third-floor apartment that he managed to steer clear of the subject. Once inside, it was easy to keep the avoidance up under the guise of an apology for the dishevelment, then again in the small eruption of chaos as he cleared the plastic sheeting from the couch and table, and offered to make Liz some tea. After a few seconds of back and forth— her protesting the extra trouble and the time it would take up, and his telling her he knew from experience that plans flowed better when hands, mouths and stomachs weren't idle—Harley thought maybe he'd dodged the need to keep being evasive.

But then, as she stood in the open kitchen doorway and watched him prepare the kettle, she said the words he'd been dreading. "I was thinking…"

He kept his reply light, but didn't turn to face her as he spoke. "Oh, yeah? Sounds dangerous."

"I was aiming for productive," she said, as he set about getting the teapot and tea bags from the cupboard.

"Better lay it on me, then."

"That logo on the white van…our best bet is to figure out who it belongs to and start there, right?"

"Yes."

"So what if we took a photograph of the drawing you made, then plugged that photo into an online image search."

He finally turned her way, impressed by her ingenuity. "That's a fantastic idea."

"Yeah?"

"Downright brilliant."

"Maybe I should consider a career change. Art dealer to superhero. Saving the day, getting the girl…" Her mouth turned up, then down. "I guess maybe I'll *need* a new career."

Harley swept in automatically, drawing her into an embrace so he could circle his hands over her back. "Hey now. Didn't I *just* give you that speech about rebuilding?"

"But it's *Garibaldi's* building," she replied, her words muffled against his chest, but still discernible.

His hands stilled. "It is."

"Harley?"

"Yes?"

"Give me the worst-case scenario."

He opened his mouth to tell her there was no way in hell he was going to even *consider* a worst-case scenario let alone posit one aloud, but he was saved by the whistle of the kettle. He dropped his arms away from Liz's body and moved back to the menial task, filling the pot with hot water, then grabbing the tray to carry it into the living room. She followed him wordlessly to the couch, quiet in a way that made him feel guilty. He kept his mouth shut, though, as he unpacked his laptop from his bag and set it up on the coffee table beside the steeping tea. Once he'd dragged the drawing of the logo from his pocket and snapped its picture, the silence finally got to him.

He cleared his throat and prepared to offer some glossed-over version of events. What came out of his mouth was something else entirely.

"He killed my father," he stated, then blinked at his own bluntness.

Liz drew in an audible breath. "Jesse Garibaldi?"

Harley continued to work on the task at hand, sending the photograph from his phone to his email address, then logging in to his account on the laptop.

"Garibaldi's the one who blew up the evidence room," he said as he waited for the picture to download, then upload. "And we've been chasing him ever since."

"I don't understand…" Liz replied. "If you *know* it was him…"

"It was a complicated thing," Harley told her, hating how banal that statement sounded. "He was a minor then. He had a good lawyer… Everything that could go wrong for the right side *did* go wrong. The only thing that worked in our favor was that my brother happened to figure out who he was. And before you ask, there's no question about whether we have the right man. Brayden saw him in court. He knew his name and his face."

Liz was quiet for a few moments, but Harley could feel her gaze on his face, and he wasn't all that surprised by how insightful her next comment was.

"So you've been waiting all this time to catch him in some other way," she said.

"And whatever it is he's been up to in Whispering Woods…is it." Harley frowned down at his computer, which was still uploading. "Don't know what's taking the stupid thing so long. When you pay for the best equipment, it should *be* the best equipment."

"It's not the equipment. It's the shoddy Wi-Fi," Liz told him, then paused before adding, "Do you know what Jesse Garibaldi's doing here?"

He shook his head, wishing he had a different answer. "No. We're sure he's using the town as a front for whatever his real business is. No other reason to ingratiate himself so thoroughly with the locals. What his endgame is—or even if he has one—is a mystery. All we know for sure is that the few clues we've managed to find all lead to something that makes no sense. Art forgery. Or something similar."

"Art forgery?" Liz echoed.

"Have any of your mom's friends who've been around a while ever told you about that explosion under Main Street?"

"Yes. Some drug addict used a pipe bomb to— Oh." She swallowed. "It wasn't the drug addict at all, was it?"

"No," Harley agreed. "It sure wasn't. The MO for that particular explosion was identical to the one that killed my dad and his partners at the Freemont PD station. But there was no reason for anyone to connect them. Years apart. Hundreds of miles apart. Totally different settings. And of course, everyone *knew* the drug addict had set off the bomb here, even though he was never convicted."

"But *you* knew it wasn't him."

"We figured it out."

"So how does the art forgery fit in?"

"Damn good question," he replied. "Before the Main Street explosion happened, there was already a warren of tunnels and crawl spaces under the businesses there. *After* the bomb, Garibaldi rebuilt them. Beefed them up. Took us a while to figure it out, but what he did was create an art-storage room. Perfect temperature, perfect air. And we found some photographic evidence that showed some big empty canvases being held in that room."

"Canvases the same size as the Heigles?"

"Safe assumption."

"But the paintings he gives me to sell…they're not worth any money. I'd never even heard the name of the artist until the man in the hood said it."

Harley sighed. "I know. It makes no sense. And I gotta say…art is my specialty, and I've been called in on some cases to help. But you don't run across related crime very often. Your average crook isn't running around stealing paintings or sculptures. There's not exactly a huge market on the street for high-priced items, and the lower-end stuff gets nothing. Couple of bucks at a pawnshop."

"So there wouldn't be a reason for Jesse Garibaldi to invest time and money in forging it," Liz filled in.

"Which is what brings *me* here," he replied. "I'm supposed to figure out what it is that's so special about these paintings."

"And that's why you're sure Teegan's kidnapping is connected to your case. But..."

"But what?"

"What made you come to me in the first place?"

Harley shifted uncomfortably in his seat, but before he could ease into an explanation, Liz's eyes widened.

"Oh, God," she said. "You thought it might be *me*. You thought I might be involved."

He didn't bother to deny it. "It was a consideration."

"But you were so *nice* to me."

"Was?"

She blushed prettily. "Are. But even when you thought I might be on the wrong side."

Harley smiled. "Flies. Honey. All that."

"When did you figure out that I *wasn't* involved?"

"Tonight."

She blinked. "Seriously?"

He shrugged. "Couldn't just come out and ask you."

"But you saved us anyway."

"We superheroes aren't that picky in who we save. Speaking of which..." He trailed off and glanced down at the laptop, which was finally doing what it was supposed to. "Look at this."

Liz leaned forward, her floral scent filling his nostrils

as she examined the search results. At the top of the page was a nearly identical logo.

"'Everlast of Freemont,'" Liz read aloud, reaching out to click on the link. "They're a contractor based in the city."

"Does it say who the owner is?" Harley asked.

"I don't see a name. You want to look?"

"Please."

He pulled the computer closer, quickly clicking through the pages of the website. It was a simple design. A standard fillable template with no added features. No contact info other than a basic email address—info@ everlastfreemont.com—and no names listed, either. It made him frown. Not because it was amateurish, but because it was so very bare. No reviews. No photos. He tapped his thumb against the edge of the laptop, thinking about it.

"Is something wrong?" Liz's voice was laden with undisguised worry.

Harley stilled his nervous twitch and turned to look at her. "Nothing's *wrong*. But something's not right."

"What do you mean? You can't have them investigated?"

"I can. I will. I'll give the station in Freemont a call and see if they can track down an address." He paused, thinking about it, then said, "Actually, I can do one better than that. I have a guy who looks into this stuff for me on the side, and I can reach out to him."

"Another cop?"

"Freelancer," he replied, clicking the construction website back to his email. "Works faster, owes me a million favors and is available 24/7." He typed up the request, then fired it off. "See? All done."

But when he turned his attention back to Liz, he found her face clouded.

"Hey," he said, "don't worry. My guy's strictly above bar. Nothing illegal. And he's the second fastest around. Right after me."

"It's not that," Liz replied.

"What is it?"

"You don't think he *will* find anything." Her words were a statement rather than a question, and Harley couldn't deny what his gut was whispering at him.

"A lot of what I do when I'm at work is this type of thing," he said. "I'm not a desk jockey by any stretch, but my specialty—after making dragon-shaped mountains out of clay, of course—is using technology to search for connections other people can't find. And I have a feeling this is one of those times when *they* would call *me* in for some expertise."

A little frown creased Liz's forehead. "So what would you expect to find?"

"I'm not sure," he admitted. "I'm used to having a few more resources at my personal disposal."

"So what do we do…just sit around and wait for your guy to get back to us?"

Harley started to reassure her that it would be quicker than she thought, but before he could speak, Liz's phone chimed to life in her bag, making her jump.

Unease filled Harley before he even knew who was on the other end. It was late. It was a weeknight. Under the best of circumstances, he would've been concerned about the call. Under *these* circumstances, it made him downright edgy.

And it only got worse when Liz retrieved the phone from her bag and held it out so he could see the name flashing across the screen in all caps.

JESSE GARIBALDI.

* * *

Liz dragged her gaze up from the phone to Harley. The blood was rushing through her so hard and so fast that she was dizzy. Even Harley's hand on her wrist offered almost no reprieve. She could see his mouth moving, but couldn't quite make out the words. The horrible sensation reminded her of the time when, as a kid, she'd taken a football to the head.

Woozy.

Faraway.

Underwater.

All of the above.

The phone continued its insistent ring, and she wondered vaguely why it hadn't gone to voice mail, before realizing that it was really only the second time the musical tone had played. The equivalent to about three rings on the other end.

Seven more, she thought. *Then it will end.*

But the dizziness worsened, and she cursed the fact that she had it set to ring so many times.

Ten rings. Who does that? Her mind was spinning, and she answered herself silently. *A woman who needs ten rings to answer sometimes, that's who. A mother. You.*

But right then, she wondered if she'd even make it that long.

Jesse Garibaldi. Her landlord. A murderer. The man who was either directly or indirectly responsible for Teegan's abduction. And either one was as bad as the other.

Liz sucked in a breath. She drew back the phone. And prepared to throw it. *Would* have thrown it if Harley's quick reflexes hadn't kicked in and stopped her. His hand slid from her wrist to her finger, forcing the phone to stay in place.

She met his eyes. Stared at his lips. And she finally heard what he was saying.

"You have to answer, honey."

"Why?" she whispered.

"If you don't, he'll get suspicious," Harley replied as he released her fingers. "And maybe act on that suspicion."

The chime started up a third time. Liz's mouth went dry.

"What do I say?" she asked.

"Play dumb," Harley told her.

"What if he's—"

"He might be. But you can't come even close to letting him think you suspect it."

She swallowed. "Okay."

"Hurry, honey," he urged.

She nodded woodenly, then lifted her other hand to tap the screen just before the final chime was about to cut off.

"Hello?" Her voice sounded fuzzy to her own ears.

Her landlord's reply was full of concern. "Liz? Are you there?"

"Mr. Garibaldi?"

She held the phone out away from her ear so that Harley would be able to hear as much as possible.

"It's me," the man on the other end said. "And I keep telling you to call me Jesse."

"Sorry. My old-fashioned manners come out when I've just woken up, I guess. What time is it? Is everything all right?"

There was a brief pause. "I was wondering the same thing. There was an incident at the store, and I thought maybe you'd been hurt."

Liz closed her eyes. There was something vaguely ominous about his words. Like he'd said "maybe" but really meant "assumed." Or worse…"hoped."

She exhaled a breath she hadn't known she'd been holding and did her best to filter out a believable level of concern. "What do you mean? What kind of incident? Is my place okay? Are *you* okay?"

"I'm fine," Garibaldi replied. "But I'm not so sure about Liz's Lovely Things. There was a bit of a fire."

"A bit of a fire?" Liz repeated, filling her voice with deliberate worry and meeting Harley's eyes as she said it; it seemed like an awfully big downplay of what they'd witnessed.

She expected Harley to react with a nod or an expression of agreement. She was surprised to see that, instead, his face was pale and still. Concern flooded through her. She reached out a hand to grasp one of his and found his fingers rigid. His gaze dropped to the spot where she touched him. It hung there for a second before he took a deep breath and offered her a nod.

What's going on in his head? she wondered, wishing she could ask.

But Garibaldi's voice jerked her attention back to the phone. "Liz?"

"Sorry," she replied quickly. "My brain's still trying to wrap around all of this. I missed the last bit."

"I was just saying that I want you to know I've got my best guy looking into it."

"What about the fire department? Isn't this something *they* investigate?" Liz blurted, then winced as she realized her tone bordered on accusatory.

"Absolutely." The reply was too quick. Too smooth. And it got worse when he added, "But my investigator has *my* best interests at heart."

His best interests. Liz shivered. She didn't want to think too closely on what his statement meant.

"Right," she made herself say.

He chuckled, which sounded utterly out of place. "Don't sound so doubtful. The civil servants have a job to do, but they don't care about my investments, or about yours. If the fire department thinks it was arson, it'll slow every damn thing down."

"*Do* they think that?" she asked cautiously.

"My guy says it was a gas issue compounded with a fault in the smoke detectors." He paused. "I take it you aren't nearby enough to have witnessed any of this?"

He didn't *quite* sound like he was fishing.

Liz bit her lip and replied with the first thing that came to mind. "No. Teegan was having a bit of trouble sleeping, which meant *I* couldn't sleep, either. So we went for an impromptu late-night dessert at a friend's and wound up sleeping there instead."

"Count yourself lucky," Garibaldi stated. "Could've been devastating for you. I do think you should get back here ASAP. There's going to be some insurance questions. The police and fire guys will want to talk to you. And I imagine you'll want to have a look at what can be salvaged."

Liz paused, then asked a genuine question, her voice soft. "How bad is it, Jesse?"

"Pretty bad," he admitted. "But it could've been much worse. The fire truck was there in two minutes. The blaze was out in five. I don't know how much of your inventory can be salvaged, but my coverage is excellent. How's your policy?"

The conversation was starting to seem far too light for comfort—far too light for the situation, in general—and Liz had a sudden feeling that it was all just preamble. Her landlord was leading up to something else.

But what?

"My policy is good," she said. "I invested everything

I had into the store, so I didn't take any chances. And my father-in-law was in insurance before he retired."

"Excellent. Or as excellent as can be, I suppose." He paused. "Actually, I was able to get inside your store for a quick look around."

Liz tensed. "You were?"

"Mmm." It was clear to her that the noncommittal noise was just a prelude to what he wanted to say next—to what he'd been leading up to all along. "Bit of a weird question."

"Okay."

"The paintings I dropped off…"

She had to make her jaw relax in order to answer in a convincingly apologetic and sympathetic way. "Oh, God. I wasn't even *thinking* about your inventory. And about *your* building."

He brushed off her feigned concern. "Don't worry about me. I just wondered if my buyers happened to have come in to buy them before you closed up."

"No. My last customer bought a sculpture for her son." It was the literal truth. "Why?"

"Not a big deal. But even with all the destruction inside, I thought it looked like they weren't there." His tone was far too casual.

The blood rushed to Liz's head again, and she could barely hear her own reply. "You don't think they were destroyed?"

"I'm sure they must've been." He let out an audible sigh. "Probably wishful thinking."

"I'm sorry, Jesse."

"Nothing you could've done. I'm just glad you and Teegan are okay."

Her heart twisted in her chest. "Thank you."

"Should I expect to see you in the morning, then?"

"I'll get there as soon as I can."

"Good night, Liz."

"Good night."

She tapped the phone off and turned to Harley with the intention of recounting whatever bits of the conversation he may have missed and discussing what would come next. But when she met his gaze, she caught a pained look in his eyes that perfectly matched the one in her heart. And instead of speaking, she threw herself into his arms.

Chapter 12

Harley hadn't expected to be hit so hard by hearing Garibaldi's voice. Or maybe he hadn't really thought about it at all, which was why he hadn't been fully prepared for it. He couldn't recall how the man who killed his father sounded fifteen years ago. In fact, at that moment, he couldn't remember if he'd *ever* heard him speak. All he knew was that the normalcy of it galled him. More than galled. Angered. Nearly infuriated. It was unfair that the man continued to exist in regular society. That he had a life. That he ran multiple enterprises and could sit down for a steak dinner if he so chose. He should've been behind bars in an orange jumpsuit. He should've been busy being reminded every day that he'd taken the life of a good man. Of multiple good men.

And not just the lives of those men...the innocence of their sons. The hearts of their wives.

As the thoughts and emotions ran rampant through

Harley's mind, a deep, searing pain built up in his chest. It was familiar, because it was the same one he'd felt when first learning of his father's death. But he'd buried it deep. Sunk himself into solving other people's crimes. And feeling it now wasn't just like ripping off a Band-Aid. It was like a fresh wound altogether.

The only thing keeping him grounded was the woman in his arms. It was almost funny. For the last few hours, he'd been doing his damnedest to keep *her* safe. To protect her from giving in to despair. Now she was holding him up instead, just by virtue of her embrace.

He pulled back slightly—he wanted to see Liz's eyes, and find the empathy he knew would be there—but he no sooner eased away than he realized the absolute last thing he wanted was to allow any space between them. And as it turned out, he didn't have to. One of her hands freed itself from his waist and came up to cup his cheek. The intimate gesture sent a new need through him. *Desire.* It coursed through him, quickly superseding the want of comfort.

Too much, too soon? asked his subconscious. *Wrong place, wrong time?*

And maybe it *was* all of that. But as Liz tipped up her face and parted her lips expectantly, Harley was sure that it was also the opposite. Just the right time. Just the right amount.

He dipped his mouth to hers and kissed. Lightly, at first. An exploration and a question. Her lips answered by parting to let his tongue slip inside. She tasted like the lightly spiced tea they'd been drinking, and she was just as warm, too. Inviting and sweet. When the tiniest gasp escaped from somewhere in her throat, it spurred Harley to deepen the kiss even further.

He brought one hand to the back of her neck and slid

his fingers into the mess of soft curls, and he brought the other to the curve of her hip. He teased her lips with his tongue and teeth, and he drew her so close that she was practically in his lap. And then there was nothing *practically* about it. She turned in just the right way, and her knees parted so that she was straddling him.

For several moments, the new position rendered Harley motionless. He stared up at her, loving the view. Her tumble of hair. Her slightly hooded, slightly glassy, oh-so-blue eyes. The flush in her lightly freckled cheeks and the swell of her lips. In that very second, he decided she wasn't just pretty. She was beautiful. Unique and sexy. Everything that captivated Harley, not just as a man, but as an artist. He had a crazy desire to ask her to pose for him so he could sculpt her. As soon as he thought it, though, he wondered if he'd be able to do any justice to her curves. They were perfect.

She had full begging-to-be-gripped hips. Her waist wasn't terribly narrow, but it dipped in and accentuated her tempting breasts.

When he still didn't move, Liz leaned down and gave his bottom lip a little tug with her teeth. It was just sharp enough to sting without really hurting, and just deviant enough to make sure Harley-the-artist took a serious back seat to Harley-the-man.

He let out a little growl and slid both hands to those grab-able hips of hers, and pulled her even closer. Her curves slammed against him—soft and firm at the same time—and she gasped. He didn't give her time to recover. He slipped his hand up from her hips to her waist, then flipped her to the couch and covered her body with his own. Then he kissed her again. Slow this time, but no less thorough.

As he perused Liz's mouth, she was anything but passive. Her hands tightened on his back, then dropped to the hem of his shirt and made their way up. The feel of her fingers against his skin was almost more than he could take. His hips thrust forward, and their jeans became a maddening barrier.

He wanted her.

All of her.

And it was that thought that at last curbed his urgency.

He wanted all of her. Not just the emotionally raw, scared-for-daughter's-life version of her. If they were going to get involved—and he hoped they were—then he didn't want it to be tainted by doubt. So he gave her one more kiss, then pulled back.

Liz opened her eyes, surprise evident on her flushed face. "What's wrong?"

Harley smiled. "A little bit of everything."

Her brow wrinkled. "What?"

He touched her lips with his fingers, then pulled her to a sitting position beside him on the couch before answering.

"I want you." It felt good and right to admit it aloud.

"And that's…bad?" she replied.

"Just the timing," he said.

The pink in her cheeks became near-crimson, and when she spoke again, her voice was tinged with a mix of embarrassment and anger. "If you think I've forgotten for even a second that we're only here because someone *took* my daughter, you're dead wrong."

He met her eyes and answered calmly. "Repeat the middle bit back to me."

"The middle bit? What middle bit?"

"You said that we're only here because someone took your daughter."

"Yes. But that wasn't my point."

"But it's mine." Harley shook his head. "I like you, Liz. I like your passion for your job and your passion for your kid. I like the way you are with the customers in your store and the way you are with me. You make a seriously good beef stew. And you're so beautiful that it physically pains me to say that we should slow things down."

"I still don't understand," she replied.

He shrugged abashedly. "I like you enough that I don't want to be the guy you were with because someone took your daughter."

Her mouth worked silently for a second, and Harley half expected her to unleash a sputtering tirade. Instead, a laugh burst out from between her lips. The sound filled the apartment, and as pleasant as it was, it puzzled Harley.

"What's funny?" he asked as her laughter finally died off.

"I think I've been checking you out every day since you came and asked me about subletting the studio space," she said.

He felt one side of his mouth tip up; the admission pleased him to no end. "You *think* you have?"

"Fine. I *know* I have." She wrinkled her nose. "You haven't been checking me out?"

"I've been doing everything in my power *not* to."

"That's a bit insulting, isn't it?"

"You forget that you were a potential suspect."

She shook her head. "You have no idea how insane that sounds from my end."

"Crazier things have happened," he said. "Trust me."

Her expression grew serious again. "I do trust you, Harley. And I like you, too. And not just because I believe your superhero powers are going to save Teegan."

He leaned back and slung an arm over her shoulders, then kissed the side of her head. "Helps, though, right?"

"It doesn't take away from the appeal, no."

"We'll be successful, Liz."

"I know. I *have* to believe that." She tucked her head against his chest. "How long until your tech research guy gets back to you?"

"I've never had him take more than an hour or two," Harley told her.

"He doesn't take time off for sleep?"

"Not sure, actually. I always kind of picture him doing that thing cats do."

"What thing?"

"They just sit there…one eye open…waiting for a mouse to go by, so they can pounce."

She laughed. "I'm not sure that's how it works."

"Sure it is," Harley said. "My mom has a big old beast named Marmalade. Lies around on the patio for about twenty-three hours a day. Only time Marmy ever blinks is when something terribly important comes along. Like a bumblebee."

Liz laughed again. "Great. Now I'm picturing the tech guy as some half man, half cat sitting at his desk, flicking his whiskers."

"That's just plain weird."

"You started it."

"Yeah, but it's the *finishing* that got weird."

"Tell yourself whatever you have to, Detective."

Harley smiled. "Right now, I'm telling myself it *isn't* sexy when you call me Detective."

She snorted, but wriggled a little closer. And for a few minutes, they sat in companionable silence.

Harley ran his fingers up and down her forearm, pleased by the way he left a trail of goose bumps in his wake.

He wondered what was going through Liz's mind. If she really believed in his abilities the way she said she did. If she was thinking—like he was—of the possibility that the intense attraction between them might grow into something more. It was a little selfish to hope that she was. He knew the thing that occupied her headspace was her missing daughter. Rightfully so. Harley didn't have any desire to take over that number one spot. He wouldn't, however, mind being on the periphery. And Liz's next words made him think that he already was.

"What do you want from life, Harley?" Liz blurted out the query without meaning to.

"From life?" he echoed.

Glad he couldn't see the red in her cheeks, she tried to backpedal. "Sorry. That sounded funny. I meant tell me more about your *current* life."

"Hmm." The noise made her sure he wasn't fooled by her lame attempt at a cover-up.

She bit her lip and cursed the fact that her mind had been quick enough to leap to the question, but not sharp enough to stop it from escaping. And *leap* was exactly what her brain had done. From the fact that Harley thought being called by his title was sexy to thinking about the sad parts of his life that led him to that role in the first place. And from those thoughts to wondering who he might've become if tragedy hadn't led him to police work. Then to who he might want to be after he got the justice he wanted. And then the final leap. A big one. Straight off the ledge. Was there a chance that he could see himself with *her* in his life after all was said and done?

She let go of her lip from between her teeth and forced a light tone. "Since I need to keep my mind from going crazy with worry about Teegan, and you won't let me kill time the way *I* thought we should."

"It's not because I don't want to," he assured her.

"I know. Superheroes are all about timing things exactly right."

"Pretty much." He slid his palm to the back of her hand and threaded his fingers through hers. "What would you like to know?"

"Anything," she replied, realizing it was true.

She wanted to hear about Harley's life *and* what he wanted from it. Both because she was interested and because she really did need the distraction. And he seemed to be very good at keeping her that way.

"Tell me more about Marmalade the cat," she urged. "Or your mom. Or what you do when you're not detecting."

"I think I pretty much covered everything there is to know about the cat. Sleeps. Pounces. Eats every now and then, which is probably why he's such a beast. And I'd tell you how great my mom is, but a lot of women think things like that are weird, so…"

She couldn't muster up a laugh. The thought of a lot of women parading through Harley's life dug at her a little more than it probably should have. And once again, her mouth wrested control from her brain.

"Are there a lot of women in your life?" she asked.

"Aside from my mom?" he teased. "No."

"No?" Even to her own ears, the parroting of his reply sounded phony.

He picked up on it, too. "Is that so hard to believe? I'm a computer nerd with a high-stress job. Doesn't exactly attract groupies."

She heard the honesty in his statement, but wanted to see it in his eyes, too, so she tipped her face up to look at him. "I think you know perfectly well how charming you are."

He smiled down at her. "Helps me in all that detecting."

"Uh-huh. Which is what makes me think you're perfectly capable of sweeping a dozen women off their feet every week."

"You'd probably be surprised at how few damsels in distress I come across. It's mostly little old ladies and big mean thugs." He lifted his fingers and pushed a few wayward strands of hair off her cheek, and she leaned into the touch as he added, "What about you?"

"Not many damsels in distress in *my* business, either," she said. "And you can't deflect me that easily."

"Okay," he conceded, then said nothing else.

Liz nudged him with her elbow. "Spill it."

"You sure you want to hear it?" he asked.

Her heart fluttered, but she nodded anyway. "Yes."

He sighed. "The truth is, there *was* a woman."

"Just one?"

"Just one. Met her at art school."

A strange stab of retroactive jealousy made Liz ask, "A model, or a fellow student?"

He smiled like he could read her perfectly. And as if it pleased him a little, too.

"I dunno…" he said teasingly. "Which answer is going to wipe that glare off your face?"

"I'm not glaring!" she protested.

"You kinda are," he argued.

She reached up a hand and ran it over her cheeks like maybe she could *feel* the offending expression, then stopped as soon as she realized what she was doing. But she didn't catch herself quick enough to stop Harley from laughing good-naturedly. She made a face at him, and he reached over to clasp her fingers in his, then settled their joined hands on top of his knee.

"She was a professor," he admitted, his voice a bit rough.

Liz was silent for a long moment before replying. "Well. That is *not* what I expected to hear."

"It wasn't what I expected to *happen*, either."

"Was she…you know?"

"Was she what?"

"Old."

He laughed, deep and low, and the sound reverberated from his body into hers. "No. She wasn't *old*. I mean, yeah. She was old*er* than I was. But only by seven years."

"That still seems like a big gap," Liz said.

He lifted an eyebrow. "You want to hear about it, or complain about it?"

She sighed and settled against him again. "Hear about it. Again."

"Well, since you're so clearly interested…" he teased.

"I am. Really."

"Okay. Let's see. Sarah had just finished her PhD, and the professor she'd been working under for her dissertation got sick. She'd been a teaching assistant in the department for a few years, and when the college decided to divvy up her boss's classes while he recovered, she was lucky enough to be assigned two. One was a painting theory class—not my best medium, by the way—and I went to Sarah for some extra help with an assignment. It started out the way you probably think it did. Getting to know each other personally. Connecting over art." He paused. "You sure you want to hear this?"

Liz nodded against his chest. She couldn't quite shake the jealousy twinges every time he said "Sarah," but she truly *was* curious about his past. Even when it sounded a bit sordid. And, of course, she had to acknowledge that it was a bit ridiculous to be jealous of a woman she'd never met—who was probably ten years in the past, anyway—over a man she'd only known for a week and a half.

On top of all that, listening to him was working as a distraction, just liked she'd hoped. The knot of worry was there in her stomach, but the rumble of Harley's voice soothed it enough that it stayed down low, instead of creeping into her chest to create full-fledged panic.

"Sarah and I had a lot of interests in common," he went on. "Although I guess that's a given, considering she'd done her doctorate in the subject I was studying. But she took me a little out of my element, too."

"Away from your family of cops," Liz filled in.

"Yes. Not to say that my life was classless. My mom is the very definition of class, and she'd slap me silly if she heard how much I curse." She could hear the smile in his voice as he said it. "But no one I grew up with understood why, when I was twelve, I dreamed about going to the Louvre instead of to Disneyland. Guess I was a weird kid to them. And I didn't outgrow it, which is how I wound up with a full scholarship for my degree. And going to college, taking the art and art theory classes, meeting people like Sarah…it was the first time my idiosyncrasies seemed normal."

Liz couldn't contain a wistful sigh. "I get it. That environment was my dream. Art history, though."

"You've never thought about going back?"

"I have. But priorities change. Especially when you have kids." Her heart squeezed painfully as her anxiety over Teegan's safety and whereabouts reared up again, and she turned the conversation back to him. "Tell me what happened next with Professor Sarah."

He didn't start up again right away, and Liz tensed,

sure that he was going to ask if she wanted to talk about their current situation instead. But, thankfully, he just cleared his throat and explained the rest of the story.

"I think Sarah enjoyed that I was a little blue under the collar," Harley said. "She liked taking me to exhibits and museums and feeling like she influenced my studies."

"Did you have to keep your relationship a secret?" Liz asked.

"Only for the semester that she taught the class I was in. After that, she took a job at an art college. People might've cared, but we didn't. We were together for four years."

"For your entire degree?"

"Yep."

"Wow."

"When I finished my last semester, I stuck around for a few months. I had a job at a community center teaching some kids' classes for the summer. I told Sarah from the beginning that I intended to join the police force after, but I guess she never really took me seriously. She was stunned when I got ready to leave for the academy."

"Was it hard?" Liz wanted to know.

"For me, or for her?" Harley replied lightly.

"Both, I guess."

But if she was being completely honest, she *really* didn't want to hear him say that it was a big regret for him. And she was extra grateful when he didn't.

"I don't know," he said, sounding completely honest.

"You don't *know*?" Liz echoed.

"She didn't beg me to stay, but she made sure I knew she didn't understand why I was leaving." He paused. "Not because I was leaving *her*. Because I was going back to my plans to become a cop. She couldn't wrap her head around the idea."

"Did she know about what happened to your dad?" Liz asked.

Harley nodded against her head. "She did. Not everything. Not as much as you know, actually."

She couldn't stop a tickle of warmth from forming in her chest. "I thought you dated for four years."

"We did," he replied easily. "But even if I *had* told her the details, she wouldn't have understood. She didn't ask for more information. She just wondered why I hadn't let it go."

Unexpectedly, a raw thickness filled Liz's throat. She couldn't imagine a scenario where she'd suggest that Harley should give up his quest to seek justice.

"He was your *dad*," she said softly.

Harley squeezed her shoulder. "He was. And if I'd had any doubt that things weren't meant to be for Sarah and me, her feelings about that wiped them away. So even after four years, it wasn't too hard to break it off. After that, I was completely tied up at the academy, then fast-tracked through the hoops to become a detective and here I am. Six years later. With you."

The way he said the last two words took the warmth in Liz's chest and fanned it out, lighting a new heat through her body. It was further reaching than the physical attraction that sparked in her each time they'd kissed. It went deeper than the tingle of desire.

The ache in her throat didn't lessen. But it did change. Warmed.

Liz turned slowly. She met Harley's eyes, which held a matching heat.

Even more slowly, Liz tilted her face toward his, her lips tingling with anticipation. She suspected that this kiss was going to be different. And she wanted to savor it. To explore what it could mean. What it *would* mean if the sensation blooming inside her continued to grow.

But her mouth barely got a chance to brush his before a jarring ring made her jerk back in surprise.

Another phone call?

For a second, she resented the interruption. Then she realized it was the *black phone* ringing. Her lifeline to Teegan. And she couldn't quite scramble to grab it fast enough.

Chapter 13

A moment after Liz snagged the phone from the table, she paused and looked up at Harley. He could read the clear need in her face, and he nodded.

"If it's her, talk as long as they'll let you. Don't worry about anything except making sure she's safe and that she *feels* safe," he said. "But if it's *him*, hand it to me right away."

Liz exhaled. "Got it." She pressed the answer button and spoke in a neutral voice into the phone, and relief flooded her features as she said, "Hi, baby. Yes, it's me."

Harley sat back, not quite tuning out the one-sided conversation but shifting it to the background so he could think. He'd just told her more about himself than he'd ever told anyone. Even his partners—his brother, Brayden, included—weren't aware of the circumstances surrounding his breakup with Sarah.

As the youngest in the group of four men, they often

gave Harley a hard time. His relationship with the older woman had been no exception. They'd teased him mercilessly about the age gap. About the taboo-ness of the teacher-student dynamic. About the fact that Sarah had a strong preference for long skirts, peasant blouses, and changed her hair color every few weeks, while Harley had sported the same look since he was about sixteen.

But when they split up, his partners had supported him. Had his back and took him for beers. Yet he hadn't felt the slightest desire to share his ex's disdain for their plan. Not even so they could unite against her.

Harley eyed Liz. Telling her had just felt right.

Just as right as kissing her. As running my hands through her hair. As sitting next to her like this, knees just touching.

Like she could feel his thoughts, she glanced his way. A tiny smile even tipped up her lips as she continued to speak to her daughter.

"Hot dogs?" she said, her voice shaking the smallest bit. "I'm glad you had something to eat. And if you're tired, you should sleep. It's way past your bedtime."

Yeah, it all felt very right. In spite of all the wrongness.

Harley suddenly felt a shift in his need to rescue the kid. It wasn't just because it was the right thing to do. It wasn't just because he liked the kid, or because he couldn't stand the thought of anyone hurting her. Or even just because it brought him a step closer to seeing Garibaldi behind bars. Those things were a given. The *new* need to get Teegan back was so Harley could take the time to pursue the burgeoning feelings for her mother. He wanted to do that unencumbered by fear, at a slow and steady pace. Pretty damn badly, actually.

She slid a hand to his knee then, her face pinching

as she said, "Okay, sweetie. Let them take the phone. I love you."

Harley put his palm over top of hers, then held out his other hand. A single heartrending tear slipped from Liz's eye, and she let out a heavy breath and placed the phone into his outstretched palm.

Harley lifted the device to his ear. "This is Harley."

There was a throat-clear on the other end. "Progress to report?"

"We'll get there."

"You'd better."

The line went dead immediately after the statement, and Harley brought his gaze to Liz, who was wiping her eyes.

"Tell me something—anything—to make me feel better," she said.

Her request was almost a plea, and Harley desperately wanted to soothe away her fear.

"We know Teegan's as safe as can be, under the circumstances," he told her. "The men who have her are cooperating with our requests, and that's a great sign. They fed her a hot dog, honey. They kept up their end of the bargain and called on time. A little early, even. They want these paintings that badly."

Liz took a breath and started to nod, but her face crumpled before she could get out a word. Harley reached out and took both her hands in his.

"We're going to get the damn things and hand them over," he said firmly. "Then we're going to take Teegan out of here. Disneyland."

"Disneyland?" Liz repeated in a wobbly voice. "Didn't you just tell me you're a Louvre guy?"

Harley couldn't hold in a smile. "All right. The Louvre.

I'll fly you both to France. We'll eat fancy cheese and take selfies at the Eiffel Tower."

"You're crazy," she replied. "But you have no idea how thankful I am for that right now."

He dropped a light kiss on her lips. "You're welcome. Ready to be off my rocker anytime you need me to be."

Her tears cleared, but her brow crinkled. "Harley… Do you think Jesse Garibaldi actually took her?"

"I don't know," he said honestly. "I was going to ask you what *your* impression was before we got…uh. Distracted."

Two spots of color brightened her cheeks. "I don't know, either. I mean, most of what he said was deceptive at best and an outright lie at worst. I *know* I saw that hooded man headed toward the shop. It would be a pretty big coincidence if the explosion was caused by anything unrelated, right?"

"Agreed."

"And if Jesse *knew* the paintings weren't there, and he'd already made arrangements for Teegan…" She paused and took a steadying breath, then went on. "Why would he call me?"

"Covering his own butt?" Harley suggested, though he wasn't sure he believed it.

Liz didn't seem to, either. "It felt more like he was trying to see if *I* knew where they were."

"Then unless the evidence points elsewhere, we'll go with that."

"Really?"

"Gut instinct goes a surprisingly long way. The clues that lead to clues."

She studied him for a second. "Your gut instinct already told you that, didn't it?"

"My gut instinct *hoped* it," he corrected. "It's sure as

hell preferable to think that we won't be a loose end for a man like Garibaldi."

She sucked in a sharp breath. "No. We don't want that."

"And it might be good in another way, too," Harley said. "Whoever took the paintings is obviously no friend of his. And whoever took Teegan is after the paintings, too. So also unlikely to be cozying up to Garibaldi."

"You're thinking that his status as a common enemy works in our favor."

"I'm thinking it doesn't hurt."

"Except that it means we definitely have three groups of people to fight against."

Harley shook his head. "We don't have to fight against Garibaldi. We just have to avoid him. And we don't have to fight against the kidnappers, either. All we have to do is get them what they want. So our focus is narrowed. We can concentrate all our efforts on Teegan. As soon as my guy comes through, we can plan our next move."

Then—like he'd cued it up to happen that way—his laptop binged with the sound of an incoming email. Certain that it was his virtual acquaintance, Harley lifted one of Liz's hands to his lips for a kiss, then dragged the computer from the table and pulled it up to rest on their side-by-side knees. Sure enough, the incoming message was the one they'd been expecting. Harley clicked it open, and they read it together in silence.

H.
No rest for the wicked, huh? Here're the stats on that company. Ten years new. Local article reported that it's financially backed by some college professor. Squeaky clean record except for one detail—their habit of employing ex-cons.

No, seriously.

Their whole docket is bad guys. Couple of petty thieves, couple of drug dealers, one guy with a record for flashing old ladies. (Scavenged an employee list. Don't ask.)

Anyway. Not exactly who I'd want renovating MY kitchen. But I'm guessing you're most interested in the stuff I've attached. Everyone's pretty little mug shots and records. Found a recent police report, too. Filed by the company, not against it.

Wait. Isn't it usually YOUR job to look up this stuff? (I kid...) (But don't say I've never repaid any favors.)

Let me know if you need anything else.

The Mighty Wizard. (I kid...again...)

J.

Harley's finger hovered over the attachments, his mind working to grasp some elusive memory. He suspected that his own exhaustion was starting to hamper him, and he wondered if he ought to have fixed some strong espresso rather than tea.

Liz waved a hand in front of his face. "As Teegan would say...earth to Harley."

He blinked to clear his vision. "Sorry, honey. Just thinking."

"Anything you want to share?" she asked.

He frowned down at the email for a second, then shook his head and clicked the first attachment instead. As promised, it was a series of rap sheets, complete with mug shots. He only had to scroll to the third before Liz let out a little gasp.

"That's him!" she exclaimed. "The guy from my store."

Harley looked from her to the picture, then back again.

"The hooded man who threatened you? You got a look at his face?"

"No. He was wearing a mask. But I could see *this*." Her finger came out to tap the screen, and Harley had to squint to see what she was pointing at.

"Looks like a smudge," he said.

She angled the computer her way, dragged the mouse to select the section of screen that held the picture, then zoomed in. The moment the man's enlarged face appeared, Harley spied what she meant. A port-wine stain framed one eye like a quarter moon.

"I thought it might be a bruise," Liz said. "But I'm sure this is him. His eyes are the same, and so is that mark."

The conviction in her voice was all Harley needed. He'd interviewed enough witnesses over the course of his career to be confident that Liz wasn't just projecting what she *wanted* to be true into what *was* true. On top of that, the coincidence would've been too much. Harley turned the laptop his way and zoomed out again to look over the rap sheet.

He read the hooded man's name and the highlights aloud. "Cameron Ruthers. Two counts of possession with intent. One count of sale of controlled substance. A drunk and disorderly and an assault charge on the same night."

"Well. He sounds like fun," Liz muttered.

"Real stand-up guy," Harley agreed with a heavy dose of sarcasm. "According to this, he had two pretty good years, but he just spent eighteen months in prison for another drug charge."

"I bet that two-year period is when he was employed at the construction contractor," Liz said.

Harley met her eyes. "That's a genius conclusion. I should get my friend to send over the employment records to confirm."

She blushed, but smiled, too. "Flattery, hmm?"

"Genuine admiration. I have a reputation at the station for being able to connect the dots pretty damn quickly, and I didn't connect those two yet." He winked. "I *would* have."

"Of course you would've," Liz said with an eye roll. "What about the other attachment he sent? The police report."

"Right. We should have a look at that first. And scroll through the rest of these rap sheets, too."

"Okay."

Harley moved through the subsequent pictures, skimming the various records in search of anything that might connect overtly to either Garibaldi or to Whispering Woods, or to his own case. He saw nothing. Liz didn't make any more comments, either, so he closed up the first attachment and opened the second. It immediately piqued more than a bit of interest. Liz's, too.

"What are the chances that's not our van?" she asked softly.

Harley shook his head. "Slim to none, I think."

Together, they stared down at the typed report. His contact was right. It *was* a report from Everlast of Freemont. A theft report, and the item stolen was a white panel van. Not just that, but the vehicle in question had a GPS tracking device installed, and the last place it had been tracked was Whispering Woods.

"Why do you think they canceled the complaint?" Liz asked.

"Usually means one of two things. Either they figured out it wasn't really stolen, or they figured out that they knew the person who took it and didn't want to press charges," Harley replied.

Liz sighed and sucked in her lower lip, chewing on it

thoughtfully. "I feel like we need one of those evidence boards you see on TV. You know...with all the pictures and red lines connecting things?"

Harley leaned over and clicked a few things on his computer, then tipped the screen her way. "Like this?"

He watched her eyes light up a little as she perused his version of the board she'd described. While the typical one wasn't used as commonly as TV would have people think, Harley liked the idea of the evidence board and had enjoyed the few times he'd seen one in action. So, he created his own. Of course, his was a digital template he'd designed himself using a storyboard originally intended for plotting movies.

"Watch this," he said, not ashamed to be showing off a little.

He tapped quickly over the keyboard, inputting bits of info they were working on and importing the attachments sent over by his online friend. In seconds, the program had a timeline down the side—starting with the smoke bomb and ending with the two of them in his apartment. Pleased with the efficiency of it himself, he expected Liz to be equally impressed. Instead, her face had grown pale.

Automatically, Harley abandoned the laptop in favor of turning to slip his hands to the crooks of her elbows.

"Hey," he said. "What's wrong? See something in there that upset you?"

Her throat worked up and down, and he suspected she was holding back more tears. "Just the timeline. I can't believe it's only been a little over *four hours* since that smoke bomb knocked me on my butt. It feels like days."

He lifted the back of his hand to stroke her cheek. "Try to think of it as a good thing. It means we still have plenty of time to get those paintings back, and we've got a good lead here."

"Do we?"

"Definitely. And the fact that it feels like it's taking so long just means we've been able to cram a few weeks' worth of getting to know each other into a few hours." He bent to drag his lips over hers. "And I can't say I'm complaining about that part."

"No," she breathed. "Me, neither."

She kissed him again, lingering a little, and Harley would've liked nothing better than to toss the laptop aside completely and drag her down to the couch.

Find Teegan first, he reminded himself, *pleasantly ravage her mother second.*

He pulled away and brought his attention back to the computer.

"Here," he said. "Let me show you something."

He grabbed the laptop again, clicked a few more times and pulled up his most-used virtual evidence board. The one that housed every detail of his and his partners' case against Garibaldi. He scrolled to the beginning, then offered it to Liz.

"Just to show you that I know firsthand what that agonizing waiting-forever feeling is like," he told her.

He expected her to turn and look his way, but what she did instead was tap on the screen like she had when she spotted the familiar mug shot.

"What's this exclamation point that just popped up?" she asked. "There wasn't one on the other board."

"It just popped up?" Harley replied, his attention now fully on the computer.

"I saw it happen," she said.

His mouth was suddenly a little dry, and he had to force aside a tingle of anticipation. "It's the signal for when the program finds an overlap between one case and another. Key people or places. Or if it reads a significant doubled-up phrase."

"So it found an overlap between your father's case and what you just uploaded about Teegan?"

"Apparently. It's set to filter out matches for Freemont, since nearly every case takes place there, but it could be as simple as the mention of Whispering Woods."

"Is that what your gut says?" She wanted to know.

"In this case," he replied, "my gut might be a little biased."

"Only one way to find out."

She leaned over, her floral scent wafting up and providing Harley with a modicum of pleasant distraction from the slight unease in his stomach. He let her take the lead in clicking on the exclamation point, then watched as she navigated the easy-to-follow prompts.

"It's the email," she said after a moment.

"The email?" he repeated.

"The one from your wizard friend. It's the phrase thing, I think. He said 'college professor,' and you've got a note on your board about a college professor being in some picture?"

"Let me see."

She moved aside so he could click through the details of the overlapped phrase. It only took a few seconds for him to find the connection, and only a few seconds more to remember what his notes had been about. He brought up the photo section from his evidence board and clicked through until he found the two he wanted. The first was a close-up of a somewhat grainy fifteen-year-old shot of a license plate. The second was a headshot of a middle-aged man, swiped from a college directory.

"Kincaid Walls," he said under his breath, more to himself than to Liz.

She answered anyway, peering down at the photographs. "That's the college professor's name? And that's him and...what? His car?"

He nodded and gave her the syncopated version of events. "My partners and I got a hold of a series of photographs, all taken by the man—Nadine Stuart's father—who drove Garibaldi everywhere for a decade. This particular shot..." He pointed at the screen. "It's of one of the cars parked at the Freemont station on the day it was bombed. I traced it back to Kincaid Walls."

"You think he's involved?"

"I like to keep an open mind. Which is why I saved this in my notes in the first place."

"So what now?" Liz said. "Are you going to email your wizard again to see if he knows the name of the college professor?"

"He'd have said if he did. He's obnoxious, but he's thorough," Harley replied with a smile. "My guess is the guy in question is a silent investor of some kind. But I do think it's worth looking into. As well as figuring out if we can access the GPS tracker for that van."

Liz's eyes filled with undisguised hope at his last statement. "Is that a real possibility?"

"I wouldn't have brought it up if I didn't think so," he told her. "I also want to take a minute to check in with my brother. Give him an update."

"In the middle of the night?"

"Trust me. He'll pick up. And I'm well overdue for a check-in."

"Okay."

"This is progress, Liz, even if it doesn't feel like it. I promise."

He kissed her, pushed to his feet and dragged his phone from his pocket. He dialed the number by memory—the line was secure, but the phone itself wasn't immune to being stolen and scrolled through—and paced the limited space in the room while he waited for Brayden's familiar voice to come on the line.

"Harley," his brother said sleepily. "Regular business hours aren't good enough for you anymore?"

"Trust me," Harley replied. "This'll be worth it."

"Better be."

Harley shot a look toward Liz. She was studying the evidence board with interest. Her lips were pursed in concentration, and she had a crease in her forehead and a strand of her thick brown hair pulled taut between her fingers. For some inexplicable reason, the pose made Harley want to scoop her up and kiss her senseless.

"Bro?" Brayden's voice cut through the fantasy, sounding vaguely concerned.

"I'm here," Harley replied with a throat-clear. "Hang on."

He stepped from the living room to the hall. Not for privacy's sake, but because he had a feeling that Liz's presence would keep him from being as efficient as he wanted to be in the conversation. And once her tumble of hair and ample curves were out of sight, it was definitely easier to focus on recounting everything to Brayden.

When he was done, his brother let out a heavy exhalation and said, "So you're forgoing the direct investigation on Garibaldi for the moment to concentrate on finding the little girl."

"Isn't that what I just said?" Harley replied.

"I dunno. I had to filter out some stuff about pretty blue eyes and the best kid *ever* to get to that conclusion."

"Funny."

"I thought so." Then his brother's tone turned serious. "You gonna be able to do it, man?"

Harley glanced up the hall and lowered his voice. "Promised her I would. So I guess I better."

"You know I've got your back, whatever you need to do."

"Easy for you to say from the sunny beaches of Mexico."

"I'm hiding in a dark bathroom at the moment, thank you very much, so as not to wake my fiancée."

Harley chuckled. "Thanks for the visual."

"You're welcome," his brother replied dryly.

"Hey, Bray? While I've got you on the line...question?"

"Yeah. Hit me."

"Have you heard from Rush at all?"

He could picture the headshake in his brother's response. "Not since we all got together to confirm that Garibaldi really was in Whispering Woods. And that was *before* I went in for my scouting mission. But you know how he is. Got a specific worry?"

Harley hesitated, his eyes once more finding the space that led to Liz. "Just worried what'll happen if my cover is compromised. With you and Anderson both away, and Rush his typical AWOL self... I don't want Garibaldi to get away again."

There was a brief pause on the other end before his brother rebutted his genuine concern with one word. "Don't."

"Don't?" he repeated.

Brayden's voice roughened. "Don't even consider that we won't see justice, Harley. Each move we've made has brought us closer to figuring out his game. Things are lining up. If you don't close the deal this time, Rush will step up."

"If he decides to show his face."

"He will. He's nothing if not consistently fashionably late to the party."

Harley sighed. "Yeah. I s'pose you're right."

"Always am, little bro," Brayden teased. "Now go back to your girl, and I'll go back to mine."

It wasn't until he hung up the phone, made his way back into the living room and found Liz curled up sound asleep that he realized he hadn't bothered to deny the claim that the pretty brunette was "his." And as he stared down at her almost-still form, he had no choice but to acknowledge that the reason for his lack of denial was that he wanted it to be true.

Chapter 14

Liz woke with a start, disoriented. She'd been in the throes of a very pleasant dream. It involved wide shoulders and strong arms, and a feeling of security. But as she blinked in the dim light, reality came flooding in, driving away any residual sensation of safety.

Teegan's gone. The thought stole into her mind and sucked the air away from her chest. *And you fell asleep.*

The only thing that kept her from losing it completely was the sight of a *real* set of wide shoulders, sitting just in front of her on the floor.

"Harley?" she said, her voice a bit of a croak.

In spite of how softly she spoke, his knees jerked up, smacking the table hard enough that it rattled, and he dropped a curse before turning to face her.

"Liz. You startled me." His voice was almost as croaky as hers—like he hadn't used it in a while.

The idea that he might *not* have spoken in some time

sent a stab of panic through her. How long had she been out? She tossed aside the fuzzy blanket draped over her body and attempted to sit up. But she did it all a little too quickly. And she failed. Her feet got tangled in the blanket, her arms flailed, and instead of making it anywhere near a sitting position, she flopped straight forward. If Harley's arms hadn't come out to grab her at just the right moment, her face would've met with a painful fate involving the coffee table. But even the feel of his capable hands on her body couldn't quite drive away the guilt and fear she felt right then.

"What time is it?" she asked. "How long was I asleep? Oh, God. *How* could I fall asleep? Why'd you let me stay that way?"

She was almost in tears at the end, but Harley seemed unfazed. He righted her and set her back on the edge of the couch, then swung an elbow around and gave her a reassuring smile.

"You were understandably exhausted, honey. And I think looking at my boring evidence board might've *put* you to sleep," he said. "You've only been out for about two hours. And I've put it to good use."

"Two hours?" She sagged back. That didn't sound so bad. Except for the fact that it was two *wasted* hours. Two hours she could've used to help Harley. Liz sat up again as her still-groggy mind remembered something else. "What about the next call? Did I miss it?"

Harley reached for the black phone, which he tapped, then held out. "No call. Just this."

With her heart threatening to make its way from her chest up into her throat, Liz looked down. It was a ten-second video of Teegan. Sound asleep. Sprawled out with a fluffy blue blanket flung haphazardly across her body and her pile of curls resting on a navy pillowcase. Her chest rose and fell peacefully, and her thumb was stuck into her mouth.

Liz's voice cracked as she said, "She only does that when she's had a nightmare."

Harley's palm met her knee. "No doubt this feels like one to her. But it'll be over soon."

She met his eyes. "Please give me some good news, Harley. Because right now, I feel like I'm failing her."

His hand slid from her leg to her face. "You are *not* failing her. You're doing exactly what needs to be done to get her back to safety. You fell asleep because you needed a bit of rest. I stayed up and worked so you could get that bit of rest. Simple as that."

She closed her eyes for a second, sinking into his warm fingers. "I should be better at this."

"Better at what? Knowing what to do when someone abducts your daughter? I don't think there's a playbook involved."

Unexpectedly, his mouth found hers. His tongue parted her lips, and for a moment, his kiss engulfed her. Soothed her. Made her feel less guilty about relying on him, because he seemed to *want* her to. Then he pulled away and spoke softly.

"I wouldn't lie to you. I wouldn't even sugarcoat it," he said. "You're doing amazingly well. In my books, you're a rock star of a mom."

She opened her eyes and found his brown gaze just half an inch from her face, and she spoke without thinking. "A rock star of a mom and a superhero of a detective. What kind of couple does that make us?"

Instead of balking at her use of the word *couple*, Harley grinned. "A damn good one." He kissed her once more, then sat back. "Let me tell you what I found."

Hope bubbled through Liz once more, guilt almost forgotten. "I'm all ears."

"So there's a bit of good news/bad news here," he stated. "But I'm erring on the side of good. I dug into Everlast of Freemont's financials—barely legal, don't ask—and found out that they're fond of creative banking. Creative billing, to be accurate. Took me a bit to figure it out, actually. Everlast pays its taxes on time. Pays its employees fairly, too, and even offers some benefits. So I had to ask what the catch was."

Liz smiled at his obvious enthusiasm for the process. He might've become a detective for the sake of getting justice for his father, but he also clearly loved putting together the pieces of the puzzle.

"My gut told me the company was a little *too* squeaky clean," he added. "So I dug a little more, and I noticed that Everlast's jobs aren't just perfectly executed... They're executed at perfectly timed intervals. One every three months, like clockwork. I took a closer look into a specific job—I just picked one at random—hoping to find something suspicious. And there it was."

"Okay," Liz said. "I'll bite. There *what* was?"

"The biller didn't exist," he told her triumphantly.

"What do you mean?" she replied. "It was a fake job?"

"*Every* job is fake," he corrected.

Even though they were sitting inches apart, she genuinely thought she'd misheard. "What?"

"I skimmed over the last two years of info. Everything is the same. Three-month intervals. Regular deposits, varying only slightly in amounts."

"But that's..." She trailed off and shrugged, unsure what the right word was.

"So slick it hardly seems possible?" Harley filled in.

"Yes."

"Someone pretty damn smart set up this operation to cover up something fairly major. And I don't think it's our friend in the hooded sweatshirt."

"I wouldn't think so," Liz agreed, shivering as she remembered the fear she'd experienced when the rough-around-the-edges man had threatened her.

"But it does bring me to my next bit of information," Harley said. "Which is *this*."

He swung the laptop her way, and Liz shivered yet again. It was a picture. Pixelated and shot from a funny angle, but still clear enough that she could easily make out the man it depicted. Cameron Ruthers. His birthmark and grimy face were unmistakable. And in the photo, he was sitting in the driver's side of a white van, which was embossed with the Everlast of Freemont logo.

"I don't think he's behind whatever scam this business is running," Harley told her. "In fact…I think it might be the opposite. I think he stole the truck and assisted with stealing the paintings, too."

Liz saw his pleasure fade into frustration, and she knew what was plaguing him. "But you still don't know why the paintings are so important."

"No. I sure as hell don't. And my request to get the GPS report for the van hasn't come through." Then he shook his head like he was trying to clear it and said, "But we're talking about the good news. And in this case, the good news is where the photo was taken." He paused to point at the screen. "You know the intersection on the way into town where the road forks after you come off the highway?"

Liz nodded. With the way Whispering Woods was nestled against the mountains, there was only one road that served as both an entrance and an exit for the town. The fork split the street in two and either direction led in a loop around the whole area. Eventually the road met up again at the very opposite end of town before leading straight into the biggest tourist hub the place offered—Whispering Woods Lodge.

But there was nothing in the photo to suggest that the picture had been taken there. When Liz said as much, though, Harley smiled.

"Doubting my superpowers?" he teased. "Have a look at this."

He reached for the laptop, clicked open the browser and pulled up the town's website. He clicked on an article near the top.

Liz gave it a quick scan. It was a piece about a group of local bird-watchers. In hopes of catching footage of some rare bird, they'd installed a camera in a tree near the intersection. But someone caught wind of the plan—which included live uploads of the camera shots onto the bird-watchers' website—and requested that the mayor have it removed because of potential privacy issues. The mayor complied.

"And the best part?" said Harley as Liz finished reading. "This whole thing took all of three days, start to finish. Day three was the day before yesterday. So some time in the last four days, Mr. Ruthers brought that van into Whispering Woods."

Liz's heart did a hopeful little leap in her chest.

"You were right," she said.

"Not that I'm arguing, but I was right about what?"

"You *did* put my two-hour nap to good use."

He shrugged. "All I did was use some facial recognition software. Easy peasy."

She started to tell him that his idea of "easy peasy" might be different than the average person's, then stopped as an awful thought occurred to her. One that probably should've been a consideration from the start.

"How do we know he hasn't already taken the paintings *out* of Whispering Woods?" she said. "Wouldn't it make sense for them to get out as quickly as possible? Oh, God. What if we can't—"

Harley grabbed her hand. "These guys are too smart for that."

"Too smart to run away?" She sounded as disbelieving as she felt.

"They know they're being watched. They know that the van is recognizable. At the very least, they would've had to find a place to stop and shuffle the paintings to a different transport vehicle. And running out of here quickly in a different van, or a cargo truck or anything remotely obvious, would just get them caught."

"Do you *know* all of this, or are you just assuming?"

"I never assume, honey. I'm telling you that I'm sure of it. And even if I wasn't… I think Teegan's kidnappers giving us that twenty-four-hour window tells us that they've come to the same conclusion. Because someone could get damn far in twenty-four hours."

Liz tried to be relieved, but couldn't quite make it happen. "So now we have to find the van. Whispering Woods is small. But it's not small enough to just walk around, street to street."

"You're right," Harley agreed. "The trick is to narrow it down. The thieves need a place where a van isn't going to stick out. Where it isn't going to be accidentally spotted and reported for any reason at all. They can't park it or store it anywhere traceable, or anywhere that some staff person might recall seeing it. Maybe *most* importantly, they can't take the van or the painting somewhere that Garibaldi is likely to find them. Whispering Woods *is* small, and there are only so many places that'll fit that particular bill."

Liz frowned, then met his steady gaze. "You already *did* narrow it down, didn't you?"

He nodded, looking strangely hesitant. "I think they've taken the van to that subdivision where the house fire was. It's unpopulated. Plenty of places to hide a vehicle. And even though Garibaldi owns the whole thing and his aim is to flatten it and rebuild, the arson gives him a damn good reason to avoid being associated with the area. And it's only ten blocks from here."

Liz stared at him for a second, then jumped up eagerly. "Why didn't you *start* with all of that? We can go right now. Why are we waiting?"

He didn't move. "Because this is where the bad-news part comes in."

Harley stood up slowly, mindful of the worried look on Liz's face. He put his hands on her shoulders, then turned her so that her back pressed to his chest, and he spoke in a low voice into her ear.

"We're going to step toward the window," he said, "and look out through the blinds. I'm going to keep holding you, and you're not going to react to what you see. But when you *do* see it, I want you to turn and kiss me."

He heard Liz's inhalation. "A kiss? I can't just tell you? I don't understand."

"You will in a second."

He slid his hands down her shoulders to her elbows, then kissed the back of her neck. He inched her forward, knowing that to an outside observer, it would look like an intimate moment. A dead sexy one. Hell. Maybe it was anyway, even if it was just for show. Lord knew it felt good and right to have her tucked up against him.

He swept the hair off her shoulder and dragged his lips down her throat a little farther. All the way to the spot where her T-shirt met her collarbone.

And he moved her closer to the window again.

He could feel the thrum of her pulse and the shortening of her breath as he dragged his fingers from her elbows to her hands, then slipped them to her stomach.

He stepped forward, propelling her to come with him. They were just a few inches from the window now, and he wanted to make sure they were above suspicion. So he ran his palm back and forth over the cotton of her shirt, then under it. Maybe it was slightly more than necessary. Maybe it was just an excuse to touch her. But it was worth it. Liz gasped as his hands met her soft skin, and Harley fought a groan himself.

He dropped his mouth to her neck again and placed a trail of kisses up to her ear. There, he paused.

"One more step," he said, his voice thick. "And you'll see what I need you to see."

Together, they made the final move. Harley didn't stop with his kisses or touches. His hands and fingers danced along the top edge of Liz's jeans. His mouth owned the exposed inches of her throat. He was almost disappointed when she eased sideways to face him. At least until her lips tipped up and found his own. Then—in spite of the fact that he knew it was the signal he'd instructed her to give—desire swept through him, erasing all else.

With a growl that he couldn't quite suppress, Harley grabbed a hold of Liz's wrists. He lifted them over her head and backed her hard into the window. The blinds protested, cracking in a way that made him sure he wouldn't get his damage deposit back. He didn't care. He drove his hips forward and swiped his lips with his tongue. She moaned something against his mouth. Maybe his name. Maybe a curse. He didn't know, and didn't care too much about figuring that out, either. Especially not after her knee came up to hook over his hip.

He'd thought earlier that he wanted her. He was sure now that that was an understatement. Whatever he felt for Liz was more than a want. It was a need. Acknowledging it drove away the reason he'd requested the kiss in the first place. If he hadn't pulled back and spotted the object he'd drawn her attention to through the blinds, he might've just lifted her up and carried her back to his bedroom. But seeing it out there was just enough of a cold bucket of water that he was able to extricate himself from the passionate moment. He dragged the blinds shut, gave her a more chaste kiss, then eased away.

"You saw it?" he asked.

For a second, she blinked at him like she had no idea what he meant. Then her face cleared and she nodded.

"The dark car with the man in the front seat," she said.

"It's been there for at least as long as you were asleep," Harley told her. "Possibly longer. I noticed it—him—when I got you that blanket. The car looked a little out of place, so I found an excuse to walk by the window a few more times, and it never moved. Only two kinds of people sit outside an apartment building like that. Cops. And stalkers. I'm damn sure it's not the former."

"Who do you think it is?" Liz asked, worry finally overriding the desire that had been in her eyes just a moment earlier.

"I *know* who it is," Harley replied grimly. "Someone who works for Garibaldi."

"What?"

"Running a plate is even easier peasier than the facial recognition. And that car is registered directly to Jesse Garibaldi."

"But…how does he know we're here? And why would he risk exposing himself?"

"Good news/bad news again," Harley said.

Liz sighed. "I don't even know if I want to hear it."

"You do," he assured her. "And even if you don't, I'm telling you anyway. The good news is that Garibaldi doesn't think there *is* a risk. Which means my cover story is holding. If he had any idea who I really am—or even had an inkling that I'm a cop—he wouldn't chance having one of his cars out there. Too simple to trace. Your everyday citizen, though, isn't going to be able to do it. And if they called in a suspicious vehicle and it came back to Garibaldi…"

"It wouldn't matter because he has a million legitimate business reasons to be just about anywhere in town," Liz filled in.

"Exactly."

"So what's the bad news?"

"Aside from the fact that we can't walk out without being followed? We know he's got a way of keeping tabs on you." He said it as lightly as he could manage, but Liz's eyes still filled with fear.

Can you blame her?

He shook off the sarcastic thought and reached for her to pull her into an embrace. Before he could get her all the way into his arms, though, her eyes widened, her face paled and she shook her head.

"My phone," she said.

"What about it?" Harley asked.

"Garibaldi repaired it for me."

"What? Why?"

"He came into the shop a few months ago and knocked it off the edge of the counter. The screen broke. He said he felt bad, but that he knew a guy who'd fix it for next to nothing. He had it for less than a day." Liz lifted a hand to her forehead. "God. I think I'm going to be sick."

Harley led her to the couch. "If it *is* your phone, this is something I can fix."

"It's been *months*, Harley. I feel so naive."

"It's not naive to assume that when you hand over your phone to someone, they're not going to turn around and use it to track you."

"I wish that made me feel better."

He grabbed a cord from the basket he kept beside the couch, plugged it into his laptop, then attached her phone to the other end. He clicked through her permissions, easily bypassing her password, and pulled up all the specs onto the screen.

Liz leaned forward. "None of that makes me feel better, either."

"Don't worry," Harley said. "I'm a little more adept than your average tech consultant. Most people wouldn't be able to find their way in."

"But can't you just pull off the back and look for…I dunno…something *extra* inside?"

"I could. But this is more efficient. It'll tell me if there's any extraneous hardware, or if there's a tracking app in place. And I'm less likely to trigger some kind of warning if I do it all remotely." He clicked a few more times. "Aha!"

"Aha?" Liz sounded less than enthused.

"It's a simple tracking app, buried under something else. The kind of thing you might install on a teen's phone if you wanted to know where they were sneaking off to."

"Take it off."

He lifted his eyes. "We can't."

"You said you could fix this." There was a desperate edge to her voice.

"I can. I will. I'm going to mask it using another app. But we can't actually remove it unless we want to alert Garibaldi to the fact that we know what he's up to."

"So just smash the phone. Drop it in the toilet. I don't care. I don't want him to be able to find me."

"We could do that," Harley agreed. "But he'll just try to find another way. With the app masked but in place, he'll think he's got the situation under control. We don't want him *working* to find that control."

Liz's shoulders sagged, but she nodded. "Okay. So what do we do while we let him think he's getting his way."

Harley glanced at the clock on his laptop. It was nearing morning. And in spite of the fact that they were literally running out of hours, he felt like they were in a good spot. He was sure he was right about the location of the van, but thought if they waited until the sun came up, his request for the GPS report might come through. Still… he knew it wasn't fair to ask Liz to wait much longer.

He sighed, and she reached out to grasp his hand.

"Whatever you're going to say that I won't like, go ahead and say it," she said.

Chapter 15

Liz didn't know what she was bracing for, but when Harley finally spoke—after scrubbing an apologetic hand over his face and shaking his head and adjusting himself in his seat, too—it was such a simple request that she almost wanted to laugh.

"I want us to sit tight until after the next call from Teegan's abductors," he said.

"That's it?" she replied.

Harley's surprised expression was practically comical. "That's…what?"

"I don't *want* to wait. I want to run straight through those guys out there. If I thought I could get away with it, I'd steal your gun and blaze into that run-down part of town and forcefully rip the paintings from their hands. Literally." Her heart ached a little as she finished saying it because she knew it was true—given the choice between action and inaction, there was no way she'd choose the latter.

"Liz…" Harley's mouth drooped as he said her name.

But she waved off his plaintive tone. "I won't try any of that. Because I know you wouldn't suggest doing anything that would harm our chances of getting Teegan back."

"It's only two hours," he replied. "Less than two, really."

"I know."

"Leaving in the night like this would be more likely to draw their attention."

"Okay."

"And if they did catch us after the sun's up, at least it makes a little sense to be out and about."

"You don't have to sell me on it."

"I feel like I *should* have to."

She lifted an eyebrow. "You feel like you want to fight?"

He sighed. "Definitely not. The opposite. I want to *not* fight. I hate the idea of arguing with you."

He said the last bit so sincerely that the dull ache in Liz's heart brightened a little. She reached out and put her hand on his cheek. It was rough with stubble, and the bristly little jabs against the sensitive skin on her palm sent a zap of pleasure through her. And when his eyes lifted to meet her gaze, the sensation grew stronger. She wondered if she should pull away. But knew already that she wouldn't.

"Harley," she said, her voice soft and unusually raw. "We have two hours to kill."

He swallowed, his Adam's apple sliding up and down in his throat. "We do."

"What you said earlier about me only being here because someone took my daughter…"

"Yes."

"It's true."

"Yes," he said again.

She exhaled. "But that's not the reason I want to ask you what I'm about to ask you."

"Okay."

"The reason I want to ask you what I want to ask you is because you're *you*."

"I'm me?" One side of his mouth tipped up, and Liz slid her hand lower so that her thumb could stroke the curve.

"You're you," she confirmed. "You're brave. And kind. And you put Teegan's needs first. And not just right now. But all the time over the last ten days. Even though—apparently—her mother was a suspect."

"Kids outweigh most everything else." He said it like a shrug.

Liz shook her head. "You realize that not every man feels like that."

"Any of the men worth knowing feel like that," he replied.

She pushed forward and tipped up her face to kiss him lightly. "You have no idea how sexy it is when you say that."

"You have no idea how sexy it is to hear you say the word *sexy*," he told her.

She laughed. "Your standards must be pretty low."

"Definitely not."

He dipped his mouth to hers for another kiss, and his attention lingered longer than hers had. But she was still regretful when he pulled away.

"Liz?"

"Yes?"

"What was it you wanted to ask me?"

Her face warmed. "Oh. Right. Did the flood ruin your bedroom?"

His brow wrinkled. "Did the…? Oh. No. As a matter of fact, it didn't."

"You wanna show me the proof?" she teased.

Harley's expression grew serious, and he reached up to place his hand over top of hers. "I want to show you the proof, Liz. I really do. In fact, I think I must be insane to be stopping and rationalizing things when all I really want to do is scoop you up, superhero-style, and take you to my very *un*-ruined bed."

"But?"

"Putting aside all the logistics—where I live, where you live—that make my already-questionable ability at romance that much *less* romantic…my preparation for this particular situation is somewhat lacking."

Liz felt herself frown as she tried to wade through his word soup. Then his intention hit her.

"You're talking about protection!" she blurted.

He chuckled. "I am."

She bit her lip. It had literally been so long since she'd contemplated going to bed with a man that she'd forgotten that particular detail. But putting aside the fact that she had the perfect everyday reminder of just how crucial birth control could be—Teegan was living proof, after all—Liz realized she had a confession to make. And she wondered if this was the right time to bring it up.

Can you think of a better moment?

She shook her head to herself. If anything, it was better to get it out of the way now. Early.

"I need to tell you something," she said, suddenly feeling awkward.

"So tell away," he replied easily.

But her tongue stuck to the roof of her mouth.

What if it's a game-changer? What if it makes Harley change his mind?

And it hit her then, that she didn't *want* him to change his mind. She didn't want a short-term fix in the bedroom. Or elsewhere. She liked Harley far too much for that. Far too much for anything that might not lead to something more.

"You all right?" Harley asked then, his gentle tone a balm against the tumble of her worried thoughts.

She couldn't suppress a sigh. "Protection didn't occur to me for two reasons. The first is that it's been a long time. A very long time. So it wasn't really on my radar."

"Ditto," he replied with a smile.

Liz couldn't smile back. "The second is that I don't actually *need* the birth-control aspect of the protection."

It only took a heartbeat for him to figure out what she meant. "You can't have any more children."

"There were some complications during Teegan's birth. There wasn't much choice about what needed to be done, and— Ugh. I'm sorry if that's a little TMI," she said, looking down at her lap.

Harley was silent for only a moment. "Does it make you unhappy?"

For some reason, the question startled Liz. Her gaze came up in a rush, and she found nothing but sincerity in Harley's face. If he was perturbed by her revelation, he showed no sign of it. In fact, the only concern he displayed seemed to be directly for *her* well-being.

"It's doesn't make me unhappy at all," she admitted. "Would I have wanted more kids? Possibly. But Teegan is enough."

He shot a crooked grin her way. "More than enough sometimes?"

She laughed. "Definitely. But in a good way."

Then Harley's face changed. It grew serious. Almost pensive. And Liz knew he was putting together a few dots in his head. Realizing more conclusively that Teegan wasn't just enough. She was everything. The *only* thing.

And when Harley spoke again, his voice was raw with emotion. "If you want me to go in there with my gun blazing, Liz, you just tell me. I'll fight for her with my own bare hands."

If Liz had thought her heart was soft toward him before, it had nothing on the way it melted now.

"But that's not what you think will work," she reminded him.

"No. But if it's what you want, then say the word. Or if you want something else, name it."

"What I want is for you to show me that un-ruined bedroom of yours."

His grin came back, and he stood up, then reached out a hand. She didn't move.

"Something wrong?" he asked.

"I was just thinking…" she said. "*Could* you do the whole scooping-me-up thing?"

In reply, he bent down, slid one arm under her legs and the other under her back, then lifted her from the couch. And a few moments later, he was showing her— thoroughly—that whatever else the flood had done to his apartment, it sure hadn't affected the mattress.

Harley sat back on the bed, admiring his view. It currently consisted of Liz in a towel, sitting on the edge of the bed, her fingers trying their damnedest to work out the last few knots in her thick mane of damp hair. The tempting curtain of chocolate hung halfway down her back, dancing along the freckles there. Harley had offered her a brush, only to remember that the only one he owned was at the studio. Not that *he* was complaining. Watching Liz's hands work through her hair was singularly enthralling.

Maybe not singularly, he corrected silently. *Just as enthralling as the rest of her.*

He closed his eyes for a moment, liking the way the memory of her curves immediately filled his mind. He smiled to himself, sinking into the pleasant recollection.

For the last hour and a bit, the outside world had nearly ceased to exist. There was just her, him and everything between them. Sweet nothings. Heady kisses. The feel of her body underneath him, and the whisper of the bedsheets.

He'd taken as much time as he dared, getting to know her body. He hadn't wanted to rush a single thing. Tasting every inch of her seemed imperative. So had memorizing the patterns of her light freckles. The minutes of exploration were more than worth it. Liz was all curves. All softness and silky dips. She had faded stretch marks on her lower abdomen, and Harley had made sure to worship them for what they were—evidence of creation. Evidence of what made her who she was. And thankfully, she hadn't shied away from the attention. She'd laughed lightly as his tongue traced the faint silver lines. Ran her fingers through his hair and teased him about spending a little too much time on the scars of motherhood.

And she was right. But only because a leisurely pace wasn't quite as much of an option as he wished. He'd still made sure she was satisfied. Pleased. *Pleasured*. Until his name was the only word escaping her lips.

When they were both spent, Harley had stood up to open the drapes of his east-facing window, then sat down and tucked Liz between his legs with her back to his chest so they could watch the sunrise together. It was a damn fine romantic setup, even if he did say so himself.

Then came the call from Teegan just a few minutes earlier.

Strangely—while it *had* forced them back to reality—listening to the little girl's brave sleep-tinged voice had somehow cemented them closer together. And reinforced the need to get her back. The fact that she wasn't where she belonged darkened Harley's mood. It dug at him. Made him feel like he was failing. After five minutes of pensive silence, the desire to win finally spurred him to make a plan that would get them out of his apartment and to their destination undetected.

While Liz had taken a shower, he'd taken care of the details. As promised, he added the blocking app to Liz's phone. He followed that with a couple of calls to arrange a few more things. In fifteen minutes, the local deli—which was more than happy to deliver for the fee Harley offered—would bring by a breakfast order. The driver had been given explicit instructions to park his well-known one-ton truck in just the right spot to block the sedan's line of sight. Harley had already stuck an envelope with payment onto the door.

All they had to do was finish getting ready and go.

Harley opened his eyes. Liz still sat on the bed. She'd finished with her hair—it was twisted into a loose bun at the nape of her neck—and was now fiddling with the clasp of her bra as she tried to do it up.

"Having some trouble?" Harley teased.

The narrow-eyed glare that Liz tossed over her shoulder was counteracted by her upturned lips. "Are you just going to sit there mocking and gawking, or offer some help?"

"Is the former an option?" he replied.

She wrinkled her nose. "No."

"How about if I forgo the mocking and stick with the gawking?"

"Still no. And I'm starting to think you *broke* my bra."

"What a damn shame."

"Shut up and help."

Harley laughed, then pushed up and slid closer. His hands took over where hers had left off. Though he suspected the job he was doing took ten times as long as it should. He had to take a few extra moments to caress her shoulder blades with his thumbs. He had to place a trail of soft kisses along the line where the two clasps would meet. And he had to laugh harder at the fact that there was evidence that he had indeed done some damage with his enthusiasm to get the bra off.

"Sorry," he said, sounding anything but, even to his own ears.

"Did you *actually* break it?" Liz asked, twisting a little.

"One of the little metal things is bent. But I can fix it."

He made short work of the assurance, pinching the clasp, then forcing it back into place. With a regretful sigh, he pressed the hook in place, kissed her back one more time, then grabbed his boots from the end of the bed.

In two minutes, they were both fully dressed. Harley had his bag repacked and Liz's palm pressed into his hand. They stood together at the front window, waiting in mutual silence. The blinds were still closed, but there was no mistaking the rumble of the approaching one-ton. When the noise heaved to a stop, Harley released Liz to steal a quick peek through the slats. Sure enough, the big truck sat outside in the spot he'd wanted it to be.

"Do-or-die time?" said Liz in a small voice.

Harley kissed her cheek, then tugged her across the room to the door. "Just go-time. This is gonna work. With any luck—and my mad-crazy superhero skills, of course—we'll have the paintings in no time. Then we'll get that kid of yours, and we'll run away to Timbuktu."

"You mean Paris?"

"That's the one. Let's go. Timing matters."

She reached for the door, but stopped just shy of turning the handle. "Tell me you mean it, Harley."

Harley didn't ask which part she meant. He didn't need to. His answer was the same for all of it. "Always."

He led her into the hall, then to the stairwell. Certain that the delivery driver would choose the elevator, he didn't hesitate to push his way through the heavy door. He didn't pause on the stairs, either. It was only when they reached the lobby floor that he stopped and put a finger to his lips to indicate a need for silence. Liz nodded her understanding, and Harley released her hand so he could inch forward and press open the door, just an inch. He peered out into the lobby. It wouldn't matter terribly if the driver did happen to see them—the guy wouldn't know them by sight—but Harley's goal was to slip out as undetected as possible. No witnesses meant no chance that Garibaldi's man would have someone to question. The only kind of collateral damage Harley wanted to allow was the sacrifice of the breakfast that would go uneaten.

From his vantage point, he could see the delivery guy make his way up the front steps and shoulder through the main entrance, bags clasped tightly in his arms. Usually Harley cursed the lack of a secure door in the lobby. Today, he was grateful for it. He continued watching as the driver walked to the elevator and pressed the button. The moment the other man stepped inside, Harley grabbed Liz's hand again, then opened the door a little farther. He leaned out.

The lobby was clear. The front end of the delivery truck was in view.

So far, so good, he thought.

Still cautious, Harley guided Liz into the open space. On the other side of the door, he immediately pulled her flush against the wall to survey the entryway. He breathed out. The truck spanned the length of the glass windows. Its height blocked any chance of being seen.

Harley breathed out a relieved breath.

"I think we've got about three minutes." He spoke in a soft, quick voice. "The clearest path is probably the one behind the truck. There's a small row of hedges we can use as cover to make our way to the end of the building. Then we can duck around the side and decide where to go from there."

"Okay."

"Ready?"

"Yes."

Holding Liz's hand tightly, Harley strode purposefully across the lobby and out the front door.

They made it down the stairs.

They made it to the hedges.

They made it to the edge of the building.

And there, they had to stop. A second dark-colored sedan was pulling around the corner, blocking them in. Moving in any direction would expose them. But worse than that was a small significant fact.

The man at the wheel was Jesse Garibaldi himself.

Chapter 16

The sight of the car scared Liz a little. Seeing Jesse Garibaldi scared her a little more. But what made her palms clammy and her heart want to stop was the look on Harley's face.

He didn't look angry. Though she would've understood if he had. Instead, his expression was near devastation. Like seeing the man—whom Liz was accustomed to interacting with on at least a weekly basis—threw him back to the moment when he'd first learned of his father's death. And Liz knew without a doubt that that was where his mind had gone. She recognized the heartbreak for what it was. She'd seen it frequently on her in-laws' faces for months and months after Teegan's dad died. She'd glimpsed it occasionally in the years that followed. She felt the edges of it herself every time she thought about what danger her daughter was in.

And seeing it now, manifested on Harley...it sent a

terrible feeling of sadness through her. If she'd had time, she would've pulled him in to comfort him. Offered him heartfelt words and true sympathy. But as it was, she knew she couldn't afford the extra moments it would take. All she could do was try to protect him.

She took a deep breath, pressed to her tiptoes and kissed him on the mouth. When she pulled back, he blinked down at her, the pain in his face lessening as his brown-eyed gaze locked on her face.

"We need to find a new way out," she told him.

He nodded, purpose taking the place of sadness as he craned his neck to look around. Liz followed his survey of the area. Through the hedges, she could see that Garibaldi was as boxed in as they were. There wasn't enough space between the oversize delivery truck and the other dark-colored sedan that he could drive through.

"He's going to have to wait it out," Liz said softly. "And when the truck does go, we'll be stuck until he leaves."

"Unless he *doesn't* leave." Harley's voice was grim.

"What do you mean?"

"He's made an effort to come this far, so he might've also come up with some excuse to pay us a visit."

Liz inhaled. "That's not good."

"It's *really* not good," the big man agreed. "If he makes his way into the building, all of our tricks are about to backfire. He'll find the bagged food outside the apartment, and when we don't pick it up or answer the door, he'll call you. When you don't answer that either, he'll force his way in. And when he finds the apartment empty, he'll know that his tracking app's been compromised, too."

"Damn."

"Yep." He turned in a slow circle, then paused with

his back to the street and asked, "Are you claustrophobic, Liz?"

"No," she replied. "Why?"

He nodded toward the back of the building. "I wouldn't want to chance running through the ground-level suites' patios because someone would probably call the police. But there's a fence back there that runs the entire length of the apartments. And on the other side of *that* is another fence for the opposite building. There's a two-foot space between them. It'll be a tight squeeze."

"I'll take that over staring down the end of a gun."

"Yeah. Me, too."

She held out her hand, and together, they made their way to the end of the building and through the narrow space between the fences. Harley hadn't been kidding about the tight squeeze. He had to walk more or less sideways just to fit, and Liz could feel her hips brushing the wood as they moved. The feeling might not have been *quite* claustrophobic, but it sure wasn't good, either. And the farther in they got, the worse it grew.

Like he could sense her increasing distress, Harley called over his shoulder. "We're almost halfway. You all right back there?"

"Not terrible," she replied. "Just busy being thankful we didn't actually get a chance to eat that breakfast back there, or I might not have fit through."

His responding chuckle bounced off the two fences. "Not gonna lie. I could actually go for an egg or two right now."

"I promise I'll make you a million eggs once this is over. Pancakes, too. And maybe some sausages?"

"You're torturing me. But offer accepted."

They pushed through the rest of the way in relative silence, but as soon as they reached the opening on the other side, Harley turned and swept her into a bearlike embrace. He kissed her face a dozen times, then leaned back and stared down at her.

"Thank you," he said, his voice surprisingly fervent.

"For what?" Liz replied.

"Dragging me back to the moment when I was busy dwelling on the past." He shook his head, grabbed her hand and started walking. "I swear. Most of the time, I think I've got it under control. It's been fifteen years, but every now and then it feels like fifteen minutes."

Liz reached up to touch his cheek. "Is that the first time you've seen Garibaldi?"

Harley nodded, blatant pain playing across his features. "First time in person. Brayden tried to explain to me how it felt. Like having that metaphorical rug ripped out from under you. But I gotta say…that description doesn't quite cut it. More like being punched in the gut ten quick times in succession."

"What can I do to help?"

"You're already doing it. In fact, I'm not sure I'd still be functioning properly if it weren't for you."

She couldn't help but smile. "I guess that particular feeling is mutual. Though I think my side is a little more warranted."

"You go ahead and believe what you like," he replied, "but I'm telling you right now…if you hadn't kissed me back there, I don't know what I would've done. Run out in front of his car, maybe? Thrown away every ounce of professionalism, years of training *and* a decade and a half of patience and planning? I'm honestly not sure. That kiss saved me."

Liz's face warmed. "You make it sound like I'm one of the magical princesses in one of Teegan's books."

"That's actually a pretty accurate description. True

love's kiss. It's been saving damsels in distress for a few millennia. The role reversal—damsels saving super-heroes in distress—is just a sign of the times."

She could hear the smile in his voice, but she didn't dare turn his way to look at his face. Because she'd also heard a far more significant word.

Love.

And while it might've been an offhand remark—a joke, even—it brought the idea to the forefront of Liz's mind. And it stuck. It made her need to think about whether or not this thing between her and Harley was heading in that direction.

You barely know him, she told herself automatically.

But really, she felt like that wasn't true at all. She might not have unraveled every detail of his life, but saying that she didn't *know* him…that wasn't quite right.

Liz made a silent mental list.

She understood what made him who he was.

She'd told him things about herself that she wouldn't even hint at with people who'd known her for years.

She could feel the tether between them—a solid bond that she couldn't imagine dissolving.

She was sure of where his priorities lay, and com-pletely certain they lined up with her own.

She knew that he was kind, good and great with Teegan, and that he was happy to let her take things as slow as she wanted to go.

And their physical compatibility was like the cherry on an already well-iced cake.

But love? asked a little voice in her head.

She gave the voice an imaginary nod. Maybe she wasn't there. Not yet. But she could definitely see herself falling. And for some reason, it didn't even scare her.

Maybe because having your daughter kidnapped

makes you realize what real fear is. And maybe it makes you extra aware that life is short and precious and sometimes the best thing to do is to jump in headfirst.

"Hey. Going somewhere without me?"

At Harley's teasing question, Liz stopped, realizing belatedly that he was a step behind her. They'd reached the end of the block, and he'd already paused at the edge of the street, but she'd been so immersed in her thoughts that she hadn't even noticed and was halfway into the crosswalk already.

"Sorry," she mumbled, her cheeks heating.

"Everything all right? That injured leg of yours bothering you?"

"I'm good. My leg's fine. I almost forgot I hurt it, actually. I just…" She trailed off and shrugged.

She couldn't very well confess that she'd been asking herself whether or not she was halfway in love with him. Could she?

"You just what?" Harley prodded.

"Never mind. It's not important."

"Your face says otherwise."

She sighed. "I've never been the kind of girl who'd be content to sit around and wait for her handsome prince to turn up."

Harley lifted an eyebrow. "Okay."

Liz made a face. "Can we walk and talk, so I don't feel like you're looking at me like I'm a crazy person?"

"I'm not looking at you like that."

"Not yet."

He chuckled. "All right."

She waited a few more moments before plunging in. "After this is over, what will you do?"

Although he didn't answer right away, his hand did tighten in hers. And after a few seconds, he let out a sigh.

"I don't know what kind of answer you're looking for, honey," he said.

"Just an honest one."

"Okay. Well. Honest, I can do. I've had one goal for as long as I can remember. Find Jesse Garibaldi, figure out what the hell he's been up to and put him behind bars. So best-case scenario, this being over means I've managed to do that."

"Do you think that's likely?"

"Another honest answer?"

"Yes, please."

"No. I might be able to do the middle bit and figure out what he's been up to. I'm pretty damn sure it's got something to do with those paintings." He paused. "Don't take anything bad out of what I'm about to say, okay?"

"I'll try not to," Liz replied, her heart skipping a worried beat.

"Once we've got Teegan back…it'll be impossible for me to operate under the radar. Garibaldi might still not know who I really am, but he'll be far too aware of my existence for me to investigate him."

"So you'll go home?"

Harley stopped walking abruptly. "What?"

Liz took a breath. "When it's over. You'll—"

"No, I heard you. I just didn't know that's what you were asking."

She didn't even realize she'd dropped her gaze to the ground until his fingers found her chin and tipped her face back up. His stare was warm. Intense. And held a hint of unexpected uncertainty.

"Liz…" he said. "What's happening between us isn't a one-off for me. I have no intention of going back to Freemont once we've got Teegan. Unless that's what *you* want me to do."

Tears pricked at her eyes. "No. Definitely not. I just don't want to ask too much."

Harley's mouth lifted up at the corner. "Pretty sure that's the mom in you. Be selfish for a minute, honey. Tell me what you'd like me to do."

"I'd like you to stay," she admitted, feeling shy about the statement.

"I'd like to stay, too," he replied firmly. "I want a chance at becoming an *us*, Liz."

Relief hit her so hard she nearly swayed. "Then I guess we better walk those other three blocks pretty quickly?"

"How about right now?"

"Works for me."

As they resumed their trek through the residential area that would eventually lead to their destination, Liz's heart felt a little more settled. Her nerves, on the other hand, grew messier and more on edge with each passing second. She sensed that Harley was growing tenser, too. She wondered what was on his mind. But she didn't ask. She was worried that she already knew.

He's gearing up to tell you that you're going to need to sit out during the confrontation.

And it was logical. Liz could reason through it just fine. Harley hadn't brought it up, but she was sure that if he was right about where the paintings were being held—and he *had* to be, because she couldn't handle the idea of starting their search over again—then the men who possessed them wouldn't just hand them over. She suspected they were armed. Organized. They'd orchestrated a complicated heist. And even if she and Harley had no idea *why* they wanted the paintings, there was zero chance of them giving up without a fight. And fighting wasn't her forte by any stretch. She would have to completely defer to Harley's expertise. She hated the helpless feeling that accompanied the fact that someone else was better suited to saving her daughter, but she trusted Harley to do everything in his power to rescue Teegan.

She opened her mouth to reassure him that he didn't have to worry about letting her down easy. But before she could get the words out, something in the not-too-far distance caught her eye. And held it.

Liz frowned. Whatever it was, it looked distinctly out of place. It was purple, and it sat at the edge of a run-down property. Liz frowned harder, something unpleasant tickling at her mind.

"We're here," Harley announced.

She looked down and saw that he was right. They'd reached the barriers that cordoned off the run-down scheduled-to-be-demolished neighborhood. But she only eyed the white-and-orange blockade for a moment before the purple object ahead drew her eyes again. And as they took a few steps closer, she finally figured out why she couldn't tear her attention away from the slip of purple for long. It was because she recognized it. Knew it well. Had purchased it herself. And before she could stop herself, she was running toward it.

By the time Harley figured out what was happening, it was too late. Liz's hand had slipped from his, and her feet were slamming to the pavement. Liz's hair flew from its loose bun and trailed out behind her.

For a second, Harley just stared after her, too surprised to give chase. Then his protective instincts kicked in, and he was on the move, too. He had no idea what she'd seen or what had spurred her sudden flight, but he did know that running out in the open was a dangerous move.

He was glad to have the advantage of longer legs. It meant it only took him ten strides to start closing the distance between them. Ten more, and he'd almost caught up. Five more after that, and he damn near overtook her, because she'd dropped to her knees and was clutching something in her hands.

Harley lurched to a stop, a question on his lips. He didn't make it as far as actually uttering it. He saw the object in her hands and knew exactly what it was.

Teegan's backpack.

The same one he'd made her pack before they slipped out of the apartment hours earlier. With his stomach churning, Harley turned in a circle, searching for some sign of why the bag had been discarded in that particular spot. A dozen questions swirled darkly under the surface of his mind. He didn't take the time to acknowledge them. His gut was screaming that they needed to get out of sight. Fast.

He dipped to a crouch and put his hands on Liz's elbows. "Honey. We can't stay here."

Liz was crying. "She was here, Harley. What does that mean?"

He shook his head. "I don't know yet. But we need to get out of sight."

For a moment, she showed no sign of budging, and Harley thought he might have to lift her from the ground and carry her. Just as he prepared to do it, she heaved a sigh and pushed up. Harley didn't pause to think about where they were going. He grabbed her hand and pulled her from the edge of the yard to the carport on the side of the house. Then he tugged her past that into the small patch of grass between it and the home beside it. And just in time. They no sooner stepped into the cover offered by the run-down home than the crunch of tires on gravel-dotted pavement carried to his ears.

Harley didn't know whether to curse or be thankful.

So he settled for both. Muttering a swear word under his breath, he pulled Liz against the prickly stucco, then flattened himself beside her. Barely breathing, he waited for the vehicle to pass. Instead, it got louder. Closer. Near enough that he could hear the chirp of something under the hood—a faulty belt, probably. Then came the squeal of the brakes.

Damn, Harley thought as the engine cut out just a few feet away. *Damn, damn, damn.*

He'd chosen the wrong hiding place. Whoever was driving the vehicle had parked it in the carport just a few feet from where he and Liz stood. Literally just feet. All it would take was a cough or a sneeze or a too-noisy breath from either one of them. Hell. Maybe even less. If the driver had a passenger, and the passenger stepped out just enough…

Harley put his hand on his weapon and held his breath as the car door slammed, then tensed as he waited for a second one to follow. His teeth gritted together as someone's shuffling gait dragged across the ground. Then he finally exhaled as he decided that the driver was traveling solo.

There was the rattle of the doorknob, an indistinct mutter, then a squeak as the door to the house opened.

Harley turned to Liz, prepared to initiate a quiet escape so they could regroup. When he swiveled his head in her direction, he found her attention elsewhere—straight over his shoulder and pointed toward the carport. He quickly adjusted his position so he could follow her gaze. It only took a second to see what she saw.

Parked at a bad angle so that the end jutted out from its spot was a white van. And Harley didn't even have to go check to be sure it was the one marked with Everlast of Freemont's logo.

Chapter 17

"We have to go look," Liz whispered.

Harley shook his head. She was right. Except for one small detail.

"*I* have to go look," he corrected softly. "And before you argue, I'm going to preemptively point out the obvious reasons. One. I have a gun. You don't. Two. I'm a cop. You're not. Three. If neither of those works, then I need you to think of Teegan. If someone gets the jump on me, you need to stay safe."

Liz's mouth turned down. "What you're saying makes sense. But that doesn't mean I like it."

He leaned over to kiss her unhappy lips. "One minute. I just want to verify that the paintings are inside. If they are, our situation just got a whole lot easier."

"And if they're not?"

"We'll cross that bridge when and if we have to."

"One minute," she said firmly.

"One," he agreed, then kissed her again and slipped away.

He slunk carefully along the edge of the house, then paused at the corner that separated the building from the open carport. Even though he wanted to look back at Liz, he didn't give in to the urge. He knew that if he saw the worry in her eyes, he might feel a need to *go* back as well as look back, and he didn't want to eat up any more of whatever window they had.

He proactively drew his weapon, inhaled and leaned around the corner. The carport was still and silent. He took a cautious step forward. Nothing changed. So he kept going. He made his way past the front of the van, then hurried to the back.

He stopped in front of the side window and tried to see in, but the paint over top of the glass completely obscured his view. He couldn't have said whether there was anything in the back, let alone something specific.

He tossed a glance toward the house. He couldn't hear a sound, so he stepped away from the window and moved to the back. Out of habit, his mind went to thoughts of fingerprints and evidence contamination. He stared at the closed rear doors, protocol fighting with the need to act.

Greater good, he told himself.

With a small nod to some vague semblance of proper procedure, he gripped the bottom edge of his T-shirt and used it as a barrier between his fingers and the door handle. He pulled, and met with resistance. A mix of irritation and disappointment trickled in.

What made you think it would be unlocked in the first place? he wondered.

Harley stepped back. His promised minute was probably already up. He could practically hear the alarm bells going off in Liz's head. Not wanting to worry her more than she already was, he stepped to the other side of the van and issued a reassuring wave, then signaled with his index finger that he needed one more minute. He didn't stop to wait for her approval. He hurried back to the front of the van. There, he spied something he probably should've noticed the first time he went by. The keys sat in the van's ignition.

A sharp stab of concern hit him in the gut. Why would the driver leave the keys in the ignition but lock the back? He didn't have time to come up with an answer. From inside the house, there was a resounding *pop-pop*, then a guttural yell. Those two sounds were followed by three more explosive pops in quick succession and then a thud.

Harley didn't hesitate. He hit the ground hard, sprinting toward Liz. He could see the fear in her eyes. He could feel her pulse thundering through her veins as he took hold of her wrist. But comfort was secondary to safety.

"Backyard," he said, the single word infused with years of authority and experience.

Liz didn't argue as he pulled her along the side of the building to the rear of it.

Harley spotted a hiding space immediately—a large low deck that was attached to the back of the house. Ducking down to avoid hitting his head, he tugged Liz into the dank-smelling space. Under the cover, he was able to stand up and take in the surroundings. They weren't pleasant. There were cobwebs coating the rotten beams overhead. A stack of nail-crusted two-by-fours leaned against one corner, and a cracked kiddie pool sat in another.

But it's better than being out there, Harley reminded himself.

As if to prove the thought true, the echo of the van

door slamming carried from the front of the house. Next came the screech of tires as it peeled away.

Sure that they were safe for the moment, Harley turned his attention to Liz.

"You okay?" he asked.

She took a shaky breath and nodded. "Fine. But was that…?"

Harley didn't sugarcoat it. "Gunshots."

"I thought… God. I can't…"

Liz shivered, and her hands squeezed Teegan's backpack. She clutched it tightly, clearly too overcome with emotion to come even close to expressing the terrible thought aloud.

Harley reached for her shoulders. "Whoever is— *was*—inside the house isn't the person who took your daughter. They're the people who stole the paintings. The gunman was driving the van used to take the paintings, and there was no confrontation when he went into the house. We would've heard it. To me, that means that the people inside must've trusted the shooter. They were working with him. I strongly suspect some kind of double cross."

Her hands loosened marginally. "You're going in the house."

"Yes."

"I'm coming with you."

"Liz."

Her face grew stubborn. "I mean it, Harley. I'm not staying out here by myself."

He ran a hand over his hair. He did need to go into the house. Not because he had to verify the truth of what he'd told her, but because he knew there could be clues inside the house. Hints at what significance the paintings held. And more important, a lead on where the white van and its driver might be headed. Because if his take on the situation was correct, he somehow doubted that the gunman would stick around Whispering Woods for long.

He didn't, however, want Liz to see the aftermath of violence. She didn't need that. No one did. He couldn't even rightly say that *he* was used to violence. Murder and mayhem weren't something to grow accustomed to. But he'd seen enough things firsthand that he had a pre-made mental shield.

"Let me go in first," he finally said. "Assess the situation and make sure it's all clear. There might be things in there that you won't be able to un-see."

Her expression didn't waver, and neither did her voice. "I don't want to be separated."

The statement softened him more than it should have. It tugged at the strings that went from his heart directly to her.

"Neither do I, Liz," he said. "Really and truly. But I also don't want to risk you getting hurt or experiencing something that there's no need to experience."

"At least let me come inside with you."

"I can't do that."

"I'll follow you anyway, whether you say yes or no. I'd just rather this not be the start of our first fight."

"Honey."

"Please." Her hand landed on her chest with the plea, and it was obvious that she ached from the inside out.

Harley scrubbed his hand over his chin and relented. "Fine. But just inside the side door, okay? And if you see a single thing that makes you nervous, you tell me."

Her eyes finally lost some of their pinch. "Thank you."

"Don't thank me yet," he said. "You might regret it in a few seconds."

* * *

In spite of the warning, as Liz leaned against the wall at the bottom of the stairs and waited for the all-clear, she couldn't make herself feel guilty for pressuring Harley into taking her into the house.

The moments after the rapid muffled gunfire had been terrifying. Heart-stopping. And not because she'd stopped believing that Harley could—and would—make good on his promise to save Teegan. Yes, for a fleeting second, she'd had to consider whether or not there was even the remotest possibility that her daughter had been on the receiving end of the horror. It was an automatic reaction. Maternal instinct. But as quick as it came, it was gone.

She knew if Harley had thought Teegan might be inside the house, he would've said. Even a shred of suspicion would've provoked a conversation about it. And there was no way he would've cared about looking for the paintings if he believed there was a way to get to her daughter instead. Her mind had made those leaps with amazing speed.

The fear was real. But it had come from elsewhere. From the still, quiet moment after the gun pops. From the seconds before Harley came bounding around the corner. Because what had scared Liz so badly that she couldn't breathe was the idea that the big self-proclaimed superhero of a man might've been the one who'd gotten shot. And that instance had sent a cold, dangerous rush through her. It slammed something home.

She could lose him. And that scared her nearly as much as the thought of losing her daughter. Never—not even *once* in the eight years since Teegan was born—had Liz ever considered someone could take up that same kind of space in her heart. But believing for those moments that Harley might not come back had utterly floored her.

So when he *had* returned, she'd known with surety that she couldn't lose him again. Not even temporarily.

"Liz?" His voice carried down the stairs, jarring her back to the moment.

"Still here," she called back. "How bad is it?"

She heard the thump of his feet, and then he appeared on the steps. "Pretty bad. Two dead. One looked a little familiar. Not sure from where."

Liz couldn't help but notice that in spite of the fact that he knew the men weren't any kind of good, Harley's voice still contained a mix of regret and sympathy. And it made her heart swell to know that he could muster up that kind of caring.

"Did you find anything helpful?" she asked. "Anything that might tell us where the van was headed?"

He stepped down so that he was standing just above her and scratched at his chin, worry creasing his brow and making his jaw visibly stiff. "Nothing like that, unfortunately. I'm going to take a second to check my—"

The muted ring of a phone cut him off, and they exchanged a look. Harley cocked his head.

"Not coming from up here," he said.

Liz stood still, straining to pinpoint the sound. "I think it might be outside."

Harley took the bottom two steps in a single stride, then brushed by her and flung open the door. He bent immediately, and when he stood, he held a gunmetal gray phone in his hand. Liz's skin prickled nervously.

"Are you going to answer it?" she asked, her throat dry.

In reply, he tapped a finger to the screen—once to accept the call, and again to put it on speaker. After a silent moment, an annoyed male voice filled the air.

"Is this some kind of joke, Ruthers?"

Liz's heart squeezed in her chest, and Harley met her eyes again.

"No joke," he replied in a roughened voice that sounded little like his own.

"So it's done?" said the other man.

"Yes," replied Harley.

"Good work. You head our way with our merchandise, and we'll make sure your bank account doesn't suffer."

"Where?"

There was a pause. "Are you kidding me? What the hell's going on with you? Are you high?"

Harley grunted. "Not high."

"Two jobs, Ruthers. Take care of business, bring our stuff to the cabins."

"On it."

The line went dead, and Liz felt a sudden need to fold herself into Harley's arms. So she did. And he took her willingly, his hands running over her back as he spoke into her hair.

"I'm sorry," he said.

The apology made her draw back in surprise. "For what?"

"I wanted to ask about Teegan, but I was afraid it would give me away."

Unexpectedly, tears seeped to the surface. Harley's fingers came up to wipe away the ones that trickled down her face.

"Every time I think…" Liz trailed off, the lump in her throat making it too hard to continue. "Don't be sorry, Harley. Please. Ever."

He shook his head. "I should've found a better way to use that conversation."

"A better way? We know where he's taking the paintings."

"The cabin? That's pretty damn vague. The whole mountainside is full of them."

"Not cab*in*," she corrected. "Cab*ins*. There might be dozens of singular cabins kicking around, but there's only one nearby *group* setup."

Harley's face filled with understanding. "The rustic ones on the way out of town."

"You know them?"

"My brother rented them as part of his cover story."

Liz started to smile, but her lips quickly dipped as she remembered something important. "We don't have a car."

"I know where we can get one," Harley replied.

And moments later, they were standing two streets over in front of a garage, staring at a vehicle with a smashed-in front end.

"Do I want to know?" Liz asked.

"It belongs to Nadine Stuart," Harley said. "She drove it into a tree while she was saving my brother's life."

"Why is it *here*?"

"Nadine didn't have a place to store it and never got a chance to see about having it fixed after the accident. My brother asked me to take care of it, so I hired a guy." He shrugged. "I normally have a few more resources at my fingertips. This was my temporary solution."

Liz eyed the vehicle skeptically. "Will it even run?"

"It got *here*, didn't it?" He bent to pull a key out from under the bumper, then opened the door and fired up the engine. "See? Purrs like a—"

"Do *not* say 'kitten,'" Liz interrupted.

"I was going to say 'lovesick wildebeest.'"

"Of course you were."

He smiled crookedly. "Get in."

Issuing a silent prayer that the wheels wouldn't fall off, Liz complied. She quickly buckled her seat belt, and though the car rattled in an unnerving way as they backed out, it wasn't too bad—all things considered—as they pulled it onto the road. Harley's explanation for their plan also provided a welcome distraction from thinking about the safety of their mode of transportation.

"So here's what I'm thinking," he said. "What our friend Mr. Ruthers pulled off back there was planned. It was cold. So he's got some cunning and a bit of patience. I'm sure he's eager to unload the paintings, but he's not completely inept. He's not going to just drive through town in a van that someone could recognize. He'll take side streets and skirt the perimeter as much as possible. Which is good, because it'll slow him down. So we'll do the opposite."

"We're going to drive straight through town in *this*?" Liz swept her hand through the air. "Won't that attract attention?"

He tipped his face her way and smiled a slightly apologetic smile. "We're not going through *town*."

Liz started to ask what he meant, then realized she knew already. Because they hadn't made their way back to the barriers that blocked the main road into the neighborhood. They were on the other edge altogether.

"You might want to hang on," Harley said.

And with that suggestion, he turned the wheel sharply and pulled the car off the road and into the grass, and pointed it straight toward the woods.

Chapter 18

For a few precarious moments after he guided the car from the grass to the brush and from the brush to the actual treed area, Harley wondered if he'd made a mistake. A miscalculation. But the dense shrubs quickly gave way to a beaten-down path, and he breathed a little easier. The off-roading trails were exactly where he thought they'd be. Right where his thorough study of the surrounding area had indicated they should be.

A glance toward Liz told him she wasn't feeling quite as reassured as he was—one hand was tight on the seat belt and the other was pressed to the dashboard so hard that he thought her fingers might snap. He reached out and gave her wrist a squeeze, then forced her hand to her lap.

"Hey," he said. "You know I wouldn't take you this way unless I thought it was safe."

"It's not that," she replied. "I know you wouldn't use

a broken-down death trap to kill me *intentionally*. But here's a fun fact. I get sick on roller coasters."

"Ah."

"What?"

"You must've been *relieved* to hear that I like museums over theme parks."

She turned a weak glare his way. "Very funny."

He smiled. "It's only a couple of miles, I promise."

"How do you even know where we are?" she asked.

He tapped his forehead with his finger. "Head for maps. When Brayden first found Whispering Woods, I did what I do best, and I researched. I looked at everything we might need, including viable escape routes. Found a pretty impressive website dedicated to the best off-roading in the area. They line the entire town, and this spot was on the list."

"Aren't the trails designed for smaller vehicles? ATVs or whatever?"

"Unfortunately. It'll get a little hairy once we're farther in, and we won't be able to get all the way to the cabins."

"Great," Liz muttered.

"Don't worry," he said. "Before the path tightens too much, we'll cut back out. There's a spot that should take us straight to the road that leads in and out of town. With any luck, we'll be able to cut Ruthers off before he even makes it to his destination."

"You memorized all of that?"

"I'm nothing if not thorough. Feel free to mock me. The guys find an endless amount of joy in teasing me about my relative nerdiness."

"I think I'll just stick to trying not to puke."

"Also a good plan." He gave her hand another squeeze,

then turned his attention back out the front windshield as they went through a particularly thick patch of trees.

He had to slow the car to accommodate the area, and his mind wandered back to the scene of the shooting. It'd been more or less what he expected to find. One dead man sprawled across the couch, two wounds in his chest. Another man, who'd clearly tried to run, was lying face-down in the kitchen. He'd had two matching holes in his back, and there was a piece of exploded wall on the other side of the room where one shot had gone wild.

There was nothing spectacular about the victims. Average height and build. Average clothes. The second guy had a generic barbed-wire tattoo on his upper arm. There'd been something vaguely familiar about the first, but even though Harley was pretty good with faces, he hadn't been able to place it. Of course, the angle of the man's head—tossed to the side and half buried in a couch cushion—didn't make ID'ing him easy.

Still... Harley performed a quick mental recap. *Dark hair that would've hung to his earlobes. Thick un-plucked brows. Thin lips and beak-like nose. Small build, height uncertain, wouldn't stand out in a lineup.*

Then, with the sudden addition of a police lineup into his thoughts, it struck him. Harley *had* seen the man before. Or at least he'd seen his mug shot.

"Everlast's employment list," he muttered, cursing himself for not clueing in sooner.

"What about it?" Liz replied.

"One of the dead men back there was on it."

"You're sure?"

"One hundred percent. Might've been one of the guys busted for possession with intent. And now that I'm thinking about it, he had a plastic baggie hanging out of his pockets, too."

"Like…for drugs?"

"Think so." He frowned. "It's strange, isn't it?"

"What is?" Liz replied.

"Low-level drug dealers and users. I feel like they keep popping up."

"Coincidence?"

"Maybe." He could hear the disbelief in his own voice. "You just don't often find art theft and guys like this in the same crowd. In fact, saying 'not often' is probably an exaggeration. It'd be different if it were petty theft. Couple of guys looking for a fix, doing a B&E to get a bit of cash. But something this targeted and this specific? And to take something that can't be fenced easily…it makes no sense."

"Even if they *were* trying to sell the paintings, they really aren't worth anything," Liz reminded him.

"I know." Harley felt his frown deepen. "Did anyone other than Garibaldi's prearranged buyers try to purchase one?"

"No. His buyers usually come in within a day of the paintings being dropped off. And even if they didn't, Jesse sets the price himself. They're by far one of the most expensive items in my shop. My inventory tends to be cash-and-carry. Tourists like to buy small pieces that remind them of their trip without breaking the bank. They'd be *really* unlikely to take a second look at anything that price or that big."

"What about Garibaldi's buyers? Are they the same guys every time?"

She shook her head. "No. Different people."

Harley's frustration mounted even more; he was sure there was something there, just out of reach. "Anything about them stand out?"

"Not really. They're usually nicely dressed and polite. But I guess that doesn't mean much."

"It only means that Garibaldi's good at covering his tracks."

Liz exhaled heavily. "I wish I was better help. But all I've got is the fact that he commissions them, drops them off, and that they have that weird texture."

Her words made Harley's instincts jump, and his mind started forcefully slamming puzzle pieces into place.

His brother and Reggie had found Garibaldi's strange underground storage room. Harley himself had determined that it'd been designed with a special air system to preserve art.

His partner Anderson and his new girlfriend, Nadine Stuart, had retrieved a series of photos that showed a group of hazmat-attired men in the same storage room, working with a series of large canvases.

All stuff you knew already, he told himself.

He slowed the car a little more. They were approaching a split in the road, and he was sure it was the place to veer off so they could make their way to the main road. He eyed the still-thickening patch of trees straight ahead, then turned the wheel to take them to the right. Twenty feet up, he could see a widening patch of light where the woods grew thinner. A few feet more, and he spied the first hint of the road in the form of a yellow street sign.

For a moment, Harley almost wished it was a little farther away. He could use the extra time to work through the details a little more thoroughly.

Garibaldi. Storage room. Canvas. Hazmat suits. Stuff you knew, he repeated silently. *But there's new information to factor in, too.*

He eased the car forward. They were at the edge of the woods now, and he needed to decide whether to hang back and wait, or to attempt some kind of roadblock. Or maybe neither. Maybe a pursuit. His mind was a little too preoccupied to make the decision right that second. It insisted on repeating the list of key elements over again, then adding to it.

Criminal records. Drug dealers and users. Strange paint and—

"It's not paint," he said, suddenly sure that the statement was true.

Liz echoed his words, sounding understandably confused. "It's not paint?"

Harley nodded. His brain was bubbling with an idea. A conclusion. Before he could tell Liz what it was, though, the rumble of an engine carried through the air.

He tensed, waiting for the white van to appear from around the bend up the road. Instead, a rusted-out three-quarter-ton pickup truck with a canopy covering its rear box came speeding out. It was traveling far faster than necessary—twenty miles over the speed limit, probably—and it burned by them in a cloud of dust, disappearing as fast as it had come.

Harley breathed out. He rolled his shoulders and turned to Liz. For a second, she looked expectant. Then her gaze landed on something over his shoulder, and her eyes widened, and her mouth dropped open as she shrieked his name.

"Harley!"

He cast a glance over his shoulder just in time to see what she did—the driver of the rusted-out truck must've slammed on the brakes just up the road. And now the vehicle was barreling toward them in reverse.

Before she had time to react on her own, Liz felt Harley's fingers slide in beside her. They slammed to her seat belt and depressed the release button. As the nylon strap flicked up, he reached across her lap and flung open the door.

"Out!" he ordered.

Liz didn't have to be told twice. She dived through the door frame and landed on the mix of gravel and pavement with a teeth-jarring thud. But she recovered quickly, adrenaline coursing through her as she pushed to her feet and whipped around to look for Harley. He was already out, too. Already striding toward her.

He reached her at the same second that the pickup reached the car. His body slammed into her at the same moment that the truck slammed into their vehicle.

Like he choreographed it, Liz thought a little hysterically as they hit the ground and rolled out of the path of destruction.

But the truck driver wasn't done with his portion of the dance.

From the corner of her eye, as Harley tugged her to her feet, Liz saw the thick raised tires start to spin again. For a moment, the truck didn't move. It was stuck to the car. Then the tires picked up even more traction, and the monstrosity was on the move again. It dug into the ground and heaved forward, stirring up a renewed cloud of dirt that made Liz choke. Then it screeched noisily and backed into the car, this time hard enough to knock it sideways.

If the driver wasn't trying to kill them, he was at least trying to ruin their chances of escape.

Or maybe he's doing both. Making it impossible for us to get away. That way, he can kill us in peace.

The idea seemed even more likely when she caught sight of the man at the wheel. His port-wine birthmark was unmistakable.

Ruthers.

The drug-dealing murderous man who'd threatened her in her shop now threatened her again.

Why did he turn the truck around? He could've just kept driving. He could've gotten away.

Liz's curiosity slipped away as Ruthers's eyes, dark and cruel, locked with hers by way of the side-view mirror. Maybe he hadn't recognized her before—maybe he'd simply attacked them because they looked suspicious there on the side of the road—but he definitely did now. Hate filled that gaze of his, and fear made Liz quake. Then the man snarled something she couldn't hear and stepped on the gas.

The truck whipped in a wide circle, then barreled toward them.

Together, she and Harley darted out of its path. The truck kept going. Like Ruthers hadn't even considered stopping. His violent onslaught backfired. Even though the brakes shrieked a protest, the beast of a vehicle continued to skid forward. Its grille smacked head-on into a cluster of evergreens.

The collision didn't do a lick of visible damage to the oversize truck. But apparently Ruthers had decided the vehicle was no longer a good enough weapon.

The driver's-side door flung out, and the man himself jumped out. He landed in a crouch, then sprang up and charged at them. Liz could see both the knife in his grip and the crazed glassy look in his eyes, and she was certain there was nothing stable or sober about him.

Harley's hand landed on Liz's shoulder then, and he issued an order to take cover. She started to argue—she'd resolved not to leave his side again, after all—but he was readying his gun, and she realized if she was too close to the action, she'd just impede his ability to take down the other man. So she turned and started to move toward the car. From there, she could both obey the command and still see what transpired. But she no sooner took a step in that direction than Ruthers veered off his path.

I'm his target, she realized.

And Harley saw it, too. He swung his weapon toward the man and hollered a warning. "Stop!"

Ruthers either didn't hear him or chose to ignore him. Or maybe he was still lucid enough to figure out that with Liz in the mix, Harley wouldn't risk taking a shot. Either way, he kept coming, his wild eyes fixed on her.

Run! urged a voice in her head.

But her feet didn't want to cooperate. They were leaden. Weighted. Like she wore gum boots full of cement. It wasn't until the sun flashed against the weapon in Ruthers's hand that her brain finally took charge again.

Liz dashed sideways, and at the same moment, Harley lifted his arm holding the gun and fired a warning. Up toward the sky. It was just enough to distract her attacker. His head swiveled. One of his booted feet caught against a rock. And suddenly he wasn't coming at her anymore. Instead, he was tumbling forward. His chin smashed to the hard-packed road in a way that made Liz shiver in a whole body cringe. The sick feeling got worse when he lifted his head, and she spied the massive split in his lip and the crimson gush that followed.

Without even realizing she was doing it, Liz stepped forward. Then immediately regretted the instinct that made her want to help the dangerous man, because in spite of the blood dripping from his split lip, he snarled, then tried to propel himself toward her again.

Equally as horrified as she was nauseous, Liz took a step back.

Ruthers managed to push to his feet. A little too late, Liz saw that his fall and his injuries hadn't managed to dislodge his weapon. And in the millisecond it took for her to see what he was going to do, her brain hit the fast-forward button.

This is what it means when they say your life flashes before your eyes, she thought.

Though that particular description wasn't quite true. It wasn't her past she saw in that millisecond. It was her future. Or lack of it, to be more accurate. When that knife left Ruthers's hand, it would hit her. Kill her.

She would never see Teegan grow up. Never watch her daughter get married. She would never get to deepen her relationship with Harley. Never see *herself* get married.

It was a terrible, horrible crash of thoughts. A millisecond of utter despair.

Then, as Ruthers drew back his weapon, a reasonable, urgent voice in her head came back, hollering at her that standing still and waiting wasn't her only option.

Dodge it!

She bent her knees, preparing to dive while also wondering if she would be fast enough. But her reflexes didn't end up mattering. Ruthers only got as far as bringing the knife to ear level before a shot echoed through the air. And the frightening man's arm flopped down, the blade toppling uselessly to the ground. Seconds later, the man followed the weapon. He landed with a dull thud, and a bloom of red seeped out across his chest.

Liz stared, her mouth open, her heart thundering. She lifted her eyes and found Harley standing a few feet away, his gun stretched out in front of him. Vaguely, she thought there ought to be smoke billowing from the barrel.

She tried to say his name. Failed.

She watched, dumbstruck, as Harley holstered his weapon and rushed forward to close the gap between them. She wondered why he was in such a hurry. Why he wasn't stopping to examine Ruthers. Then felt herself sway. Thankfully, Harley got there before her body actually gave way. She collapsed against him, inhaling his masculine scent. Feeling his strength. She didn't cry, but she knew her body was shaking.

Harley's hands soothed a circle across her back. "It's okay, honey. You're okay. I'm here."

She tried to answer him. She *did* answer him. But what she said out loud wasn't what was in her head. "Is he dead, Harley?"

"Yeah, honey."

"Check."

"What?"

"Please."

His hand slowed, then stilled. "All right. Let's find a place for you to sit down."

"I'm fine," Liz said, but as soon as Harley eased away, she realized she wasn't; her body immediately started to wobble.

"Come on," Harley said. "There's a big rock over there. Looks like an armchair if you squint."

She couldn't manage a laugh. She let him lead her—half carry her, really—to the boulder-sized stone in question and sank down gratefully. The rock was cold and hard, but it was solid and reassuring as well.

Harley kissed her forehead, then her mouth, then moved back to Ruthers's prone body.

Though part of her felt like she ought to watch—ought to verify for herself that the man wasn't going to magically come back to life—Liz's eyes closed as Harley knelt down to check Ruthers's pulse. She'd never seen a dead man before. Never attended an open-casket funeral, never been in the room during the passing of a loved one. And even though she had every reason to hate the man on the ground, there was a large human part of her that mourned the loss of life. She understood now why Harley had seemed sad and sympathetic at the run-down house where the other two men had died.

"I'm sorry," she murmured.

She didn't realize she'd spoken loud enough to be heard until Harley answered her.

"What for, honey?" he asked.

She looked up. Harley was upright again, and moving back in her direction.

"That he died," she admitted, feeling a bit embarrassed. "That you had to shoot him."

"You or him, Liz. No contest, no choice." Harley's voice wasn't *quite* matter-of-fact, and in spite of his words, Liz knew he didn't take what he'd done lightly. His next statement, spoken in a softer tone, confirmed it. "I'd have aimed for his arm, if I'd been closer. But I wasn't quite close enough to guarantee the shot. Or to be sure he wouldn't move too quickly and leave a path for the bullet to get to you."

"I know. I'm grateful you saved me. I just…" She trailed off, wishing she couldn't feel the tears forming.

"Someone died," Harley replied. "It's right to feel bad."

Liz nodded and breathed out. "Thanks for not making me sound like a crazy person."

"Here to help." He stretched out his hand. "Speaking of which…"

"Teegan." Saying her daughter's name as she took his hand was almost like a reset—a reminder, at the very least, that for all her regret in the current moment, there was a reason the man had died.

"Teegan," Harley echoed. "And I think if we look in

the back of that truck, we'll find the paintings we need in order to get her back."

Liz took a breath and stood. "Okay, then. What are we waiting for?"

And she was pleased that her voice was firm and determined.

Chapter 19

As they made their way toward the jacked-up truck, Harley hazarded a single look back at Ruthers's body. It was far enough back from the main road that no one would spot it by accident. They'd have to be actively looking or coincidentally in the same spot. He still felt a nagging need to alert the authorities to its presence. It felt wrong to leave the man lying there.

No time, he told himself. *You'll have to take care of it after.*

He glanced down at Liz, who was leaning on him. He suspected Ruthers's death had shaken her up badly.

And that surprises you?

He shook his head at himself. It didn't surprise him. Not at all. It was the very thing he'd been trying to protect her from—that violence.

But he couldn't dwell on it. Couldn't let guilt creep in. In the moment when the other man had drawn his knife, then readied it, the world had slowed. Harley had felt only two things. First: a need to protect Liz. And second: a fear that he might not be able to. The latter had nearly overwhelmed him. The mere *idea* that the creep on the ground might take away the woman he cared so deeply about… It'd been more than Harley could handle. A world where Liz was ripped away from him wasn't a world he wanted to be in. It would be like having his heart forcibly removed. So he'd taken aim. Kept his heart intact. Kept *Liz* intact. Then realized that, really, they were one and the same.

So it wasn't just two things you felt, was it? There was a third.

He stopped with his hand poised on the handle of the truck canopy. He spun so quickly that Liz stumbled back with wide eyes.

She started to ask a question. "Harley! What are you—"

He didn't let her finish. He swept in with a kiss. Firm. Thorough. Possessive. He crushed her body to his, then turned to press her to the raised tailgate. He kissed her and kissed her. Then kissed her some more. When he finally pulled away, he ached to keep going. Longed for the nightmare to be over, so they could just be *them*. Harley and Liz. No. Harley, and Liz and Teegan.

He pressed his forehead to hers, met her unblinking blue gaze and laid it out in a raw voice. "If he'd killed you, it would've killed me, too."

She drew in a small breath, clearly surprised by the vehemence in his words. "Harley…"

"Hear me out."

"I'm not going anywhere."

"Ever."

"What?"

"I don't want us to be separated. Ever."

Thankfully, she didn't look at him like he was crazy. In fact, a little laugh escaped her kiss-swollen lips.

"Funny…" she said softly. "I had the very same thought."

He touched her face. "Did you?"

She leaned into the caress. "Yes."

He stared at her for a moment longer before plunging in with what he really wanted to say. "I don't know how it happened, Liz, but in the last few hours, you've carved out this enormous spot in my heart."

Her hand came up to press to his chest—like she was trying to find the spot he meant. She dropped her gaze to the place where her fingers had landed. Then her palm flattened, and warmth seeped through.

"Here?" she asked.

"Somewhere in there," he agreed. "But far, far bigger than would fit."

"You're in my heart, too." Her eyes came up to meet his again, a hint of uncertainty playing through her stare. "Sharing a spot with Teegan."

Harley felt a wide smile crack his face. "I don't think I've ever been so honored." He dipped down to kiss her again, then spoke against her mouth. "I've got three little words in my head, if you're ready to have them."

"Yes, please," she breathed.

"I love you, Liz."

"I love *you*, Harley."

He wondered if he should take a moment to relish it. To talk about it. To reaffirm his need for forever. But he didn't feel a need. Instead, he felt spurred to act.

"Good," he said. "Let's finish this."

He kissed her once more, then released her so he could open the hatch at the back of the truck. He pushed it up and leaned in. Just as he'd suspected, three large framed paintings sat in the truck bed. They clearly hadn't been secured during Ruthers's violent attack, and they were spread out unevenly.

"Are these the Heigles?" he asked.

Liz pressed in beside him, nodding her head before she'd even looked all the way in. "Yes. Definitely them."

She reached out and slid her hand to the nearest painting. Rather than pulling it closer, she just ran her fingers over top of it. So Harley did it, too, recalling his earlier conclusion about the paint not being *just* paint. As his fingers slid over the texture, Harley saw immediately what Liz meant. The paint felt off. Grainy, but not in a way he would've expected.

You need a sample.

He pulled his hand out of the truck, considering the best way to get one. He couldn't very well take a chunk of the canvas itself.

But a scraping, maybe?

"What do you think?" asked Liz.

Harley started to tell her his opinion, then stopped. He'd fill her in after. For now, he knew the men who had Teegan would be waiting. In fact, they'd rounded the corner of another three hours, and he was sure the phone should be ringing any second.

Come to think of it...

"Why don't you grab your bag from the car?" he suggested. "I'm going to check the truck for a piece of paper so I can try and get a sample of the paint."

"A sample?" Liz repeated. "Because it's not just paint, you mean?"

"Yeah. You were right. It *does* feel weird. So the best thing to do is send it to the experts for analysis." He stepped back from the rear of the truck and nodded at the shattered car. "You're probably not going to want to miss that call."

"No, definitely not."

She pushed to her tiptoes to kiss him, then slipped off in the other direction. Harley turned his attention to the task at hand, climbing into the cab to search for something he could use. He winced at the sight of the exposed ignition box. Ruthers had obviously stolen the vehicle and made short work of hot-wiring it. Harley didn't relish the idea of cruising around in a pilfered piece of property, and it wasn't exactly subtle, either.

"But beggars and choosers and all that," he muttered.

He dug through the glove box until he found a suitable sheet of paper, then quickly folded it into a makeshift envelope. He grabbed a pen from the console, too, and pulled off the end to expose a rough edge. Then he hopped out and moved to the truck bed again, where he dug into a particularly thick glob of dried paint. He quickly swept the chips into the envelope, folded it up as securely as he could and jammed the sample into his pocket. It wasn't exactly uncontaminated evidence. For his purposes, he didn't need it to be. All he wanted was confirmation of his suspicions.

Satisfied, he started to turn in search of Liz. A shuddering crash greeted his ears, and his slow pivot in the direction of the car became a quick spin. Liz stood on the side of the road, both her bag and his slung over her arm, and the black phone in one hand. She had a stunned look on her face, and the car was nowhere to be seen.

She gestured a little helplessly over her shoulder, and when Harley took a few steps closer, he saw why. The already-crushed vehicle had somehow rolled back into the wide ditch between the road and the woods. More startling, though, was the way it had *folded*. Almost into a

V. Like the frame had taken all it could take and just collapsed with the final impact. The tall, thick grass made it almost impossible to see.

"Well," Harley said dryly. "At least we don't have to worry about anyone stopping to offer roadside assistance."

Then he shrugged and pointed to the truck, and Liz hurried toward it without looking back.

Liz held the little black phone in a death grip, silently willing it to ring. Even though she knew they were just a few minutes out from the cabins, the fact that the kidnappers hadn't called filled her with dread. They'd been on time or early for each check-in. Even when Teegan had been sleeping, they'd sent the video clip. They'd kept their word.

So why not now?

She held the phone even tighter and forced herself not to check the screen again. She'd already scrolled through and verified that the settings were correct. She'd checked the signal five times. There was no reason for a call or message not to come through.

Unless something's wrong.

She swallowed nervously and tried to shake off the thought. She turned a quick look in Harley's direction. His jaw was stiff, his hands tight on the wheel. He looked as worried as she felt. But she knew he wouldn't begrudge a request for comfort. He loved her. *Loved her.*

Liz tried to focus on that. To hold on to the all-over warmth she'd experienced when he said the words. It had felt so right. Perfect, in spite of every other imperfect thing happening to them. It should've seemed like an impossible thing, to fall in love in the height of danger. How was there even time for it to happen, when her mind was so preoccupied with finding Teegan? But part of her knew that was exactly why it *had* been able to happen. She wasn't bogged down by overthinking. Her emotions were out. They were raw. Some might say it made her vulnerable. Or that she'd somehow mixed up the feeling with another. Liz knew better. She wasn't vulnerable. She was just more open. More willing to accept the head-over-heels feeling than she would've been under any other circumstances.

"Just a few more minutes," Harley said.

She nodded, but she couldn't shake the fright. "Why haven't they called?"

"Could be anything, honey. Didn't keep a close enough eye on the time. Had to deal with something else."

His words made sense, but Liz wasn't buying it.

"Or they don't think they need us anymore," she said softly. "Because they think they have Ruthers."

His hand snaked across the console to close on her knee. "Listen to me. Even if that's true—even though they probably do think he's on his way right now—they're not just going to give Teegan up."

Even though his voice was even, Liz heard the dark undertone. *Give Teegan up*. It wasn't what he meant at all. The kidnappers needed her as a backup plan, so they had to keep her alive. Which should have been at least a little bit reassuring. Instead, it just gave her yet another chill.

She bit her lip and did her best to keep her chin up— figuratively and literally—by staring out the front windshield. She watched the trees whip by, and noted when Harley veered from the main road onto the side one, which was made of packed dirt. Overhead, the morning sky had grown darker, making it seem much later than it was— more like dusk than like midday. Liz knew that at some point over the last few minutes, clouds must've rolled in, unnoticed until that moment. But the somberness seemed more connected to her mood than to the weather. And it only added to her sense of foreboding.

As they got nearer to the cabins, Harley slowed the truck. There wasn't anything to be done about the roar of its engine, but Liz guessed that it was better to roll in with a warning than to swoop in without one.

What will they do when they see us inside instead of Ruthers? she wondered.

Without the phone call, they had no way to tell the kidnappers to expect them. And in her head, things should've played out the way they did in the movies. A drop location. A furtive exchange. Stealing away with Teegan in her arms and Harley at her side. No faces seen, of course. But this changed all of that. And she suspected it wasn't in a good way.

Then Harley answered her silent musing by bringing the truck to a stop and turning in her direction to say in a firm voice, "I want you to get into the back."

Liz automatically started to shake her head, but Harley spoke again before she could even form the word *no*.

"They're expecting one man," he said, "so we have to give them one man. If the two of us pull up in the truck, they might react badly. I'll get out, hands up, and explain."

She couldn't really argue against that. After all, she'd just been worrying about the same thing. So she nodded and let him help her out of the cab, then into the back.

Once Harley had given her a kiss, a reassuring promise, then closed the door, Liz scrunched her legs up between the side of the truck and the paintings, feeling strangely repelled by the art. Maybe she was transferring her anger onto the flowing rivers and trees—she wasn't sure. Either way, she felt a need to keep her feet as far away from them as possible. She closed her eyes and pulled back even farther.

She waited for the roll of the tires to start up again. But instead, the canopy flap squeaked noisily. Her eyes flew open, and she found Harley standing at the end again, his weapon held out, butt-end first.

"Do you know how to fire one of these?" he asked.

She eyed the weapon, wishing she could say no, but had to be honest and nodded. "Yes."

"Take it."

"But then *you* don't have it."

"They're not going to let me take it in," Harley told her. "This way, at least one of us has it."

Liz couldn't help but hear the words he'd left out. *One of us has it...in case something goes wrong.*

She didn't want to believe everything wasn't going to go smoothly, but she reached out and took the gun anyway. It was better to assume the best while planning for the worst.

"Two minutes more of driving," Harley added. "A couple more to make the exchange happen. Then we'll be on our way to the future."

He started to close the canopy door again, but Liz felt a sudden need to stop him.

"Harley?" she called.

"Yeah, honey."

"I love you."

"I love you, too."

Hearing the words again—and the smile in his voice as he said them—eased the dull ache of worry. It made the click of the latch seem less final, too. She even leaned back and let the tips of her toes touch the edges of the frames. She closed her eyes again. And this time, the truck did start to roll underneath her.

Holding an image of her daughter in the front of her mind, she counted off sixty-three measured breaths before they came to a halt. She counted nine more as she waited for something to happen. But aside from the engine noise, she heard nothing. She could picture Harley in the cab of the truck, waiting for someone to acknowledge his presence. Were the abductors inside one of the cabins, peering out? Was there some sort of prearranged signal that they weren't aware of?

Liz counted four more breaths, and then the truck bounced and she waited for Harley's door to slam. But the expected noise didn't come. She did hear his voice, calling out a greeting. But she couldn't tell if his words were a reply to someone else, or just a verbal announcement of his presence. Her ears strained to hear something. The engine remained the only sound.

It's almost over, she told herself.

But unease filled her. She tried to shake it by counting some more, but her desire to know what was going on outside—or what *wasn't* going on, as the case seemed to be—made it hard to focus. So she gave up trying, and instead bent her knees and pushed her torso over top of the paintings so she could steal a peek through the tinted window of the truck canopy.

Even though there was nothing truly odd about everything in front of her, Liz felt even more unnerved. In search of some real reason for the gut churning, she inventoried what lay in her field of vision. Harley had left his door wide open, but she couldn't see the man himself. There were two other vehicles in sight—a dark-colored late-model minivan and a generic hatchback—but no people. She could tell that the truck was angled in front of the main cabin, which was set up a little higher and quite a bit bigger than the secondary ones just below. But they were parked in a way that didn't actually let her set her gaze on the log-sided house. The woods, dark and somehow dangerous looking, were just in view. And it seemed far, far too quiet outside.

Liz was sure there should've been *some* kind of noise. From the abductors. From Teegan. Or at least from Harley. Where were they?

Worry growing tenfold, she wondered what to do. Climb out? Call to Harley? Sit tight? She started to sit back, but a flash of movement outside caught her eye. She froze. The flash came again. Whatever it was—*whoever* it was—was skulking through the forested area beside the cabins. Liz's heart rate skyrocketed, and she wished she hadn't set down the gun before taking a look. Could she reach it without making a noise? She felt like she should try.

Slowly, she eased from her all-fours position to a crouch. Without taking her eyes off the window, she stretched out her hand and felt around on the truck bed. When her fingers found the cool metal, she wanted to sigh with relief. And even though the engine would've muffled it, she made herself hold it in, just in case. *No chances.* Her pulse was already thumping so hard that she wouldn't have been surprised if the whole truck started to rattle.

Slightly reassured by the weapon in her hands, she pushed forward again, her gaze on the woods. They were still now, but that didn't mean anything. Liz *knew* she'd seen something. Holding her breath, she waited for another stir. Then it came. A shuffle and a bump and a muffled curse. But from the side of the truck instead of near the woods.

Liz's head whipped to the side. *Harley.* He was just in view, but bent down. It looked like he was tying his shoe. *Really? Now?*

And she no sooner had the incredulous thought than

yet another flash from the forest drew her attention. Only now it was more than a flash. It was a man. And he was headed straight for Harley.

Chapter 20

Harley's fingers wiggled uselessly once more over his already-secure laces. His legs were bent, ready to spring. His hands prepared to coil into fists. When he heard the rush of air and the stamp of approaching feet, his ruse gave way to action.

He jumped up and sprang forward, fully intending to take down the unknown attacker who'd been stalking him as he'd examined the exterior of the cabin in search of a sign of life. He'd felt the eyes on him. Been aware that the watcher was just waiting for him to come out in the open to make a move. So he'd set up the opportunity— a false one for the man on the edge of the forest, and a real one for himself. And his plan might've worked if it hadn't been for the sudden scream of his name from the general direction of the truck.

Liz.

Hearing her voice—trying to issue a warning, he was

sure—threw him off just enough that instead of taking down the other man with a full-on body check, he simply clipped him, shoulder to shoulder. His attacker stumbled, but didn't fall.

Damn, damn, damn!

Harley fought to recover from the glancing blow and cursed his own stupidity. He'd assumed Liz wouldn't be able to see him from the back of the truck. He'd intended to take down the assailant so quickly that Liz wouldn't even know what happened until it was over.

Time to adjust the plan.

He stabilized his footing and turned to face the other man, who was also trying to find firm ground. As Harley's fingers curled, he made automatic notes on the guy's appearance. He was taller than him, but not as wide. He wore a black ball cap, dark-tinted sunglasses, and his face was covered in a full beard. Long sleeves covered his arms, but a ring flashed on one hand, and a tattoo poked out from under one cuff. All in all, rough around the edges. The kind of man who needed a swing-first-ask-questions-later kind of tactic.

Harley drew back a fist and prepared to deliver a blow. He hesitated, though, when the bearded man raised both hands in a surrendering gesture and opened his mouth.

"You gonna hit me?" he asked, then nodded to a spot over Harley's shoulder. "Or is your girlfriend gonna shoot me?"

Harley might've thought it was a trick or distraction. Except for one thing. He *recognized* the voice. It was one he knew as well as he knew his own.

"What the *hell* are you doing here?" he demanded, his tone as stunned as his thoughts.

"Trying not to get shot, apparently," the other man replied dryly. "You might want to have her put that thing down before she maims me."

Harley turned sideways. Liz really was standing behind him, her delicate hands clasped around his service weapon. She had an uncertain look on her face, and her eyes flicked from him to the other man, but she didn't lower the gun, and her hands didn't shake.

Harley was impressed.

"Liz," he said. "You don't have to shoot him. Not today, anyway."

She exhaled and asked, "Are you sure?"

He couldn't help but chuckle at how serious she sounded. "Yep. I generally try to keep my partners from getting shot. When it can be avoided, of course."

"Your partner?" Liz echoed, the gun finally sinking down to her side.

He nodded. "This ugly hairy dude is Rush Atkinson. Normally, he's a little more presentable. Ish."

In response, Rush tipped up his sunglasses and grinned. "Thanks, little man."

With an eye roll, Harley stepped back and slung an arm around Liz's waist. "Should I bother pointing out that I outweigh you by twenty pounds, or…?"

"S'okay," said the other man with an easy shrug. "You're young. There's still time to cut back on the doughnuts."

"Funny."

"I thought so."

Harley studied his longtime friend for a moment. Something was off. He just couldn't put his finger on what. He frowned, trying to figure it out. Then he did.

Rush is nervous.

It was an odd realization. One that almost made him blurt the observation aloud. Rush Atkinson was a lot of things. Good friend. Rogue cop. Heartbreaker. Thrill seeker. One thing he wasn't, though, was nervous. So seeing the hint of it now…it made Harley wonder.

"Seriously, man," he said casually. "As awesome as it is to see you, what're you doing here?"

"At the moment?" Rush replied, somehow sounding evasive and aloof at the same time. "Looking for a little blonde girl."

Liz gasped. "Teegan?"

"Didn't catch her name before she bit my hand and ran off."

"Ran off?" Liz repeated. "Ran off where?"

"Into the woods." Rush eyed her up and down. "Oh. Damn. I take it you're her mother?"

As soon as the question was out of his friend's mouth, Harley was sure it was subterfuge. Rush *knew* that Liz was the kid's mom. For some reason, he wanted to play that he didn't.

What the hell are you up to, my friend? Harley thought.

Whatever it was, Liz bought it. She disentangled herself from Harley's arms, her attention fully on Rush.

"Where?" she said, her tone a mix of excitement and worry. "Which direction? Was she hurt? Please tell me."

Rush took his sunglasses off completely and stuck them on top of his ball cap, then pointed behind the cabin. He didn't look Harley's way as he answered, and Harley suspected it was deliberate.

"She was fine," the other man said. "Or I think she was, anyway. She jumped out of a closet—"

"She was in a *closet*?" Liz interjected.

"It's actually a good thing, in this case," Rush told her. "But are you looking for a discussion about it, or do you want to go find her?"

"We want to find her," Harley said evenly, giving the other man a warning look.

In addition to being all the other things he was—minus the nervousness, of course—Rush tended to be impatient, gruff and blunt. And that was at the best of times.

His friend sighed, then started again. "Okay. Skipping over the currently irrelevant details, I heard thumping, so I unlocked the closet—and please don't interrupt to confirm that the closet was locked. Or to ask why. It just was. And then the kid came out screaming. I tried to grab her—nicely, so don't make that face—and she bit my damn hand, then went tearing out the back door and into the woods between the two big rocks."

"The big rocks…" Liz swung toward Harley, her expression tinged with barely suppressed hope. "Can we go?"

He was hesitant to say yes. He had the distinct feeling that they were being *herded* to do the very thing she'd just suggested. He didn't like the sensation at all. Could he come up with a valid reason not to? He didn't think so. Not without drawing attention to the fact that he knew his friend had some game in play.

But Rush wouldn't put you in harm's way, he told himself.

Biting back his real questions, Harley nodded at Liz, then directed a different query toward Rush. "How long ago did the kid run off?"

"I've been looking for her for about ten minutes, give or take," his friend said. "Couldn't have gotten too far. She was in bare feet. My bet is on a hiding place."

"Anyone else around that we should know about?" Harley asked.

Rush shrugged. "No one breathing. Couple of kidnappers who got on the wrong end of a gun."

Harley thought the reply was a little too flippant, but

he refrained from commenting. "You want to wait here in case the kid comes back?"

Rush shrugged. "Not that it'll do any good. Kid'll probably scratch my eyes out if she sees me again."

"If you see her," said Liz, "just start yelling 'tacos.'"

"Tacos?" Rush replied.

At the same moment, Harley said, "What?"

Liz sighed. "It's our code word. Trust me. Please. Can we go?"

"Tacos," Rush said again. "Got it."

Harley shot a questioning look at his friend. "We'll talk more about whatever the hell's going on when we've got the kid?"

Once Rush nodded, Harley grabbed Liz's hand and ran with her to the back of the house.

Liz wanted to tear frantically into the woods, screaming Teegan's name at the top of her lungs. She wanted to hear Harley's bass-filled voice doing the same. But as they reached the rocks described by Rush, and her mouth dropped open in a yell, Harley tugged her arm.

"We need to do this methodically," he said. "Call her name. Just once. Then we'll both listen for a reply. It'll be better than hollering until we're hoarse. Plus, we know she'll recognize your voice. She might not respond at all to mine."

So in spite of the half-frantic, half-anticipatory feeling in her chest, Liz deferred to his expertise.

"Teegan!" she called, then turned to Harley.

He stood still, a hand cupped over one ear and pointed toward the woods. Held up his other hand and slowly lifted each finger and his thumb.

Once.

Twice.

Liz's own body was rigid with how hard she was listening.

A third time.

Then Harley dropped his hand and shook his head, and Liz felt her shoulders sag in defeat.

"It's all right," Harley said gently. "That's just the first attempt. Rush said she's been on the move for a few minutes. She's a tough little monkey. I'm sure she wouldn't have hidden this close to the cabins."

Liz swallowed against the threatening tears, then followed him a few steps up the path into the woods, where he stopped again and nodded at her.

Liz took a breath. "Teegan!"

Harley cocked his head, and she did the same. Liz closed her eyes, too, hoping that cutting off the one sense would help fuel the other. But she heard nothing except the slight breeze rustling the branches overhead. Then Harley touched her arm, and when she opened her eyes, he motioned for her to move forward. She obeyed silently, not trusting her voice for anything but calling her daughter's name.

A few steps up, they stopped again.

"Teegs!" Liz yelled, trying to sound more positive than she felt. "If you can hear me…olly, olly, oxen free!"

This time, Liz counted off the seconds herself. And when she got to fifteen, she could feel the desperation coming back. It grew worse as they continued their walk. What if Teegan *hadn't* stopped and hidden? What if she'd just kept going? The forested area around the cabins only grew denser farther in, the terrain rougher. The path had already narrowed, and though Liz knew it branched off for various hikes and for ATV routes, too, it was no place for a child to be alone.

Without warning, Harley's arm shot out, stopping Liz

midstep. He pointed to the ground to the side of the path where a few branches had snapped, looking like they'd been trampled on.

"Maybe our monkey decided to skip the path?" Harley suggested.

Liz's hope spiked, then dropped again. Leaving the path for better cover would fit just right with Teegan's personality. But it didn't take her out of danger by any stretch. In fact, it would just make her harder to find. Especially if she really had kept going.

"Call her again," Harley said.

Liz nodded. "Teegan! Teegs!"

She waited. She wished she expected a response—tried to grasp at one mentally—but she didn't have too much belief that she'd get one. And her low expectations were met. There was only silence.

But Harley didn't seem worried. He just reached for her hand and helped her step from the path into the bushes. A few feet in, they stopped for Liz to call out. Teegan didn't answer, but just a short distance in front of them, Harley pointed out a thick fern, which sat crushed to the ground.

"C'mon," he said. "I'm sure she came this way."

The certainty in his voice buoyed Liz's spirits. How much ground could Teegan and her short legs cover, anyway? Sure, she was a wily, wiry acrobat of a kid, but she was also probably exhausted. Emotionally and physically. It was remarkable, really, that she'd managed to get away at all. The fact that she'd *bitten* a man in the process...

Liz wondered if she should feel bad about it. She *was* regretful that it'd happened to be the *wrong* man. And that the man was Harley's friend and partner. But aside from that, she was just proud that her daughter had seen an opportunity to escape and that she'd done everything she could to take it.

"Look there," said Harley, pulling her from her thoughts.

She dragged her attention to where he now pointed—a broken-off branch near the bottom of a particularly wide tree trunk. Hanging from that was a small piece of blue fabric and a single blue sequin.

Proof. Concrete proof.

Liz's heart didn't just skip a beat. It skipped four. Or maybe five. She clutched her hand to her chest and pressed down, relieved when she felt the thud there.

"Teegan!" she called, less shrill and more excited now. "Teegs!"

She let Harley's hand go and stepped to the tree to pull off the familiar fabric. She stopped just short of lifting it up to inhale and see if she could catch a whiff of her daughter's scent.

"Teegan!" she yelled again. "It's safe to come out!" Her gaze whipped back and forth, searching. "Teegan!"

Harley appeared at her side, his finger lifted to his lips. Liz immediately clamped her jaw shut.

"I thought I heard something just then," Harley told her, his voice barely above a whisper.

Liz strained to hear something—anything—too. The forest was frustratingly quiet. The only new sound was the *tick-tick-tick* of a drizzle starting overhead.

"Try again," Harley urged.

Liz took a breath and dragged her daughter's name out, long and loud. "Teeeeeeeeeegaaaaan!"

Then she heard it. Not a reply in words. A rush of wind that carried in a rustle. The gust died off and so did the rustle.

Liz exchanged a look with Harley.

Was it just the wind itself? She saw the same question on the big man's face, and she shook her head as she decided. *No.*

Though the noise was in the distance, it had the quality of…something else. Something bigger moving through the trees, breaking branches.

She concentrated. Tried to will the wind to move in their direction again. It didn't.

She met Harley's eyes again, then started to holler before realizing it wouldn't do much good. She wouldn't be able to hear any better—*please, please let it be Teegan*—if she stayed in exactly the same spot. She broke away from Harley's gaze. And she ran.

She crashed through the woods, tripping over roots and rock. She tried to slow down. Tried to reason with herself. Rushing the way she was only put herself at risk for falling and getting hurt. But all the reason in the world couldn't stop her.

Harley was behind her every step of the way, anyway. If she faltered, he'd pick her up. She was sure of it. So she kept going until she was *just* certain she hadn't gone far enough. Then paused and gripped a nearby tree.

She'd only been running for thirty seconds—her lungs didn't burn enough for it to have been much longer—but it *was* enough for the rain to pick up. Overhead, it beat down on the high-up branches. It filtered through the greenery and hit Liz in a thick drizzle. She wasn't going to let it deter or discourage her.

She lifted her face into the wetness and prayed that the weather wouldn't drown her voice. "Teegan!"

For a second, she heard nothing. Then came another rustle, louder than the one she'd heard before. The fact that they'd come closer made her want to cry. She forced back the tears.

"Teegs!" she yelled. "Please, Teegan!"

Why wasn't her daughter answering? She was sure—so sure—that Teegan was the source of the noise. She could swear that she could *feel* her daughter's presence. Something had to be wrong.

There are a hundred *things wrong*, her conscience reminded her. *Why is this any different?*

Liz didn't know the answer. She just knew it was true. Something felt very, very off.

"Teegan?" she called, this time so softly that the wind and rain just carried it away.

But there was a response. Or a noise, anyway. A branch breaking in the woods. Like a dire warning, straight out of a horror movie. And when Liz turned toward the sound, things only got worse.

A man in a suit stepped out from behind a tree.

And Liz realized three things simultaneously.

One. She knew him. Or knew who he was, anyway. One of Garibaldi's men. The same one who'd been sitting in the sedan outside Harley's apartment.

Two. He held a gun. Its barrel was pointed straight at her chest.

And three. Her favorite pair of blue eyes—the ones that were so very like her own—were staring down at her from a tree just a few feet behind the gunman.

Chapter 21

Harley could read the soaking wet, suited man perfectly. He had that smug smarter-than-you look on his face that all criminals got when they thought they had the upper hand. When the man narrowed his eyes, Harley knew the crook wasn't just content to feel that way; he wanted to talk about it, too.

It was what stopped Harley from diving like a madman between the weapon and the woman he loved. The movement would only startle the gunman. Maybe provoke a shot that wouldn't have otherwise come right away. Instead, he'd look for a subtle way to get in the middle of things. Move slowly and worm his way into the shielding position. So the only change in posture that he made was to press a reassuring hand into the small of Liz's back.

"Who are you?" The man directed the question Harley's way. "I sure as hell know you're more than some oversize painter."

"Sculptor," Harley corrected mildly.

"Same thing," the guy scoffed.

"To you, maybe."

"Irrelevant, anyway."

Harley took the smallest step forward, his palm staying where it was. "You brought it up, not me."

The man's near-black eyes flashed with irritation. "I'm guessing you think you're pretty clever. And maybe you are. I actually told Jesse you were too damn organized to be who you said you were."

"Jesse?" Harley echoed innocently, dropping his hand to his side and moving forward a bit as he spoke. "You mean Mr. Garibaldi, Liz's landlord? What does he have to do with anything?"

The guy flicked his sopping hair off his forehead and glared a little harder. But Harley had spied a flash of doubt. A distinct sign that the man wondered if he'd made a mistake, and if his own words were only making things worse.

"We're just here trying to save Liz's daughter," Harley added.

The crook's face cleared a little. "Right. By using Jesse's paintings as a down payment."

Liz spoke up then, her voice soft but clear. "Did *he* take her?"

The guy snorted. "Hell, no. Jesse's hardly in the kidnapping business."

"What kind of business *is* he in?" Harley asked.

The question made the other man's face change, and too late, Harley realized he shouldn't have been so direct. Cursing his lack of subtlety, he angled sideways. He was just ahead of Liz now, though not quite in front of her. Unfortunately, the suited man noticed.

"Stop," he said, his tone brooking no argument, his

eyes far too assessing for comfort. "You're not an artist at all, are you? You're a damn *cop*."

As soon as the words were out of the other man's mouth, Harley knew he only had a moment to act. Even if he'd wanted to deny the statement, he was sure there was no time. He started to move. To dive toward the other man's knees and forcefully take him down. Throw the inevitable gunshot wild.

But he no sooner crouched down than *Liz* tackled *him*.

What in God's name—

The thought cut off abruptly as he landed on the ground and his gaze shifted up.

Teegan.

The kid was above them. Way above them, her curly hair visible in the high branches. In just the right position that a wild shot could've had devastating results.

Harley didn't have time to do anything but be relieved. The gunman, who'd jumped back in surprise at Liz's seemingly strange pounce, was now trying to recover from his initial surprise. The water and the surprise seemed to have made the weapon slippery, though, and he was fumbling to get on target once more.

Harley was thankful for that, and also for the fact that— at least for the moment—the man seemed to have chosen him as the primary concern rather than Liz. The criminal's dark eyes didn't move from him. Clearly, he saw Harley as the biggest threat. Which was fine. He'd gladly take a bullet if it meant she could get to safety.

But she won't run, he said to himself. *Not with Teegan up there.*

If he wanted to save them both, he was going to have to do something a little more complicated than making himself a martyr.

Thinking quickly and working with what tools he had

at his disposal, he rolled sideways and reached out. His hands closed on a rock.

Better than nothing.

He yanked it from the ground, ready to take aim, and prayed that his throw would be faster than the other man's ability to fire his weapon. In the end, though, Liz's voice was quicker than either of them.

"Stop!" she said.

The single word was infused with far more authority than Harley would've expected. Even more surprisingly, the man with the gun obeyed her. He had one arm stretched out toward Harley, the weapon in his palm, but not quite poised to shoot.

"Now drop it," Liz added. "Please."

Harley pushed up to one knee and risked turning his gaze from the gunman to Liz. He immediately spied the reason why she was so calm. She held Harley's service weapon in her hands, and he realized he'd all but forgotten that she was still in possession of the gun. He'd been too caught up in his concerns about Rush and the search for Teegan to notice what she'd done with it. Then too busy acting defensively to think about it. Right then, he was glad to see it and also glad that the rain didn't seem to be making *her* grip any less steady.

"I'd do what she says, if I were you," he told the other man.

Dark, angry eyes tipped his way. "I doubt she'll shoot me."

"You wanna take that risk?" Harley asked. "You're potentially standing between her and her kid."

"I don't *want* to shoot," Liz said. "It's kind of a last-resort thing."

The crook turned his gaze back in her direction. "You think you're fast enough to fire before I shoot him?"

"As a matter of fact…" Liz replied. "I think I *am*."

They stood like that for several long moments. Almost in limbo. The other man continued to hold his weapon in Harley's general direction, but made no move to get a better hold on it. Liz was unwavering, too. Harley wondered how long they could continue with the stalemate. Could he do anything to hasten it along in Liz's favor? Was there a way he could get the gun from her and take over? The dark-eyed man might not believe that Liz would shoot at him, but Harley was sure *he* would inspire a fair amount less doubt.

He didn't get a chance to address any of these thoughts. A resounding crack echoed through the woods, carrying above the rain and the wind. It only took a moment to pinpoint the source of the noise. A breaking branch from the exact spot where he'd spied his favorite blue-eyed, blond-haired kid.

The sound distracted the gunman. His eyes were darting around, confused and concerned. His weapon dropped. Maybe Harley could've—maybe he *should've*—used that to gain an advantage. But he didn't even consider it. His entire focus was on making sure Teegan didn't plummet to the ground.

He strode forward as another crack sounded. This one was sharper, and followed by a muffled shriek and a crash. Harley reached the clearing underneath the tall evergreens just in time. He tipped his head up, slid a little to the left and shot his arms out. Not a heartbeat later, fifty-five pounds of solid kid slammed straight into him. He curled his hands around her and pulled her close to his chest.

"Hey, monkey princess," he said softly. "I've got you."

For a worrisome moment, she didn't react. She was utterly still. Then she drew in a shaky breath and flung her arms over his shoulders, burying her face against him.

"Right here, sweetheart," Harley murmured. "Hold on as long as you need to."

He swung toward her mother, fully expecting to find her rushing toward them. He only made it half a spin before figuring out that while he hadn't taken advantage of the situation himself, Garibaldi's lackey *had*. The other man had finally gotten a proper grip on his gun. He was swinging it toward Liz, whose eyes were fixed on her daughter.

No!

Panic took a hold of Harley. No matter what he did, he wouldn't have time to stop the man from shooting. He couldn't put Teegan down quick enough. He couldn't charge at him in time with the little girl in his arms. He started to try anyway. Then froze as a new sound rang through the forest. A bang.

In a surreal blur of rain and worry, Harley saw the gunman jerk. For a second, the criminal seemed to be suspended in place—like his body hadn't quite caught up to what had happened. At last, his weapon-holding hand dropped. His chin drooped. And he folded backward and landed on the wet ground in a heap.

Stunned, Harley lifted his eyes. A figure blurred through the woods just past Liz's shoulder. Then Rush's familiar voice carried out from the trees.

"Try not to shoot me," he called. "I think I just saved your butts."

Harley exhaled and took a step toward Liz, her daughter held out like an offering. But instead of just scooping Teegan away, Liz folded herself into the two of them in a three-way embrace.

Liz wanted to hold on to Teegan forever. Or maybe to look her over again and again to make sure she was okay.

And thank God, she really seemed to be mostly unhurt. A few scrapes and bruises from her flight through the woods, and a small tear in her shirt, but other than that, the only damage was the emotional trauma. And remarkably, even that seemed to be as minimal as it could be.

"Mom," she said when Liz finally pulled away long enough to let her talk. "I was *just* kidnapped."

And in spite of the absurdity of the statement—or maybe because of it—Liz burst out laughing. Harley chuckled, too. But his friend groaned, and when Liz turned to look at him, she realized the bearded man was in far worse shape than her daughter.

A mottled black-and-purple bruise decorated the top of his cheekbone and went all the way up to his eye. He had a bloody gash over his brow on the other side of his face. His shirt had a giant tear in it, revealing another bruise. And on top of all that, a piece of shredded twine adorned one wrist.

Liz took an automatic step toward him, and at the same time, Harley said, "What in God's name happened?"

Rush brought his fingers to his bruised face. "Couldn't convince Amos I was on his side anymore."

"Amos?" Harley repeated.

His friend nodded down at the man in the suit. "Friendly neighborhood thug."

"Okay," Harley said. "That's *really* gonna need more of an explanation."

"Any chance we can do it from the comfort of one partially destroyed cabin?" Rush asked.

Liz jumped in to answer. "Yes. I think it would be good for everybody."

But as they made their way back through the woods—with Teegan still tucked into Harley's strong, capable arms—it was a little slow going, and Rush offered a glossed-over version of events from his end. He explained that he made his first move when Harley's brother, Brayden, had confirmed Garibaldi's presence in Whispering Woods. Using his shady connections from the extended time he'd spent undercover in vice, he set himself up with a low-level enforcer role on Garibaldi's team.

"Also known as 'security' in nicer circles," he told them dryly.

But he'd quickly made it clear to anyone who would listen that he was willing to go the extra mile. Which meant something different in the *not* nicer circles. And Garibaldi gave him a few chances to prove himself. So he did. Over the last few weeks, he'd earned some trust. So when the explosion in the store happened, Garibaldi asked Rush to help Amos—one of his preferred underlings—in the search for the missing paintings.

"I don't normally consider chasing down someone's pretty little decorations as a good time—no offense to you, my artsy friends—but Garibaldi was fixated on the damn things. Figured out pretty quickly that my new boss wasn't the only one obsessed with them. Chased down the group of drug-guzzlers who'd taken them, but they were…uh…" Rush glanced at Teegan. "*Gone*…when we got there."

"You mean dead?" Liz's daughter piped up.

"Very little gets by this one," Harley told his friend.

"I see that." Rush looked like he was trying not to laugh. "Anyway. Amos and I put some stuff together and figured out one killed the other two."

"Ruthers," Liz interjected. "He stole the van from Everlast—a construction company in Freemont—then double-crossed his friends."

Rush stopped so hard in the path that Liz bumped into him.

"Everlast?" he repeated.

"That mean something to you?" Harley asked.

"Yeah. Came across them half a dozen times when I was in vice. The company's a front for a bunch of drug dealers. Wished a few times that someone'd give me the all-clear to investigate them, but it never came across my doorstep." He paused like he was going to say something else, then changed his mind. "After we found the two guys who'd met their demise at the house, we got a tip from an associate of Garibaldi's that some of his rivals were holed up here in the cabins. So we made the trek out. Took one step out of the car, and two guys came out, guns ready. Amos popped them both off without even blinking."

Liz glanced over to Teegan, expecting another comment. But her daughter's eyes had drifted shut, and her head lolled just enough that she had to be asleep.

They reached the cabin then, too, and put the conversation on hold for a minute while Liz tucked her daughter into the bedroom. She made triple sure that the window was locked and left the door open, just in case. Once Teegan was settled, Harley sat on the couch and patted the spot beside him. Liz was more than happy to settle in beside him. Rush, on the other hand, prowled the room like he *couldn't* sit still. Liz wondered if he was in a permanent state of restlessness, or if it was just his current mood. She decided not to ask, and instead went back to the previous conversation.

"So Amos killed the two guys, just like that?" she asked.

"Said he knew exactly who they were—old rivals of Garibaldi's or something—then told me I'd graduated to the big time. And lucky me. I got to help him drag the bodies to the woodshed. Then we went inside the cabin, expecting to find the paintings. Instead, we found the locked closet and you-know-who." He inclined his head toward the bedroom door. "Chased after her for a few minutes, then came back here to regroup. And then you showed up."

"So then what?" Harley replied. "You just let us tear off after her, knowing your good buddy would follow, too?"

Rush paused in his pacing to shoot him a glare. "No. I told him I'd come out here and deal with you. Pointed out that your girlfriend is well-known in town and that since she rented from Garibaldi, it would be better to give her a hand rather than get ourselves in a situation we couldn't get out of."

"How'd *that* go?" Harley grumbled.

"Just fine until he decided to have a look inside that big truck you rolled up in. Then he kinda lost it. Said he *knew* you guys had more info than you were letting on. I tried to reason with him. He turned it around on me, saying I was too friendly with you. Which, to be fair, was true." He resumed his attempt to wear a hole in the floor. "Next thing I knew, Amos coldcocked me, tied me to a chair in the cabin, said he'd let Garibaldi decide how to deal with me, then took off. Luckily, he was stupid enough to leave my gun behind. And you're welcome, by the way."

"Thank you," Liz said, before Harley could throw in any more sarcasm. "Really."

"My pleasure," Rush replied. "Can't let my friend have *all* the superhero fun."

"Speaking of fun…"

"What's on your mind, my tiny friend?"

"Drugs."

Rush stopped his pacing. "Well. That's a first."

"Seems to be a repeat offender these last few hours, actually," Harley said.

"All right. I'll bite. Explain."

Liz was genuinely curious, too. She was more than aware of how often the drug users and sellers had cropped up as they'd searched for Teegan, but she hadn't really put together what was going on. She wanted the big reveal as much as Rush did.

"Okay," said Harley. "Here's my theory. They're in the paintings. In the *paint*. I took a sample and I plan on dropping it off with a friend at the crime lab, who I'm sure will confirm my suspicion. The solution is paint mixed with some kind of narcotic."

Rush let out a low whistle. "Holy crap. That explains the Everlast construction connection. And why those drug addicts were willing to kill to get a hold of them."

"He was using me to transport his *drugs*!" The horrified words burst out of Liz so loudly that she half expected to wake Teegan. When there was no sign of stirrings from the bedroom, she tried to calm her voice as she added, "So what are you going to do? Bust him? I mean, we've got the paintings, right? And people are dead. That's all evidence."

Rush shook his head, and Liz started to argue, but Harley cut her off gently.

"Garibaldi is too smart to let himself get caught that easily," he said.

"This was *easy*?" Liz replied disbelievingly.

Harley lifted his palm to her cheek. "Not for us. But if the paintings were that easy to trace back to him, he wouldn't last long, would he? We need something more concrete."

"I'll find it," Rush promised darkly.

Harley scrubbed a hand over his chin, started to speak, then stopped as Liz's phone came to life in her pocket.

"Sorry," she said. "I didn't even know I had it in there."

She pulled it out to shut it off, but froze when she saw the name.

"Liz?" Harley prodded, his voice filled with worry.

"It's Garibaldi," she whispered.

Harley and Rush exchanged a look, and then Harley said, "Answer. Be vague. Ask about the shop and make a good excuse for not checking up on the so-called fire. If you can, think of something that could give you a bit more time. Nothing else. Think you can do that?"

Liz forced herself to nod, then tapped the screen. "Hello?"

Jesse's reply was immediate. "Liz. I was expecting to see you this morning."

She took a breath. "I know. I'm so sorry. I should've called. Teegan wasn't feeling stellar, and I didn't want to leave her."

"Ah. So you're still at your friend's?"

"No." Liz thought quickly, well aware that he knew she'd been at Harley's apartment. "I actually got called away for a family emergency, so we're on the road."

There was a pause, and she thought he might be trying to decide if her story didn't add up. She braced herself for a comment about her not caring quite enough about the destruction of her livelihood. Or maybe a question about why, if Teegan was unwell, she would take her on a road trip.

Instead, he let out a dry chuckle. "They say bad things come in threes, so I guess this means you've met your quota."

Liz forced a responding laugh. "Yes. I guess it does.

I'm really sorry about not calling. But at least I know things on that end are in good hands."

The flattery he seemed to buy right away. "They sure are. I'll take care of any paperwork that needs to be taken care of, and you just worry about your family."

Liz swallowed. Just a day ago, she would've appreciated the words. Taken them as genuine. Now she knew it was all a front. A way to keep her—and, she suspected, everyone else in town—not just complacent, but *happy*. Now that she knew better, it just made her feel sick.

It took her a second to realize that Garibaldi was still talking. He was waiving two months' rent and asking if she needed any other kind of support.

She exhaled. "We'll be fine. Truly."

"All right, Liz," he replied. "Take your time. It'll be three weeks before the building is back in action, anyway."

She started to sign off, then stopped. "Mr. Garibaldi?"

"Jesse," he corrected.

"Sorry. Jesse."

"Yes?"

"Did your investigator ever figure out the problem with your paintings?" Liz asked.

There was a brief pause before he answered. "I was trying to get a hold of him right before this call, actually. But I'm starting to think they were destroyed."

"That's too bad."

"You have no idea." He paused. "Take care, Liz."

"You, too." She clicked off the phone and brought her attention back to Harley and Rush. "So. What now?"

"I'm gonna head off Garibaldi's call," Rush said. "Give him the bad news about Amos and the good news about the paintings. Should give me a fair number of brownie

points. We can talk again before you two decide to do…
whatever it is you two do."

He shot them a wink, winced as the gesture scrunched
up his bruised face, then moved toward the front door.

"Wait," Harley called after him. "You're seriously not
going to give me a hint about your plans?"

"You know me. Less you know the better."

"That always makes me assume you're planning on
breaking a few laws."

"Bending. Not breaking."

"Could you at least try not to get killed?"

"I'll do my best," said Rush, and then he slipped out.

Liz started to turn to Harley. But he was quicker. He
brought both hands to her face, then bent to give her a
warm, sweet kiss. He tasted like heaven. Like rain and
a hint of salt, and like coming home. Liz was regretful
when it was over, but she couldn't complain about the
affection in his eyes as he pulled away.

"I would *really* prefer not to have such a long break
between kisses again," he said, his voice utterly serious.

"Me, neither," Liz replied breathlessly.

"Wanna hear my proposal?" he asked.

She knew he didn't mean the word in *that* way, but it
still made her heart skip a beat. "Yes, please."

And he grinned back like he could read the automatic
train of her thoughts.

"Not quite that kind of proposal," he teased. "Yet."

She gave him a playful swat, her face warm. "I know
that. Tell me what you want to do."

"I did say 'yet.'"

"I heard you."

"I want to take you away from Whispering Woods
until Garibaldi is behind bars."

"You don't want to hang around and see it through yourself?"

He shook his head and kept his gaze on her. "I meant what I said before, Liz. I want there to be an *us* for the long-term. And I want to keep Teegan out of harm's way." He paused and got a considering look on his face. "Actually, maybe we should ask *her*. She probably still thinks I'm the weird artist next door."

Liz's heart swelled the same way it did every time he put her daughter's needs ahead of all else. "There's a strong chance she's almost as in love with you as I am. Though maybe in a monkey-bars kind of way."

"So…is that a pending-Teegan-approval yes?"

"Definitely."

He kissed her again. Long, slow and full of promise for the future.

Epilogue

Two days later...

"Teegs! Seriously?" Liz said. "We've already stopped twice since lunch."

"It's not *my* fault you guys bought me such a big slushy drink," her daughter said.

"It's not *my* fault, either," Liz grumbled, shooting Harley a glare.

He seemed completely impervious to both her narrowed eyes and Teegan's never-ending need to use the bathroom.

"Aha!" he said. "I see a rest stop up the road. It says it's got a playground, too. Almost as awesome as a toilet."

Teegan giggled. "Gross."

"Bodily functions," Harley replied agreeably. "One part yuck, one part *hilarious*."

"You're a terrible influence," Liz said.

"I know."

He flicked on the turn signal then and guided the car off the road. Liz smiled. The last forty-eight hours had done nothing but affirm her choice—with Teegan's enthusiastic approval, of course—to leave Whispering Woods together.

Harley's various connections had helped them along. From the vehicle where they sat now, to the hotel rooms where they'd stayed the last two nights, to the rush passports they were picking up hundreds of miles away in another two days' time, their plan had gone off without a hitch. He'd even helped Liz make sure Teegan would successfully graduate from third grade while missing the last few weeks of class.

It felt completely natural to rely on him. To treat him as a partner. Even lying in bed together each night, with Teegan squished between them reading aloud, felt normal. Like they'd been together—as a family—for years. And maybe it should've felt weird. But it didn't. And Liz wasn't going to fight it.

She worried a little about leaving things unsettled. But he'd repeated what he'd said from the outset—the only thing they needed on their minds was the next three weeks. That was the time frame Liz had given to Garibaldi, so they'd use that as their measuring stick. They'd decide what to do next when they *had* to. And for some reason, every time he said it, it seemed a little more plausible to Liz. This was her actual life. A dream at the end of a nightmare. And already the bad was fading away.

"Stop making that face," Harley joked as he pulled the car to a stop. "You're going to give all three of us a headache."

Liz stuck out her tongue—which made Teegan giggle—and sighed. "Okay, fine. No more overthinking."

He grabbed her hand. "I don't believe you. You've got far too much mom-ness in you to stop overthinking completely. But I love you anyway."

"You guys are so gross," Teegan said.

"And we love *you*, too," Harley said.

Her daughter rolled her eyes in a pure, sassy eight-year-old fashion, but Liz saw the smile that was trying to tip up her mouth as she asked, "Can we *get out* now?"

Liz swung open the door. "Are you coming, Harley?"

"Catch up with me at the playground," he replied.

She gave a swift kiss—just shy of gross, she hoped—then climbed out and took Teegan's hand, knowing the big man would keep an eye on the bathroom door. Her life felt impossibly, perfectly complete.

Harley waited until Liz and Teegan were in the bathroom before dragging his phone from the console. He didn't want to worry either of them, or to make Liz think he was having second thoughts, but he did feel a brotherly obligation to check up on his friend.

After another quick glance toward the washrooms, Harley dialed Rush's number. The other man picked up on the third ring.

"Make it quick and make it good," he said.

"Quick and good, huh?" Harley replied. "You got some unwanted company?"

"Yeah. I can't hear you. Hang on." A shuffle and a muffled conversation carried through the line for a second, and then Rush spoke again, his voice a little less rough. "Sorry, man. I've got about two minutes before these jerks start wondering why I'm locked in a wheelchair bathroom to take a call."

"Just following up to make sure you're not dead."

"Far from it. Garibaldi was abso-freaking-lutely *de-*

lighted to have them back. Bought me a bottle of scotch and promised me great things."

"I hate to have to point this out, but the man who killed our fathers *might* have a different idea of 'great things.'"

Rush grunted. "I sure hope so. I want to use his 'great things' to put him behind bars."

"Any progress on that front?" Harley asked.

"Word is there's something big about to happen. Don't know what yet. But I'm sure as hell hoping my loyalty gets me in. I think that—" A startling bang and a curse in a feminine voice interrupted, and Rush muttered something about crime really *not* paying, then cleared his throat and said, "Sorry, man. Duty calls."

"Duty is a woman?" Harley replied skeptically.

"Don't ask," said Rush.

Then the line went dead, leaving Harley shaking his head. He had no idea what his friend was up to, but he'd been trusting him for over a decade and a half, so he wasn't going to stop now. Especially not when he had the best woman and the sweetest kid in the world waiting for him.

* * * * *

*If you're looking for more stories from
Melinda Di Lorenzo, be sure to find these titles:*

Undercover Protector
Captivating Witness
Silent Rescue
Last Chance Hero
Worth the Risk

*Available now wherever
Harlequin Romantic Suspense
books and ebooks are sold!*

ROMANTIC suspense

Available December 4, 2018

#2019 COLTON'S FUGITIVE FAMILY
The Coltons of Red Ridge • by Jennifer Morey

Demi Colton—fugitive, single mom and bounty hunter—has finally found refuge in a cabin in the Black Hills. But when Lucas Gage comes to help clear her name, he brings the notorious Groom Killer on his heels.

#2020 RANCHER'S COVERT CHRISTMAS
The McCall Adventure Ranch • by Beth Cornelison

When PI Erin Palmer investigates the sabotage at Zane McCall's family's ranch, Zane must battle betrayal and danger—and his own stubborn heart—in order to claim a forever love.

#2021 WITNESS ON THE RUN
by Susan Cliff

After witnessing a murder, Tala Walker hides in a nearby semitruck. Cameron Hughes just wants to be alone, but he can't just leave the pretty waitress to fend for herself. And they both have secrets as they set out on Alaska's deadliest highway.

#2022 SOLDIER FOR HIRE
Military Precision Heroes • by Kimberly Van Meter

Decorated military veteran and current mercenary Xander Scott is on the run, and the woman who's supposed to bring him down, Scarlett Rhodes, always gets her man. Can a shared history—and passion—overrule a search warrant?

ROMANTIC suspense

*Decorated military veteran and current mercenary
Xander Scott is on the run, and the woman who's
supposed to bring him down, Scarlett Rhodes, always
gets her man. Can a shared history—and passion—
overrule a search warrant?*

*Read on for a sneak preview of the first book
in Kimberly Van Meter's brand-new
Military Precision Heroes miniseries,*
Soldier for Hire.

She wasn't accustomed to sharing a bed with anyone.

Irritated, she flopped onto her back, trying to find a comfortable position.

"Are you going to do that all night?" Xander asked.

"Sorry. I'm not used to having company in my bed," she groused. "And you take up more than your share."

"I promise I don't have cooties."

"I know that."

He chuckled. "Then relax."

"It's not that…" She risked a glance toward him. "It's because…there's history between us."

"One time does not history make," Xander said. "Or so I'm told."

She wasn't going to argue the point. Exhaling, she deliberately closed her eyes and rolled to her side, plumping up her pillow and settling once again.

A long beat of silence followed until Xander said, "Do you really regret that much what happened between us?"

That was a loaded question—one she didn't want to answer. She regretted being messed up in the head, which made it impossible to trust, which in turn made her a nightmare to be in a relationship with. Not that she wanted anything real with Xander.

Or anyone.

Her silence seemed an answer in itself. "I guess so," Xander replied with a sigh. "That's an ego-buster."

Scarlett turned to glare at him. "Did you ever think maybe it has nothing to do with you?" she said, unable to just let him think whatever he liked. For some reason, it mattered with Xander. "Look, aside from the fact that I'm your boss…I'm just not the type to form unnecessary attachments. Trust me, it's better that way. For everyone involved."

Every time she ignored her instincts and allowed something to happen, it ended badly.

"I'm not cut out for relationships."

"Me, either."

His simple agreement coaxed a reluctant chuckle out of her. "Yeah? Two peas in a pod, I guess."

"Or two broken people with too many sharp edges to be allowed around normal people."

"Ain't that the truth," she agreed, the tension lifting a little. She turned to face him, tucking her arm under her head. "Maybe that's why we're so good at what we do… We can compartmentalize like world-class athletes without blinking an eye."

"Mental boxes for everything," Xander returned with a half grin. They were joking but only sort of. That was the sad reality that they both recognized. "I know why I'm broken, but what's your story, Rhodes?"

This was around the time she usually shut down. But that feeling of safety had returned and she found herself sharing, even when she didn't want to.

Don't miss
Soldier for Hire by Kimberly Van Meter,
available December 2018 wherever
Harlequin® Romantic Suspense books
and ebooks are sold.

www.Harlequin.com

Need an adrenaline rush from nail-biting tales
(and irresistible males)?

Check out **Harlequin Intrigue®**
and **Harlequin® Romantic Suspense** books!

New books available every month!

CONNECT WITH US AT:

Facebook.com/groups/HarlequinConnection

 Facebook.com/HarlequinBooks

 Twitter.com/HarlequinBooks

 Instagram.com/HarlequinBooks

 Pinterest.com/HarlequinBooks

ReaderService.com

**ROMANCE WHEN
YOU NEED IT**

SGENRE2018

Love Harlequin romance?

DISCOVER.

Be the first to find out about promotions, news and exclusive content!

Facebook.com/HarlequinBooks

Twitter.com/HarlequinBooks

Instagram.com/HarlequinBooks

Pinterest.com/HarlequinBooks

ReaderService.com

EXPLORE.

Sign up for the Harlequin e-newsletter and download a free book from any series at **TryHarlequin.com.**

CONNECT.

Join our Harlequin community to share your thoughts and connect with other romance readers!
Facebook.com/groups/HarlequinConnection

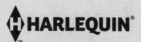

**ROMANCE WHEN
YOU NEED IT**

lover in you!

Earn points on your purchase of new Harlequin books from participating retailers.

Turn your points into **FREE BOOKS** of your choice!

Join for FREE today at
www.HarlequinMyRewards.com.

Harlequin My Rewards is a free program (no fees) without any commitments or obligations.

MYR18

THE WORLD IS BETTER WITH

Romance

Harlequin has everything from contemporary, passionate and heartwarming to suspenseful and inspirational stories.

Whatever your mood,
we have a romance just for you!

Connect with us to find your next great read, special offers and more.

 /HarlequinBooks

@HarlequinBooks

www.HarlequinBlog.com

www.Harlequin.com/Newsletters

 HARLEQUIN®

A *Romance* FOR EVERY MOOD™

www.Harlequin.com